CITY OF LOONS

T.D. FOX

CITY OF LOONS. Copyright © 2021 T.D. Fox. All rights reserved. Printed in the United States of America. For information, address Acorn Publishing, LLC, 3943 Irvine Blvd. Ste. 218, Irvine, CA 92602

www.acornpublishingllc.com

Interior designed by T.D. Fox
Cover design by Damonza

ISBN-13: 978-1-952112-51-5 (hardcover)

ISBN-13: 978-1-952112-50-8 (paperback)

Library of Congress Control Number: 2021904709

www.tdfoxbooks.com

PRAISE FOR THE WALLS OF ORION

"An exciting debut that will ensnare YA readers and leave them wanting more of this intricate, intriguing world where nothing is quite as it seems. Fans of science fiction, dystopian and superhero fiction will fall in love with this story."

—K.A. Fox, USA Today Bestselling Author of *The Devil's Own* and *Judas Kiss*

"Original, dark, and gritty, Fox's debut novel beautifully marries the complexities of forbidden romance and moral gray areas. The pages practically turn themselves."

—Jessica Therrien, Bestselling Author of *Children of the Gods*

"A fun, inventive urban fantasy debut with plenty of atmosphere and a swoon-worthy antihero. Kept me turning pages late into the night!"

—Kat Ross, Bestselling Author of *Some Fine Day*

"T.D. Fox has crafted a gripping and gritty fantasy with the perfect combination of suspense, twists, and self-discovery. *The Walls of Orion* will have you on the edge of your seat!"

—Dennis K. Crosby, Bestselling Author of *Death's Legacy*

"The mystery woven into every scene of this debut is riveting! Fox is a master at building suspense. The Walls of Orion will capture you with its charm, then drag you deep into a world that feels all-too-real. I'm so in love with this book!"

—Danielle Harrington, Bestselling Author of *The Diseased Ones*

"WOW! A debut novel? I would never have guessed. The writing is perfect, the world building beyond imagination with truly exceptional characters. Stand aside, Roth! Fox is in town."

—D. Fischer, Bestselling Author of the *Heavy Lies the Crown* series

To my Friends
Who remind me how lucky I am
To have Loons in my life

CONTENTS

PART I:
THE LEAP

1. THE DUGOUT

THE MORE MILES these ancient tires put between herself and her crumbling Westside apartment, the lighter she felt. Like she was shedding a skin, leaving Courtney Spencer behind. Gone was the disillusioned, med-school-dropout-turned-barista struggling to survive in the shadow of the Wall. Someone else sat in this cracked leather passenger seat of W's Cadillac. Someone she didn't know yet.

C.

W's single-letter nickname for her rippled through her head. She chewed on it, rolling it around behind her teeth. If she spoke it aloud for herself, she sounded silly. But when he said it, she felt bigger than just *Courtney*. She became an enigma: packed full of unseen potential, a dark horse, marked not by a label, the name she'd always known, but by her ability to inflict change on the world. The hum of excitement under her skin, coursing through her veins burned fiercer. Dina would understand. She'd have to. If Courtney sat stagnant any longer, she'd ignite.

A spark in dry grass.

Her heart thumped, racing ten times faster than her thoughts, so far ahead she hoped her brain never caught up. She didn't want room to think about what she was doing. To think about the chaos rumbling behind her, the face her best friend would make when Dina found out she was running off with a killer. Orion City's Public Enemy Number One, the man they called the Whistler. The one who'd terrified her, challenged her, saved her, and opened the door to a frightening, electrifying unknown.

Jasper would be looking for her. She winced at the thought of her now ex-boyfriend, Detective Wade, combing through the clues she'd left behind, putting two and two together with a horrified sense of betrayal. She hadn't meant to hurt anyone. She could only imagine what he thought of her now; maybe she was already lumped in with the criminals, one more shadow in the dark he'd been trying to fight since the day he arrived in Orion City. But there was no controlling that. She had only her own next step forward.

And her choice was made.

The minute she'd shut the door to her apartment behind her and stepped out into the frigid street, she'd known. There was no going back. Once she followed W, she'd begin a reckless freefall she couldn't rewind. Consequences blurred together in a funny stream of irrelevant white noise at the back of her mind. All she had seen was the rain-soaked concrete in front of her. W's even, sure strides clipping away from the tiny corner of Orion City she knew. Away from the Wall, away from Westside, away from everything that was normal. So horribly, wrongly normal.

Adrenaline seared under her skin. After today, *normal* was a foreign word.

So, of course, she should've been prepared when the man walking next to her had suddenly transformed himself into a completely different person.

Courtney had blinked once when W's six-foot-four frame shrank to something only a few inches taller than herself. An older, unassuming gentleman with dark skin and thinning hair walked beside her. She'd almost laughed. He looked like a sweet older man she might hold the door for at a shop. Nothing like the sharp-edged, imposing man she'd grown used to, with his striking pale eyes, dark unkempt hair and hollow cheeks that undercut his youth in a way that unnerved most who held his gaze.

W didn't glance over. Just kept walking. She wasn't sure if he was waiting for her to voice her reaction or simply didn't care if she had one.

She fell into step beside him, grateful that his strides were shorter now. Of course, it made sense for him to Change. Come to think of it, she wondered how often he actually wore the face she knew when he roamed the streets. Maybe someone had seen him, earlier, when he'd fled wherever he'd gotten shot. Maybe the shooter knew his other face. That thought hit her with a twinge of regret. She hoped she wouldn't have to get used to looking at a new face whenever she looked at W. Despite what she knew, mentally, it would still feel like someone else.

It was hard to believe it had only been a few days since he'd appeared on her doorstep, drenched in blood and swaying on his feet, before collapsing across her threshold without a word of explanation. Harder still, to believe that her own reckless decision to rob a hospital for the medical supplies she needed had saved his life. Now her face was no doubt plastered over some wanted poster on an OCPD bulletin board right alongside his. She'd tried not to let that thought catch up to her as he'd stopped beside a car tucked into the shadow of an alley: an ancient-looking Cadillac with a faded gray paint job.

"Where are we going?" she'd asked as she slid into the old leather seat. It smelled like gasoline, peppermint and cigarettes.

"First stop would be the Dugout." He slipped the car into gear without bothering with his seatbelt. She moved to snap hers on, but discovered she didn't have one.

"The Dugout?"

"Home. For the time being. You'll meet the others—whoever's left."

His voice sounded weird, thinner than usual, but she couldn't tell if that came from the rougher vocal cords of the old man whose face he'd stolen.

They drove in silence for what must've been twenty minutes. Orion was a big city; she'd never travelled across the whole thing in one sitting. The gloom of the Wall's close shadow faded as they left Westside behind.

Now, she couldn't say she knew where they were. She caught her own dark eyes looking back at her in the window's reflection, and stared for a moment. She looked different. Copper-blonde hair chopped short, skimming her chin, a fading scar on her temple. Her mocha brown eyes looked older, somehow. Sharper. Like they carried the same kind of blade behind them now that W's did.

She didn't like that thought. Tugging her gaze away from the rain-streaked glass, she focused on the building thunderheads in the snatches of sky she got between looming scuffy buildings.

The downpour increased to a steady drum on the roof. W didn't turn on the windshield wipers. Courtney found herself wondering if they worked, or if he just rejected conventional things like *wind-*

shield wipers, when they pulled into the lot of a run-down apartment complex.

W killed the engine and slid out of the car. Courtney took that as her cue to follow. She squinted through the rain, lifting a forearm over her eyes.

The ancient complex looked abandoned. Condemned, even. Cracked red brick, black spider webs of mold climbing from the sprouting asphalt. Several windows were shattered on the lower levels. The upper ones were opaque, caked with grime.

She realized W was already walking toward the building, so she jogged the few steps to catch up with him. He grew taller, lankier with every stride. When he stopped beneath a rusty fire escape and turned back to her, she felt a flood of unexpected relief to see his normal, harsh-angled face.

"You're gonna need a boost."

She blinked and looked up at the lowest rung of the fire escape, hanging two or three feet above her head. Silver-white droplets clung to the gleaming metal. "You can't be serious."

"Used to be a lot more of a jump. We tugged it down for Margo's sake."

"Are you kidding? Margo can get up there?" The strange, non-verbal little girl who sometimes followed W around barely cleared Courtney's waist.

"She's got a jump rope, tosses a loop up and over, but I can't remember where she stashes it. Come on, up you go." He made a V-shape with his interlaced fingers and leaned down, as if expecting her to step into them.

"This is ridiculous." Even so, Courtney stepped up before she could lose her nerve. She swallowed an embarrassing yelp when he vaulted her upwards, with much more force than she expected. Her fingers slipped on the rung. Water showered down onto her face, but she managed to catch hold with her other hand before she dropped back down. For a moment, she dangled there, fighting to pull herself upwards. She'd never been able to do a pull-up, and always knew it would come back to bite her.

W laughed. Just before she let go in frustration, he caught her around the waist and pushed her up. She clumsily scrambled onto the first level, the front of her shirt soaked with water. Pushing herself to her feet, she glanced back down to see W reach up with one hand, kick a foot off the wall and pull himself up in one fluid move. She glared at him.

"Why don't you just pull it all the way down? Or use the *door*?"

"Discourages squatters from setting up camp. Also keeps the police from checking out any obvious signs of habitation."

Following him up the metal stairs, Courtney wondered how many people stayed here. If they'd all have to uproot when the time came to raze the place, or if he'd cut a deal with someone.

W stopped three stories up, next to a shattered window. The shattering seemed almost intentional. The jagged glass shards stuck up around the edges everywhere except the bottom, leaving enough room for a person to slide through without slicing themselves. W paused and looked down.

"I'd say ladies first, but they might shoot you." With a wink, silver tooth flashing in his grin, he ducked through the window.

Courtney hesitated. She squinted through the gloom inside. All she could make out was a wall a couple of feet away. A hallway, maybe. Pulling in a breath of stale air, she stepped through.

She wasn't nearly as graceful about it as W. By the time she regained her balance, he was out of sight, and she stood alone in a short, dark hallway. A bar of golden light spilled around the corner. And voices. On slow, cautious feet, nerves tingling like a group of wild animals waited around the corner, she headed toward them.

The huge, brick-walled room would've fit her entire apartment inside. Wooden floors, scratched up and bare of any rugs. Couches with torn cushions stood in odd places around the room. Naked yellow bulbs hung from a high ceiling. Tables shoved up against a back window, no chairs.

She stole a few seconds to take in the room, before registering the sudden silence. A dozen sets of eyes flickered over her. Thankfully, half the room went back to their activities, bored in half a heartbeat with whatever they saw in her.

A dark-skinned girl lay with her half-shaved head in a man's lap, tossing a knife in the air and catching it. She stopped mid-throw, knife dangling between her third and fourth fingers. Both she and her partner eyed her. At least, the man did to the best of his ability—a leather patch covered his left eye. Burnt salt-and-pepper hair, too old for his young face, hung down over a silver scar that skimmed the ridge of his cheekbone, disappearing beneath the patch. Beside them, a skinny, bored-looking young man with mousy brown hair and glasses sat reading a book. He didn't look up. Behind that couch, a few people stood practicing what looked like a martial art, barefoot and breathing hard. Two guys and a girl, each not much older than herself: mid-twenties, maybe. They glanced her direction for only a second, and then the girl took a swipe at one of the guys, and the spar continued.

Just past them, below the window, several more individuals sat cross-legged on the ground. Cards, dollar bills and a few candy bars lay scattered in front of them. Beyond their game, a young woman sat with her back to them, rocking back and forth with her hands on her knees, muttering to herself.

"Everyone, this is C." W's sudden voice behind her made her jump. She hadn't realized he was there. The occupants of the room snapped to attention, activity paused. "C, everyone."

He walked past her into the room. As he passed the couch where the couple lounged, the man with the eye patch lifted a folded paper over his shoulder.

"Everything's set to blow. Here's the layout of the first level."

W took it. "The Triads on board?"

A snort. "They were ready to go yesterday. Last year. Hell, Li Zhao wants to run the whole op himself."

W rapped him on the head with the paper. "I hope you told him our timeline was delicate. If he jumps the gun…"

"Yeah, yeah, Boss, he knows the drill. He's on board."

With a short nod, W walked away, studying the paper. He strode through a doorway to a stairwell Courtney hadn't seen and, with a subtle flutter of his long fingers in her direction, waving her toward the strangers… he left her alone with the ragtag troupe.

The half-shorn girl draped over the eye-patched man sat up. A thick cascade of braids fell down over the shoulder of her hoodie, crimson strands woven with black. The close-shaved half of her head sported a dyed red stripe to match, vivid against her dark skin. A strange leather brace shielded her left forearm. Twirling the knife, she started cleaning her fingernails while she watched Courtney, poking at the inside of her cheek with her tongue.

"So," she drawled. "What's your story?"

Courtney must've hesitated a beat too long, because the guy with the glasses looked up from his book. Keen blue eyes swept over her.

"She's a Changer," he said in a monotone. "Fresh, by the look of her. Lost somebody. Typical trigger, another blue-collar nobody, probably figures she's not leaving much behind."

The girl with the knife laughed at the look on Courtney's face. "Sorry. This is Books. He reads. Pages, people, everything *except* social cues."

Books wrinkled his nose and went back to his paperback. The girl waved the knife.

"You can call me Red. This here's Deadeye. I'd tell you everybody else's names, but you'd just forget on your first day. I did."

"Um." Courtney glanced to the doorway where W had disappeared. "I'm Courtney."

Red measured her. She went back to picking her nails. "Won't remember that, because you'll probably get a new name before breakfast tomorrow. If you want to settle in, we've got an opening upstairs. First door on the left. Your roommate's up there sleeping off a grouchy day, so I'd be quiet."

Roommate? Courtney hovered at the edge of the room for a minute, taking in the group. Nobody seemed interested in her presence any longer. Red soon rolled herself up into a sitting position and began making out with Deadeye, so Courtney took that as her cue to leave. She walked to the stairwell where W had disappeared.

The first cold trickle of doubt seeped in. A faint, musty chill leaked off the walls around her as she climbed. The stairs themselves were rotted in places, the wood munched through from years of feet. Everything about this place spoke *condemned*. A dead end for the building itself as much as for the people inside. The lair of runaways, criminals, vagabonds. What was she doing here?

Pausing in the stairwell, Courtney fought the sudden rush of second thoughts and fear. She'd followed a man she knew next to nothing about, into a world she had no idea if she could even survive. A flinch jerked through her as the memory of this morning replayed in vivid sensory detail: the coldness of W's lips under hers, the lack of response as she'd thrown her feelings out there in the open, reckless and exposed. He'd given no indication that he returned her feelings. In fact, his cool demeanor suggested the opposite—a distant respect that suggested he'd rather give her the dignity of pretending her wordless confession this morning had never happened, lest she be embarrassed further.

Her inward cringe smarted, but the levelheaded side of her brain pushed another detail forward. *You didn't follow him because of those feelings.* Sucking in a deep breath, she forced the heat in her cheeks to cool and climbed the rest of the stairs.

She'd made the choice to follow W for the answers he could provide. For the chance to enter the fight against the monster she was only just learning lurked beneath her city.

She'd be damned if she let a schoolgirl crush distract her from what really mattered.

Priorities refocused to ascertaining her next step, Courtney hit the first floor and found herself gripped with the unexpected urge to explore. She paused on the landing before the hall. Should she climb further? Maybe she should find W. Curiosity discarded that thought, lingering on the instructions Red had given her. *Roommate.* With quiet steps, she slipped into the hallway and headed to the first room on her left.

The door was cracked. She pushed it open, pleased when it didn't creak. A rickety old bed frame stood in one corner, thin mattress bare of any sheets. On the other side of the room sat an identical bed, this one with a woolly red blanket stuffed up against the wall, a thousand pills of dark fuzz marking its age. No windows.

"What did I tell you about knocking, Margo," growled a voice from above.

Courtney looked up. Someone hung from the ceiling, knees locked around a beam nailed from wall to wall. Knuckles pressed back to back in a zen-like pose, silky black hair hanging down in a ponytail. The girl opened her eyes.

They recognized each other in the same instant.

"Strings?"

"Coffee-waster." Upside down, that smooth round face looked even younger, dark eyes full of mischievous reflections. Strings swung down, landing neatly on bare feet. "I see you didn't get toasted."

Courtney frowned at her, before she remembered the cryptic warning this girl had given after Jasper ran off for his 'Code Sigma.' "There was a fire," she realized. "You knew it was going to happen?"

"I knew *who* was going to happen. Boss left to spring his right-hand man, and Reggie was sure going to be feeling his oats after two years cooped up inside a fireproof cell." At Courtney's blank stare, Strings huffed and rolled her arms into a deltoid stretch. "Y'know, the Torch? Burned up half of Westside this weekend? Don't you watch the news?"

"I had a busy weekend."

"Never mind. What are you doing here anyway?"

"I'm…" *Asking myself the same question.*

Before she could struggle out an answer, Strings dropped her hostile stance. "Wait, really? You're a Changer?"

How did everybody seem to sniff it out of the air? Did she smell different? Could Changers sense one another? "What makes you think that?"

"Only reason you would be here. No way. And you were with a cop!" Strings guffawed. "Right under his nose. Ballsy! What's your name? Wait—did they give you one yet?"

"I'm Courtney."

"Ha! I never beat them to an alias. Okay, we gotta pick a good one for you, before they give you something awful you'll *never* shake."

"How'd you get the name Strings?"

"Boss thought it'd be funny to toss a ball of yarn at me when I was in form. Never lived it down. Damn feline instincts." With a grimace, Strings waved an arm. "Anyway, welcome to the Loons."

"The Loons?"

"S'what we call ourselves. Or at least, what I call us and nobody around here's thought of anything better. It fits us. Stick around any longer, and you'll see why." Strings turned and pointed to the empty bed. "That'll be you. My old roommate left some stuff behind, so I shoved it under the bed. Blankets, shoes, old clothes. Help yourself to whatever fits."

Courtney wandered toward the bed. "She... doesn't need it?"

"Well, not really, since she got shot in the head during the AITO raid."

Her drawl was so nonchalant, Courtney almost didn't register the horror of the words. "She's *dead*?"

"We lost a lot of people. I don't think Boss was counting on the cops showing up in such large numbers."

"What happened? What *is* AITO?"

"Dang, you really are green." Strings plunked down on her own mattress. The bed springs squeaked. "The cliff notes version? An organization of evil scientists slunk in after the Wall went up. They say they're state-run, but they're military. The mayor tells people they're working on a cure, keeping the dangerous Changers off the streets, but actually they're just rounding up test-subjects to work on a super serum that went wrong a decade ago. And they're holding the whole city hostage until they get it right."

"The people outside have no idea?"

Strings laughed. "If they did, would they care? The government outside won't let the Wall down until AITO gives them the green light that we're not contagious. That's not gonna happen, because AITO doesn't *want* it to happen. They've got the perfect little lab rat factory, right here, without the accountability of the government sniffing around their affairs—and everybody outside's too scared to do anything but take their word for it." She shrugged. "We're freaks. That's something older than Quarantine—freaks get left to fend for themselves."

Courtney sat down on the bed. "Earlier, you said something about a serum."

"Yeah. Boss knows more about it, but from what I've pieced together on facility raids they're studying every Changer they catch, trying to isolate the genes that make them do what they do. It was never a virus. It was an experiment that got out of control. Now not only are they trying to cover up their mess with Quarantine, but they haven't given up trying to perfect the serum that could give human beings the potential to be limitless. To become anything. They could make soldiers literally invisible, a cat like me who could slip behind enemy lines, or crazy powerful, like a two-ton gorilla who won't go down till he's hit with a hundred bullets."

"That's..." Courtney shook her head.

"Insane? Impossible? Evil?" Strings shrugged. "Whatever it is, it made us what we are. Only thing to do now is poison them with their own medicine."

"How?"

"Simple. Make more freaks like us. Turn their sea of guinea pigs into an army."

"*Make* Changers?"

Strings grinned. "Don't worry. Boss'll get you up to speed. If we decide to trust you."

2. THE RINGMASTER

ONCE THE BRIEF novelty of her roommate faded, Strings let the conversation die and looped herself up over the ceiling beam again, striking some acrobatic yoga pose. Courtney hadn't brought anything to unpack. So, after making the bed with the few linty blankets left behind by the old roommate—she shivered at the idea of sleeping in a dead girl's bed—a fidgety restlessness pushed her into the hall again.

What was she doing? The thought was a needle in the back of her brain. Of course she hadn't brought anything to unpack. She'd come here with nothing. Not the same kind of nothing it seemed the others had arrived with. She wasn't starting from scratch. She still had Dina. Still had a job, maybe. Or maybe not, after all her hours MIA. She had Michael. Her throat throbbed.

What had she been thinking? She hadn't been. She'd jumped,

before her brain could catch up to her feet, and now the wind was screaming in her ears and she was starting to see the ground. Coming up fast. A hard slap, the bone-shattering crunch of reality. It was coming; she could feel the cold dread of it, knotted in her stomach.

This wasn't a coffee shop conversation. Pale eyes and grand, sweeping ideas pulling her into a world she'd never imagined. A flickering, shadowy world... in which she didn't belong. Who was she fooling? Herself? W? Red, Deadeye, even Strings had a hardness in their eyes. A chilly steel she could never possess. Yet here she was. Something had made her follow him into the dark. The fierce, intoxicating idea of getting caught up in something bigger than herself. Something beyond the little world she knew.

And... Her mind drifted back to that strange feeling at the door of her apartment, that sudden burst of emotion when she'd tried to stop him from leaving. Something else had driven her to follow him. Something that scared her too much to try and identify.

The smoky scent of food pulled her from her thoughts. She let the hollow growl of her stomach tug her back downstairs, but checked herself at the doorway to the common room.

More people had stacked up in here since she'd left. Twenty or thirty of them spread about the room, lounging on couches or standing and talking, eating pizza from boxes on the far table. Most looked her age or a little older—twenties, thirties. A handful looked to be teens, with one exception. Courtney's eyes locked on a small form sitting cross-legged in the corner. Tangled dark hair, huge brown eyes, olive skin showing through the holey knees of her overalls. Margo. It felt funny, the warmth that filled her at the child's familiar face, even though she and Margo had never exchanged a word. She made up her mind to go and sit near her.

Courtney started into the room—and found her path blocked

by a huge chest. She looked up. Wild orange hair, a scruffy beard, and a too-wide grin that sent a warning through her bones.

"I *thought* I smelled fresh meat."

She took a step back. The hulking man seemed to think that was funny, and followed with a widening grin. Within two steps, she was back in the doorway, and he was far too close.

"Skittish, aren't ya? Boss must be scrapin' the bottom of the barrel since I left, if he's haulin' in twigs like you."

Adrenaline speared through her—she recognized those yellow-tinged eyes. A mugshot flashed through her mind, along with grisly photos of burnt corpses splattered over the news.

The Torch.

"Leave her alone, Reggie," snapped a voice from the couch.

"Aw, will ya look at *that*," the man sang. "Even Lil' Red's gone soft. How long have I been gone? Two years and this whole place goes to shit."

Over his shoulder, Red climbed to her feet. "Hurt her and you'll have to answer to the Boss."

"Oh, he'll thank me. This is quality control. If she can't stand a little heat, she won't last a day in here anyway."

A metallic *click* beneath her chin made Courtney freeze. She expected a knife, but a searing heat licked her skin so sharply she yelped, jerking back. Her head hit the door jamb. Reggie laughed.

"You're cute. I barely touched ya. Betcha *this*'ll get me a real scream."

He lifted the lighter again, and Courtney struck out. Her fist clipped his chin, knocking him back a step. He cackled in surprise. Before she could strike again, he lunged, curled a fist in her hair, and yanked down hard. Pain exploded in her scalp. Her back hit the wall, and his breath was on her face, hot and sour and shaking with laughter.

"Y'know, Boss is gonna reel in a dozen more recruits by the end of the week, and I'm itchin' to butcher a blonde. My pretty little Doc's holed up in her concrete fortress, so I guess you'll have to do for now."

Courtney clawed at him, reaching for his eyes. He dodged and yanked her head back further. Her neck joints popped in warning.

"Excuse me," said a voice from the stairwell.

The air at her back shifted. A blur of motion, too swift for her to make out at this awkward angle. A scuffle, a guttural howl—and Reggie released her. Courtney righted herself to see a tall figure striding away, while Reggie doubled over, clutching his ear and spitting curses. Speared straight through his earlobe, jutting out between bloodied fingers was… a pen.

"Dammit, W," he spat. "Use your *words*."

Red smirked from across the room. "Actions speak louder."

Swearing, Reggie yanked out the pen and jammed a palm up against his bleeding ear. Courtney's stomach lurched at the sight of crimson leaking through his knuckles. He turned and gave Red a one-finger salute, then shoved past Courtney and stomped up the stairwell.

"Don't mind him," Red called. "He likes to pick on the new recruits. But since he's had a particularly crappy week and you made the offense of being blonde…" She shrugged. "He won't bother you again. Want some pizza? There's a box left."

Forcing her wobbly knees to straighten, Courtney exhaled, banishing the image and smell of blood from her mind. She glanced up to where W now stood beside the table at the far wall. Half a dozen others stood around him, looking down at a spread of what looked like maps or blueprints. He was back in his long gray coat. He looked all business, not glancing back at her once as he discussed whatever was on the papers with the others. With a casual flourish, he tugged a handkerchief from a coat pocket, cleaned a trickle of the Torch's blood off his left hand while he spoke.

Her insides rolled again. Fighting to ignore it, Courtney crossed the room and glanced around for Margo, but found that the little girl had taken her pizza upstairs after the violent episode. Hesitating for a second, she spotted Red waving a hand on the couch. She dropped onto a tattered cushion beside her. The girl passed her a half-empty box of pepperoni pizza.

"Don't do blood?" Red chuckled. "Boy, you're gonna be fun to break in."

Courtney swallowed, taking a slice.

"So what's your shift?" Red asked, mouth full.

"My what?"

"Y'know, your form. I'm a lynx. Deadeye's an owl. We're good for reconnaissance. Torch is our resident pyromaniac, a mutant giant lizard who's pretty much fireproof. Daisy over there—the one talking to herself—she brings the brute strength. She's a gorilla."

Courtney blinked. "That skinny girl can turn into a gorilla?"

"Yeah. We had two on the team, but Donavan got cut down in the AITO raid. Daisy didn't take it well. The Change was hard on her mind before. But now…"

They both looked over to where the teenager sat rocking herself on the floor, arms around her knees, staring out the window. Her lips moved in a faint, unbroken murmur.

Red waved her pizza slice. "So what's your trick? You a regular tooth-and-claw, or you got something cool up your sleeve? Don't tell me you're another Orion Giant. We get enough grief with just one trying to ruin our operations." She laughed, referring to the city's most well-known vigilante who could double his size at will, remaining human: a Changer with a freak mutation. At least, more freakish than the rest of the freaks. He tended to target the city's organized crime groups. Which might prove concerning, if Red was implying he targeted *this* group's operations.

"Um." Courtney realized Red was expecting an answer. "I guess... I'm a wolf."

"You guess? Haven't used it much, eh? Hm, well, a wolf's versatile. Stealth, speed, a nice sharp offense."

Offense. Here it came, the question she dreaded to ask. "What do you... do with them? Your forms. You call this a team. Do you... fight?"

"When necessary." Red wiped her lips with the pizza crust, then popped it in her mouth. "*You* won't, at least for a while. Boss has to train you, and then you'll go on your first job, with one of us veterans to watch you in case you go loony. The Change is hard to handle on a regular day, but under pressure, some people just *pop*," she said, her crimson lips popping around the 'P.'

Courtney glanced again at Daisy. "What kind of jobs?"

"Mostly low-profile stuff, destabilizing AITO's smaller bases around the city. You know how they seem to swoop in from anywhere and everywhere when a Changer appears? They've got stations all across Orion, upwards of a hundred posts. We go in and steal their supplies, knock out their com systems, and otherwise mess with their game. We can't do much more than that, or they get reinforcements sent in from the outside."

Courtney frowned. "This last AITO raid sounded like more."

An edgy glint lit Red's eyes, reminiscent of the light shining off a blade. "Yes. Because it's the beginning of the end. Finally. We're done lighting sparks. After ten years, the Loons are ready to burn that Wall to the ground or go down in flames trying."

Courtney's gaze slid to the table again, resting on the back of W's head. From the couch where she perched with Red, she could sort of make out snippets of their discussion. One man pointed to the spread of papers. W shook his head, muttered something about a back door, and pointed to a different spot.

Across the room, a scuffle broke out. Some of the Changers sitting on the floor, playing a game of poker, stood up. One guy punched another. A girl stood up, scowling, and yanked on his shoulder. The stricken man, reeling from the punch, righted himself. He pulled a gun from his belt.

"Hey—!" The girl's yell was cut off by him firing, point-blank, into the other man's chest.

Courtney gasped. The man staggered backwards. He swayed for a moment. Then he dove clumsily for the shooter, who stepped aside as he pitched forward and fell flat.

"Hey, idiots!" Red barked across the room. "Don't waste tranqs."

The girl snatched the gun from the shooter, shoved it into her own belt, and sat back down to the poker game. He joined her. The body lay behind them. W hadn't looked up, as if the whole thing were background noise as normal as the dishwasher, or the sound of the heater running.

"Did they just…" Courtney squeaked.

Red glanced at her, then laughed at the look on her face. "Oh! No. That was a tranquilizer gun. We're *supposed* to use them for facility raids, if we're recovering a feral Changer or something. He'll wake up in an hour or two." When Courtney continued to stare, Red nudged her arm. "Go on, eat your pizza. There's a lot weirder things you'll see in this circus before the day's done."

Courtney did. The food tasted like cardboard on her tongue. *Circus.* Red's description felt disturbingly accurate. Acrobats, lions, clowns. Her roommate hanging from the ceiling. A man with a crazy orange mane and bared yellow teeth—her chin still burned from the fire. A burst of laughter erupted from the game of poker across the room. The man who'd shot the tranq reached back and slapped the unconscious man on the back, holding up a trio of cards in triumph.

And the ringmaster stood across the room, his back to it all. Letting them run wild.

A woman entered the room. Courtney glanced over to the new-comer—and found herself unable to look away. Something flitted through her brain, an old adage about beauty so stunning it sparked a physical ache. This woman had that. She moved more gracefully than any human Courtney had ever seen, making her wonder if maybe she borrowed an inhuman grace from some hidden Changer ability. Satin black curls cascaded down her back. Deep olive skin, full red lips, a tall regal stance. She moved through the room like she owned everything and every*one* in it.

"Who is that?" Courtney whispered.

"Cassandra Silver." Red's voice had a tinge of awe in it, mak-ing Courtney suspect the woman had that effect on everyone. "Once the de-facto queen of the underworld. She's W's... well, I don't know if second-in-command is the right word. She basically owned all of Eastside before W came along. Us Loons all answer to him, but I don't know if she really does."

Courtney watched Cassandra cross the room, pulling the eyes of several people as she went. The Changers on the floor quickly went back to their game of cards. The ones on the couches went back to their pizza. Cassandra approached the table. She slipped her arms around W's waist from behind. Leaning her cheek against his shoulder, she peered down at the mess of blueprints.

"James." Her low voice carried. Dark and dusky, with the hint of a complaint. "You've been at this all day. Give it a rest, and come upstairs."

He murmured something in return. Courtney didn't catch it, but it made Cassandra shake her head and laugh. The sound floated on the air like the notes of a song.

"Hey, you alright?" Red's voice cut through the awful, beautiful melody. "You don't look so good."

Courtney wrenched her gaze away from the two of them. She set down her pizza. Her sudden nausea flushed out any hunger she'd felt.

"Sorry, I... think I might actually head back to my room. It's been a long day." She stood. "Thank you for the pizza."

Red looked down at the uneaten slice. She lifted an eyebrow at Courtney, then shrugged and scooped it up herself. Courtney didn't look back toward W's table as she hurried from the room.

She stopped to breathe in the middle of the stairwell. Her chest was tight, her stomach tighter. Cursing herself over and over, she marched up the stairs to the room she'd been assigned.

Stupid. Impulsive, reckless, unthinking idiot. Courtney shoved open the door to her room, at the same moment a raspy melody hit her ears. She didn't know how she hadn't heard it on the stairs—maybe the roaring in her head had drowned it out.

Strings sat on her bed, legs crossed in a lotus position, eyes closed with her cheek on a violin's deep red wood. The high, husky notes swirled out across the room. She didn't look up as Courtney froze in the doorway. She was lost in the eerie song. Dipping and bowing close as she swept the bow across the strings, which sang as if from her own breath.

Courtney watched. The rough, haunting melody sealed off the back of her throat. She didn't move from the doorway until the song reached its end. Strings tapered off the final note, letting it sigh away into the air. She lowered the violin. Her eyes opened.

"Thanks for not interrupting."

Courtney didn't know what to say. She entered the room and sat down on her borrowed bed.

"What were you?" Strings asked after a silence. "You know, before."

Courtney knew what she meant. Before the Change. "A nobody."

Strings nodded. Her eyes looked far away, her voice soft. "You don't really get to keep pieces of yourself. After the Change, it's a fight just to remember that you're *you*. I was a concert violinist before my parents kicked me out. After the Change, it seemed like I had nothing left that made me *me*. No family, no music."

"Your parents kicked you out for being a Changer?"

"Not that uncommon." Strings set the violin aside, delicately, like it might break. "I went from a somebody to a nobody. Now I don't play to crowds. I play to remind myself who I am." She looked up and met Courtney's eyes. "Maybe it'll be different for you. The Change could take you from a nobody to a somebody."

Courtney shook her head. "I think I'm more of a nobody here than I ever was."

"You want to leave."

Courtney looked down. That ache in her chest, edged and deep, knifed its way inward.

"Why did you come here in the first place?"

"I don't know."

"The hell you don't." Strings' voice gained an edge. "This dump is full of freaks and psychopaths, geniuses and lunatics. We don't have a lot of good people. I knew from the moment I met you in the square you were different. So don't walk away. Tell me. What brought you here?"

Courtney sank back against the bed, letting her head thump the wall behind her. She looked up at the beam on the ceiling. She imagined balancing on it. Feeling the world tip one way or the other beneath her feet, urging her to pick a direction to fall.

Why did she have to always fall?

"I came because someone told me I was bored," she said. "And I realized they were right. Then it became so much more. I got sick of waiting on the edges, ignoring the monsters in the shadows. I wanted to do something. And so... I followed the only person I knew who *was* doing something." Courtney hesitated. "I still don't know if I did the right thing."

She looked down to see Strings' dark eyes measuring her. An odd light gleamed in the girl's gaze.

"We need more people like you," she said. "Stay."

That sick feeling twisted again in her stomach. Courtney grimaced. She remembered her thoughtless move in the doorway of her apartment earlier that day. The unreturned kiss. Then the sharp memory of Cassandra, so casually sliding her arms around W. Her face burned. She'd been a fool, certainly, for revealing her naïve feelings. But that wasn't all that had driven her across the city into this condemned building.

Strings was right. She had to stay. If not for her pride—the pathetic, ragged scraps of it that were left—then for that old spark that hadn't wavered.

Strings left the room, mumbling about idiots eating all the pizza before she got down there. Courtney curled up on the covers, staring at the violin under the opposite bed.

The spark was deeper than W. Deeper than the Change. Something she'd brought with her. Something that had driven her out of her empty life into a world that terrified her, thrilled her. A spark that was growing. She had to figure out what it was.

3. ALL'S FAIR

I T WASN'T PERSONAL.

No, it wasn't. That wasn't the reason Jasper Wade was standing outside Commissioner Van de Graaf's office, about to ask to be put back on the Whistler case. With what he knew, it was his duty as an officer. Feelings aside, he could no longer sit on the information.

He hadn't heard from Courtney since she'd left him in the café—since he'd accused her of helping *him*. Reeling from the breakup, her goodbye kiss burning on his cheek, he'd struggled against his pride for too long before going after her.

But he was too late. A bloody handprint stained the door to her apartment. Inside, more rust-colored stains darkened the carpet, the couch, the coffee table. Panic had blasted through him, until his eyes fastened on the makeshift IV stand behind the couch.

Fear. Confusion. Then the horrible gut-twist as logic pulled the pieces together.

Her voice rang in his head. *Maybe the law's not enough.*

Are you saying you'd break the law?

To protect someone I care about? I'd snap it in two.

At that moment in time, he would've given anything to step out of his detective's brain. But the evidence stacked, dropping like rocks into his belly. Her lies about knowing the Whistler. The growing cracks in her moral compass. The fierce, reckless streak he'd discovered she possessed, which had only sharpened at his efforts to curb it.

He hadn't wanted to believe it. But—as the closest responding officer to the robbery at St. Barnabas—he'd seen the CCTV footage of a Changer. A Changer with short copper-blonde hair.

The realization forced past every denial, settled like that final boulder onto his chest, pressing down. The stubborn traces of hope he'd clung to vanished.

She'd helped him. Jasper had grasped the chance to end the Whistler, had sent him bleeding on the run, and his own girlfriend had helped the murderer escape.

Jasper paced in front of the wide mahogany door. He couldn't avoid it any longer. Evidence like this couldn't be fought. Duty first. Always, duty first.

"Miss, you're not allowed back here—"

"I'm here to see Detective Wade! Get your grabby hands off me."

"—Patton, some *help* over here—"

"Jasper!"

The familiar voice rocketed through the precinct, and Jasper turned to see a tiny figure marching toward him, dodging a harried-looking officer who zeroed in on him in the same moment Court-ney's best friend did.

"Wade," the officer barked. "This one of yours?"

"Ah…" Jasper stepped back from the commissioner's door. Dina Ramirez's dark eyes blazed into his. "Yes?"

"Control your witnesses." his coworker scowled. "This isn't a visitor center."

"Sorry, sir. I'll talk to her."

Ignoring the part of himself that felt relief moving away from Van de Graaf's office—he'd be back, soon—Jasper stopped in front of Dina. He waited until the officer grunted and strode off, before looking down at her. "You know, if you need the police, there's a number to call."

"I don't need *the police*." Gnawing on her full lip, Dina cast a narrowed glance around them, deep brown eyes flashing. "Can we go outside?"

Jasper frowned. Studying her flushed copper cheeks, the dark bob of hair tousled around her small face as if she'd jogged here, he nodded. His colleagues stared, none too polite, as he guided her outside. He'd be hearing about his unruly "witness" later.

Out on the sidewalk, Dina's arms went instantly around her middle, and Jasper felt the wind tugging through his black curls. The promise of snow nipped the air. He sighed, and watched his breath rush away in a thick white cloud.

"Is this about Courtney?" he asked.

Dina hesitated. Ever since the weekend his girlfriend—*ex*-girl-friend—had gone missing that first time, he and Dina had forged an alliance of sorts. They were working together against all the people who didn't care whether their friend lived or died. Struggling to find her as the time ticked down, while his department would've swept her under the rug. "How much do you know?"

Suspicion flared. "Enough. Did you come to fill in the blanks?"

"No," she said, adding quickly, "I mean, I don't know anything. But I'm worried. Her apartment's empty, she left me the weirdest voicemail, then when I stopped by the café, her boss told me she didn't know where she was. Courtney never skips her shifts. I've tried calling her, but she just sends these vague texts asking me to check in on Michael for her, like she can't."

"Maybe she's with her *friend* again." Flinching at the bitterness in his own voice, Jasper ran a hand through his hair. "When was the last time you saw her?"

"I was hoping to ask you that."

"I don't think I'm the best source of information."

"What? You're her boyfriend, *and* a detective."

"We broke up. At this point, I know less than you do." Leaning back to slump against the station wall, Jasper glared down at a puddle on the sidewalk slowly turning to ice. His own blue eyes reflected back at him, narrowed and harder than he'd ever seen them. "Besides, I think we learned from the last go-round that I'm not the best detective when it comes to this city."

Dina inhaled, then caught her words before they escaped, silver breath sliding out in Jasper's peripheral vision.

Footsteps scuffed on the sidewalk. Jasper looked up. Oliver Lee approached, lifting a hand in quiet greeting. His best friend's footsteps never scuffed; he was giving them a heads-up before he startled anyone.

"Sorry, didn't mean to interrupt," came the soft voice. "Was just stopping by to see if Jasper wanted to grab lunch. My shift's over."

The black security guard uniform from Zhao & Huang's firm looked neatly pressed as ever, as if he'd just put it on instead of walking around in it all night. In contrast to the suit, his sleek black hair was ruffled, faint circles under his dark eyes, and he looked paler than normal. Jasper wondered if he'd had a hard shift.

"Oliver, this is Dina," he said, nodding to the girl who'd stiffened beside him. "Dina, Oliver."

"Pleasure." Oliver dipped his head. Dina relaxed a fraction. Oliver's short, wiry stature and quiet voice put most people at ease—a combination Jasper knew not to underestimate, since Oliver's mixed martial arts background made him a coveted asset for security details across the city.

"I couldn't help but overhear," Oliver added. "You're looking for Courtney again?"

His gaze flickered from Jasper to Dina, and the latter straightened, tensing again.

"Yes," Jasper said. "You haven't seen her, have you?"

Oliver shook his head. "She hasn't been at the coffee shop the last few times I've dropped in. Was starting to wonder if she found another job." He studied Jasper's face. "Is everything… okay between you two?"

"They broke up," Dina huffed.

Jasper sighed. Oliver's eyebrows lifted.

"I don't want to get into it," Jasper bit out. "But pretty soon, we won't be the only ones looking for her. I need to find her before this gets any worse."

"Wait." Dina's small fingers tightened on his sleeve. "You didn't turn her *in*?"

"I will." At her shocked glare, he gritted his teeth and passed his other hand over his face. "What would you have me do, Dina? Let her loose on this city when she's conspiring with a *psychopath*? A deranged killer at large who's probably brainwashed her? The longer we do nothing, the more danger she could be in."

Dina's mouth fell open. "You have *no* proof of that."

"I don't need it. She broke the law, that's enough to bring her in."

"Whoa," Oliver said. "Slow down. You realize all you have to go on in a couple of photos, right? You're accusing your girlfriend of conspiring with the Whistler."

"Photos?" Dina echoed.

"She's not my girlfriend," Jasper said. "She's someone I don't even know anymore."

"Look, I'm not saying she doesn't have some major explaining to do." Oliver's low voice carried an urgency that surprised him. "But even if she wasn't telling you the whole truth, she's still the same person. You said she was frustrated with how this city deals with injustice, right? Maybe she's fighting for justice, the only way she knows how."

"The way to real justice doesn't involve skirting the justice *system*," Jasper retorted. "Those vigilantes, the Orion Giant and the Bird-Man, fight for justice the way they '*know*' how—and undermine the real arms of the law. Are you going to tell me next that the Whistler's fighting for justice the only way *he* knows how, too?"

Oliver's faint frown looked stung for a moment. An apology jumped to Jasper's lips—he couldn't take this out on them; they weren't the enemy here—but then Oliver said:

"He might be."

"Come again?" Dina interjected.

"Jasper and I met because, a few years ago, I was part of the Eastside Triads." Oliver paused only a second at Dina's startled intake of breath. "I always wished I were bigger as a kid. I joined the Triads at fourteen to be a little bigger. Big enough to protect my family, and fight for change on my street—the only way I knew how. I got sick of how they ran things pretty fast. When I realized they weren't gonna help me make the kinds of changes I wanted to make, I became Jasper's street source. Started working against them, instead. But not everybody gets there." His eyes returned to Jasper's, glinting with an unusual, hard light. "When there's a vacuum for real justice, it's going to be filled by whoever has the *cajones* to step into it. This city needs fighters, and it'll fall behind whoever's fighting for change, whether or not they're doing it the 'right' way."

"You think the Whistler's fighting for a cause?" Dina asked. "I thought he was a madman."

"Maybe," Oliver conceded. "But his madness seems to have a method behind it."

"He still needs to be stopped," Jasper said. "Before he takes anyone else down with him."

"No arguments there." Hands in his pockets, Oliver turned his gaze to the hard, black shadow of the Wall beyond the precinct. "Just understand what he's fighting for. If you don't, taking him out won't matter—it won't be long before someone takes his place."

Dr. Jeanine Campbell stared at the shattered fragments of her plaster cast, holding her arm still while the nurse fitted a new casing around the reset bones of her wrist. The old cast lay strewn across the med table: a few clean-cut pieces among the mess of jagged, torn edges. The doctor hadn't had to do much cutting to get it off her.

This cumbersome thing had saved her life.

The day she'd broken her wrist in the Torch's cell felt distant.

Her pounding heart, the cold grip of shock at the violence exploding before her dimmed to nothing in comparison with the horror she'd just experienced.

Evan had saved her, then.

Bitterness swept in with a force that squeezed her lungs, tugged a startled breath from her chest. Hatred wasn't something Jeanine felt. Conviction, determination, perhaps zeal on her more passionate days—these drove her toward progress. Fear, desperation, a thirst for revenge: none of these existed in her repertoire of emotions.

Yet he'd made her feel all of them.

Jeanine glanced up, catching her own gaze in the mirror above the med table. The fine lines around her eyes looked deeper, her usual pristine blonde bun frayed loose in several places, the thin red line of her mouth pressed thinner. She swallowed. The tendons in her neck jerked.

Evan Grimes.

How had she been so blind?

This whole time, the one closest to her, her assistant in every level of her work here at AITO—was the Whistler himself. The brilliant, infuriating specimen she most wanted out of all of them: right under her nose, mocking her, manipulating her to his own ends, knowing full well his exceptional genes were the ones she'd been searching for all along.

She hated him. But she hated herself more for relying on him. Fed up with the muscle-headed orderlies her superiors sent her for backup, with no reverence for science, no regard for the higher mission at hand—she'd thought she'd seen a kindred spirit in Evan, someone whose thirst for knowledge almost rivaled her own. Someone who yearned to *understand*, like herself, who knew the nobility of the cause and the sacrifices required. Someone who didn't gain respect from throwing his weight around or from hard-earned titles, but from the soft, unyielding power of his voice. She'd let her guard down. Relying on his eerie ability to calm the storms on the lower wards, she'd gone against forty years of life lessons proving she could only rely on herself—and sure enough, *he'd* become the storm once her guard fell.

She'd been lucky to escape with her life.

The chaos still echoed in her ears. When Evan—when the *Whistler* had set the theriomutants loose on the staff, filling the compound with a bloody cacophony of screams, rabid laughter and gunfire, Jeanine had been in her office. Signing the final paperwork for the F-Ward's euthanizations. The alarms had erupted with just enough forewarning for her to activate the lock-system on her office door, scramble beneath her desk and dial the emergency line to Commissioner Van de Graaf.

She'd stayed in that office until the bedlam faded down the hall. By the time she'd unfolded herself from her cramped position under the desk, the thick bulletproof glass of her office window held tiny freckles of drying crimson.

Minutes felt like hours. After she'd waited as long as she could stand, cheek pressed to the cold steel of the door, the distant tinny alarms all she could hear, she dared emerge. Bodies littered the corridor. Swallowing the bile that lurched in her throat as she tiptoed around the carnage, she headed for the private elevator at the back of the hall.

The deep, guttural wail drove her flat against the wall. Lungs frozen, she'd slid down until she was partially shielded by the large carcass of a deceased... *something*. The hot stench of blood attacked her senses. Across the hall, a shape sprung into view. Great humanoid hands and feet, thundering forward on all fours: a gorilla skidded to a stop in front of a hulking, crumpled form—a second gorilla, a still island in a shimmering red pool. The moan rattled across the hallway again. Sputtering into a squeaking, half-human sob, it broke off entirely as the living gorilla shrank. The theriomutant reverted to human form in a graceless series of jerks. Jeanine had seen much smoother transformations from test subjects, but she didn't recognize the teenage girl dropping to her knees beside the other beast. Weeping echoed off the concrete walls. Jeanine watched, silent, while the girl collapsed forward onto the side of the dead gorilla, face buried, hands fisting in the blood-matted fur.

Two more shapes pounded around the corner. Gray jumpsuits, one armed, one empty-handed. A short, muscular woman covered in scars, a tall man with a ponytail. They froze for half a second, before sprinting forward.

"Daisy, come on." The male's voice carried, ragged and pained. "There's no time."

"I won't leave him," came the muffled shriek.

"Carry her," the armed female ordered.

The weaponless man strode forward, grabbed the girl by the armpits, and hoisted her over his shoulder. Her scream ripped across the hallway.

"No!" Legs flailed, fists pounded. "We're not leaving him! We're *not!*"

"Don't make us tranq you, Daisy." The woman's voice cracked. "We have to go."

They carried her back the way they came, the hysterical sobs fading down the corridor beyond.

Jeanine pushed herself upright. Knees shaking beneath her, she tripped past the final obstacles before the elevator and ducked inside.

Four floors up. Sixteen agonizing seconds. By the time she reached the sixth level, thirty paces from the control room, she watched the green numbers above the elevator doors flicker and freeze, and suddenly wished she'd grabbed a gun from one of the fallen officers below.

The doors opened with a sickly-sweet *ding*, almost drowned out under the blaring alarms. Jeanine hugged the wall of the elevator, inched around the corner.

Stillness.

The red lash of the emergency bulbs scraped over a lifeless hallway, scattered with dark, unmoving heaps like the second floor. Wobbling on her heels, Jeanine plunged a hand into the pocket of her lab coat, gripped the little syringe she kept there—no good against more than one person, but she had to have *something*—and took a step.

The owl attacked her halfway to the control room. Talons ripped down her arm—raised to shield her face a blink before those wicked claws drove into her skull. They bit into the cast instead, and the plaster shield crackled, crushed inward. Jeanine's own shriek joined the raptor's as she felt that bruising grip pierce the flesh beneath—the thunder of its wings cleaving the air in front of her face—and then a high-pitched whistle, unearthly and piercing, echoed from the hallway beyond.

The owl released her with a jerk. Stumbling back against the wall, Jeanine's head hit the concrete. Stars blurred her vision as she fought to make out the theriomutant's shadow gliding down the hall, toward the source of the whistle. It disappeared into the flashing scarlet lights.

Ten steps to the control room.

The world swam back into focus, and she saw the door stood half ajar.

Then, she'd known.

The memory flickered, and Jeanine forced herself to play it

out; to see the faces of her fallen colleagues again, in full detail, bloodless and open-eyed on the slick floor.

Dr. Davies. Dr. Meyers. Dr. Woodford.

There was... no one left.

She'd stopped at the body of Dr. Green, the tips of her shoes inches away from silver-white hair stained red. The stern lines of his face hadn't relaxed even in death. Opaque gray eyes stared up at her, through her, as they always had—as if her four PhDs could never make up for the fact that she was a woman in a man's field. Jeanine studied the pale face of her old mentor: this man who'd always stood in her way, an archetype, an obstacle. Now at her feet.

Like all of them.

The realization bled into her slowly, pounding colder and louder, until it drowned out the pulse of alarms.

She was the highest-ranking member of AITO remaining.

"Finished, Director Campbell." The nurse's gentle voice yanked her back to the present, echoing in her ears as she moved back to let Jeanine examine her newly casted wrist. *Director.*

Distant, dazed, Jeanine's fingers skimmed the new plaster. Her fingertips trembled.

"Your wrist was broken once before, I noticed," the nurse said. "From your X-rays."

"Yes." The whisper left her lips involuntarily. "A long time ago."

Thirty-two years ago, to be exact. When six-year-old Annika Campbell had missed a branch in their favorite climbing tree, and eight-year-old Jeanine had lunged down to catch her by the arm. Her own arm had bent backward over a limb, wrist bearing all the weight of her little sister, but she hadn't let go. Even when the tears stole her vision, blinding white pain exploded up her forearm, she'd held tight until her parents arrived below, shrieking in horror, to catch their youngest daughter.

She'd made it down the tree by herself, cradling her arm. Tears held firmly behind her lashes, she'd watched her parents hug a sobbing Annika. Only later had they realized the horrific angle of Jeanine's wrist.

It would be the first, and last, time she was the center of attention in the doctor's office.

The memories invaded, sharp and hard to fight in the sterile, bright quiet of the med room. Jeanine let them take her for a moment, closing her eyes. The familiar ache spread behind her sternum.

When Annika's bone disease first appeared, the doctors had called it growing pains. As it progressed, they'd been stupefied, diagnosing and re-diagnosing in vain from every corner of the medical books. But of course, the books were faulty. Incomplete, hollow. As Jeanine grew older, and Annika weaker, her indignance mounted in tandem with her sister's deterioration. By age thirteen, she'd begun her own research, and slammed up against so many brick walls she'd finally ripped up and burned a two-hundred-dollar medical book in the family fireplace, watching the flames eat the pages through blurred vision and silent sobs.

Only a handful of people in the whole world had bothered studying this disease. Of them, none had received grants, funding or support of any kind. The condition was too rare, too strange, too scientifically baffling. The medical world's resources were devoted to the more universal pursuits: discovering the cure to cancer, or researching the more common conditions like heart disease or diabetes. Her sister's disease was virtually nonexistent as far as they were concerned.

And then, finally, her sister was as well.

She still remembered the family doctor's words to her family, in the final week of Annika's life. *I'm sorry. Some things, there's just no cure for yet.*

Yet.

Yet, as if they ever planned to develop one.

How could they live with themselves? How could the scientists and doctors of the world be content to accept their own ignorance? To let the mysteries of science go unsolved, knowledge left undiscovered, because some things seemed too bizarre, too obscure— too *inconvenient* for them to try to understand?

How many other families had suffered—*would* suffer—the way hers had? Because of the complacency of the so-called experts?

Twelve years later, Jeanine did discover the cure. She even won an esoteric award for it. But it didn't satisfy. Over the next decade, she earned three more degrees, found the cures to ten other rare diseases, and would've cured twenty more if not for the brick walls of law, "ethics," and thinly-veiled complacency standing in her way.

You have a drive beyond anything I've ever seen, Jeanine, her old mentor had said to her, the day she'd graduated with her fourth degree, a doctorate in biophysics. *Your sister's passing created in you a thirst for knowledge deeper than your colleagues can experience. Remember this, as you endeavor forward through failure and success. Even the loss of human life can produce great things.*

The words had stung, when she'd first heard them. But as her years and experience mounted, Jeanine discovered he was right. The truth was often chillier than expected. A tragedy for one could mean salvation for many others. Her research deepened and expanded, until she soon found herself sunk into the heady current of fringe science, hunting the elusive cures to humanity's most irremediable weaknesses.

AITO had approached her, then. Finally, she discovered her vehicle for change. The bio-regenerative qualities of theriomutation—when a person changed back and forth between animal and human—could be revolutionary in healing across all fields of medicine. Once they learned to replicate the phenomenon happening in these subjects' genes, they could redefine the boundaries of life for the entire human race.

Of course, Jeanine's colleagues and higher-ups, attuned to AITO's military sponsors, intended to take the project in other directions. All of the mutations created unlimited potential for weaponizing the human body. Rewriting a subject's DNA to make them stronger, faster, or smaller, stealthier, within a few seconds—or letting them transform completely for espionage or other arts of war—Dr. Green and the others had planned it all.

And now, they were dead.

Only she remained.

Only *Director* Campbell. No glass ceilings, no roadblocks left standing in her way.

Except one.

He was still out there.

Even if he was dead, like she desperately hoped—she'd seen the footage, read the report of the OCPD officer who'd shot him—his *people* were still there. All of what he stood for, the monsters crawling up to take his place, loomed like a thunderhead on the horizon. She couldn't tell which way the wind was blowing. But she'd be damned if she let it take her unprepared again.

"Director?"

The voice came from the doorway, over a soft knock Jeanine barely heard. She turned to see two young men in lab coats hovering in the doorway, a burly orderly behind them. All three looked uncertain, hesitant to approach or address her.

"We, uh, wanted to know… what you had planned, next."

A pressure tightened in her shoulders, a building weight. It wasn't just her, here. Taking up the mantle of her fallen colleagues, she now bore the staggering responsibility for everyone left. A fish bowl full of frightened survivors, trapped within a larger, hostile fish bowl of monsters that had just proved capable of breaching their defenses.

They should've been safe. The location of AITO'S compound—butted straight up against the Wall, covering the only opening to the Outside—should have been the most secure position in the city. But the Whistler had learned every inch of it from the inside. It didn't matter whether the rest of this godforsaken city still thought of their building as a compound full of heroes, risking their lives here in the trenches within the Wall to save them from the "virus." The Whistler knew the real story. Dead or alive, he was still a threat. He could have leaked his knowledge to any and all of the theriomutants he'd absconded with; they could be planning a mass attack right now, preparing to strike while her team was still reeling from the last blow.

Three anxious sets of eyes watched her, waiting for her direction.

"Gather everyone in the conference room." Jeanine lowered her cast, straightened her shoulders, and stood. "Ten minutes."

The men nodded and scurried off. She listened to their quick footsteps receding.

Glancing down at the stiff plaster of her cast, she tightened her fist, ignoring the pain tingling up her wrist.

No. The monster at the head of the pack would not get the best of her this time. He couldn't ruin what she'd come so far to build. This was war. She'd stand between him and this compound if it took her life.

Her life—any of these small lives—were nothing in comparison with what this breakthrough could do for countless others. For all the little Annika's out there, without the strength to break their own falls alone. She'd break herself again and again to save them.

And she'd break anyone who tried to stop her.

4. ONE OF US

COURTNEY WOKE UP with a band of sunlight on her face. The dream was fading—the familiar, foreign open road she'd never seen in real life, the salty tang of ocean she'd never smelled, the wind tugging at her hair. It took a few minutes to remember where she was. Then a few minutes longer to beat down the panic that came with that realization.

Dina. She'd called Dina. Then Michael, although she'd gotten her little brother's voicemail—which the still gun-shy part of herself was thankful for. How was she going to explain this to him? She'd have to. She refused to disappear on her little brother again. Even if the other time hadn't been on purpose, after the Change had first ripped through her and W had taken her in, Courtney had battled the guilt of knowing Michael had both his remaining family members vanish on the same night. Their father was either still out there somewhere in the brutal hands of AITO, or...

She stopped the thought. She wasn't brave enough to confront the idea of her eleven-year-old brother being orphaned.

Flat on her bed, she watched little floating specks of dust glitter above her. Struggling through an explanation would be hell, even harder than telling her best friend she'd officially jumped off the deep end—but telling Michael was something she had to face. She'd entered this odd little underworld of her own volition; she was confident W wouldn't keep her here against her will if she needed to see her brother. He wouldn't, right?

A quick rap at the door made her jump. Strings didn't strike her as the knocking type. It was the teen's room first after all. Red, maybe?

She sat up, wary. "Come in."

The door swung open. It wasn't Red.

W stood in the doorway.

Courtney straightened, suddenly—stupidly—conscious of her bed hair sticking up in all directions. She forced herself not to smooth it down. He had someone here; he didn't look at her like that. Still, her face flushed.

"If you're done sleeping the day away, I've got something to show you."

He walked away. Courtney slid out of bed and straightened her rumpled T-shirt. She'd slept in yesterday's clothes, unwilling to rifle through the box of hand-me-downs under the bed just yet. She still wasn't sure if she'd decided to stay.

Slipping out of the room, she spotted W standing a few yards down the hall. He began walking. She followed.

She hadn't taken the time to explore yesterday. The hallway stretched far beyond Strings' room. They passed a dozen doors, paint peeling off chipped wooden numbers. Behind a few of them, she heard voices. Laughter echoed behind one. The feverish, unnatural cadence of it raised the hair on the backs of her arms. She hurried to catch up to W.

He stopped in front of a room at the end of the hall. Lifting a hand, he rapped with the backs of his knuckles in the same short way he had on her door.

Courtney looked up at him. At her unspoken question, the corner of his mouth lifted. He stepped back. She started to as well, but then the door opened and a hoarse voice she would recognize anywhere gasped, "Court?"

She looked up just in time to be knocked off her feet by a rib-crushing hug. Red hair obscured her vision. Her nose pressed into a shoulder that smelled like coffee, rain, and something that only lived in her childhood memories.

She fought for air. "Dad?"

His whole body shook. Her arms went around him on instinct. Wet, gasping sobs puffed against her hair. "Court, I'm sorry. I'm so sorry, for everything."

She pulled away and looked back. W was gone.

"How—" Her own throat closed, turning back to her father. "How are you here?"

Her father's face was thinner than she'd ever seen it. Red cheeks sunken in, his beard too long, eyes framed with lines that weren't there before. His eyes, once a warm brown like her own, looked glazed over and dim. He'd never been a big man, but his shoulders had a new frailty. Bent low under some invisible weight.

He shook his head, back and forth, so many times she had to grab his shoulders to get him to stop.

"You know what—you know what I am, don't you?" he hiccupped.

"Yes, Dad. You're a Changer, like me. I saw you on the news.

Did they rescue you from AITO?"

He stared at her. "You're… you're one of them?"

"It happened to me right after it happened to you. Only AITO didn't get to me."

"But wha… what about Mikey?"

"He's safe, he's normal. Staying with his friend Joey. I've visited him, he's all right."

He broke down all over again at that, blubbering and gasping things unintelligible. Courtney kept her hands firm on his shoulders.

"Dad, listen to me. None of it was your fault, all right? You never meant to Change. You didn't abandon us. Understand?"

He wept harder. She yanked him into a hug, feeling her eyes burn and spill over. "I'm sorry," she whispered. "It was my fault you broke in the first place. I pushed you. I blamed you and I hurt you, Thanksgiving night, and I'm so—" she choked. "I'm so sorry, Dad."

"No, you were right. Everything you said, I… I've been a terrible father."

She clutched him tighter. "You started trying again, and I stood in the way. I was stuck in the past, and I wanted to make you hurt like I hurt, even if it hurt us all. I was so…" Her throat squeezed off the words. "Can you forgive me?"

He shuddered. "Only if you'll forgive me."

They stood like that for an age, both crying, both unable to speak. Courtney had no idea how much time passed before he finally pulled away. He looked smaller than she remembered. More like an old man, fragile and bent. She touched his arms with a new worry.

"Have they been starving you?"

He shook his head. "Actually, I've been gaining weight back

since AITO. They put me on some sort of termination list there. When this group broke me out, I was due to be euthanized that same day. Can you believe it? Put down like a stray cat."

Ice trickled through her. "They *saved* you?"

"Yeah, me and forty others. Most of us are staying here now. Learning how to control it." He said *it* with a shiver, like he'd swallowed something he wanted to cough back up. "I can't go back to Michael. Not until I know I'm... stable."

Courtney nodded. Before she could tell him about her similar struggle, offer help or advice, his face changed. He gripped her arms.

"Court, these people—they're not good. You have to get away from them. They may have saved me, but *they're* the ones causing this mess. They've got... *drugs* that trigger the Change. They're dispensing them throughout the city. To innocent people—nobodies on the streets, like you and me. In the coffee, in the food, slipped to shady contacts working at cafes like *yours*. Any one of us could've ingested it, at any time."

Strings' words flashed in her head. Courtney stared into his brown eyes, seeing herself reflected back in them. *Nobodies.* "Why?"

"They're trying to create *more* Changers."

Her head spun, sifting through snippets of old conversations, memories of the cryptic files she'd read in W's apartment—nothing added up. No sane explanations surfaced.

"I don't know how you got mixed up in this," Conrad went on. "But you've got to get out. Fast as you can."

She pulled him in for one more hug. "I've got to go. But I'll see you soon, okay? We're in this together now. We'll figure this out."

He stiffened as she pulled away, but didn't protest. She gave his worried look the most reassuring smile she could manage. Then she turned and walked with fast strides toward the stairwell.

She didn't know where she was going to find him. But she *would* find him. And she would get her answers. She'd search this whole building if necessary.

In the end, she didn't have to. The apartment complex had four stories. Three floors of hallways and endless doors—which she dreaded knocking on, for fear of meeting someone like Reggie again—and the main floor, which held the common room where everybody met to eat and scheme and play poker. She found Red lounging with Deadeye in the common room. Everyone had burgers this time. Fast food seemed to be a constant; quick and dirty calories to fuel a group of Changers who burned through them like paper.

"Where can I find W?" she asked Red.

The girl lifted a pierced eyebrow. Deadeye watched her with suspicion.

"Fourth floor, end of the hall," said Red.

"Thank you."

Courtney climbed the stairs. The burn felt good by the time she reached the fourth floor, her muscles grateful for some place to put the adrenaline. When she reached the last door, she hesitated. It was open.

Steeling herself, she walked inside.

She saw Cassandra first. The woman was hard to miss in any setting, but here, in the golden spill of the window's dusty light, she looked close to regal. She looked up at Courtney's entrance, and the corner of her full red lips turned up. Not in a friendly way.

W stood next to her, a pen in one hand, drawing a bold line over another set of blueprints. This room had a table setup like the one downstairs. Only here there were more stacks of papers, messy and disorganized, and a trail of cigarette butts littered the floor around them. Beyond that, a doorway hung ajar to a single bedroom. Courtney swallowed. W didn't look up until she cleared her throat.

"I'm… sorry to interrupt." She tried to keep her voice level. "I have a question to ask you."

Cassandra chuckled, a musical, humming sort of laugh. Placing a hand on the table before W, she leaned into him. "Call me when you're done babysitting." Then she stretched up and kissed him full on the lips.

Courtney winced. W didn't react, merely set down his pen as she walked away. She passed Courtney in the doorway, close enough that Courtney looked up to meet her eyes. They burned. The smile was still there, but Cassandra's gaze froze the inside of her stomach. Courtney stepped aside.

The sharp staccato of heeled boots faded away down the hall.

"Yes?" W asked.

Courtney swallowed. She couldn't tell if he was annoyed at the interruption. His pale eyes gave nothing away. She struggled to bring back the nerve that had brought her here.

Her father's frantic warning. Strings' words about an army. Drugs. Max, all those months ago, his face bashed into a counter. Her resolve thickened.

"You're *making* Changers," she accused.

He rolled up a sheet of paper on the table and set it aside. "Yes." The repeated word was so matter-of-fact, so emotionless, that she felt rage explode inside of her.

"How long?" she spat. "Did *you* start this entire epidemic?

Were you responsible for the Quarantine? Are *you* the one feeding AITO all their guinea pigs, only to break in and save them like some backwards hero?"

He smirked at that. "I knew you'd start piecing it together, but that's the most entertaining conspiracy I've heard yet."

She crossed the room. Her hands started to shake. There was... *so* much she didn't know about him. Her mind tripped over a dozen half-formed questions she craved answers to. The drugs. His history with AITO. The files on his father, J.W., back in his apartment. Jessica, the faceless girl from his past he'd refused to talk about.

"I left my whole life behind to follow you here." Her voice slid out low and calm, despite the quake in her hands. "If you're a liar, I want to know right now."

"I believe I told you once before that you're the only person I've never lied to."

She wanted to believe him. So, so badly. But he had a crimson smear of Cassandra's lipstick on the corner of his mouth and she felt like she wanted to run out of the room.

"You're right," he said. "I am making Changers. But not in the way you're thinking."

From an inside pocket of his coat he pulled out a tiny bottle. It looked like a pill container. But instead of pills, it held a fine white dust. Her stomach dropped further.

"The drugs," she said. "When you first came to the café with a different face. You shot that guy, beat up Max. You said he stole from you."

"Yes. Maxwell signed on to distribute a tasteless powder into every drink he sold. It was why I frequented your little café in the first place. To make sure he was doing his job. He thought it was just another street drug he could fence—which put my entire operation at risk. The point of avoiding the street scene was to fly under

AITO's radar."

"But AITO has the drug already. Isn't that the serum they're trying to test?"

W frowned. "No. That disappeared over a decade ago."

"What?"

"This powder does nothing more than enhance what's already inside. You've learned emotion triggers a Change. Well, this drug triggers emotion. Deepens it, intensifies it until it overwhelms the chemistry of a Changer. It awakens the ability that would've otherwise stayed dormant for years longer."

"But... if you're just triggering the Change, that means all these people had the Changer genes inside them already."

"Yes."

"How? Who created that serum? Where did you—" She caught her tongue before the barrage of questions drowned her, and sifted for the most important one. "How many people has it affected?"

"Everyone. And only a few." He sighed. "It's a complicated process, that would take too long to explain, even if you had the background to understand."

Courtney crossed her arms to hide the shaking. "Try me."

She couldn't tell if his face twitched with annoyance or amusement. He unrolled another large paper on the table and began to look over it.

"You remember Freak Week," he said. "The first weeks of chaos following Quarantine, with Changers popping up all over the city and the military flooding in from outside to scrape back control."

She nodded. How could she forget? She'd lost her mother that night.

It had been a horrible coincidence. After a nasty fight with their father, Melody Spencer had packed an overnight bag and slammed the front door behind her. Maybe she'd planned to come back, after cooling off. Maybe she'd gone to her sister's in Chicago, and escaped the chaos that followed. Or maybe... she'd been lost in it. Either way, the insanity that exploded on the streets that night prevented not only her return, but any hope of searching for her. So many had disappeared that week. Screams in the streets, sirens and helicopter blades beating the air. The Wall had gone up like a great black tidal wave against the sky, poised to sweep over them, erase them from existence. It may as well have, so far as the rest of the country was concerned.

Maybe her mother had gotten stuck on the other side. Maybe she was still out there.

But Courtney had lost her grip on hopes like that a long time ago.

"General consensus says that's where it all started," W said, tugging her back from the hollow memories. "But they'd be wrong. The first Changer appeared a long time before then. In a padded little cell buried beneath a military compound."

She remembered the files in his apartment. Her lips burned to ask about the failed trials, the subjects who'd died, but she waited for him to continue.

"The project was shut down thirteen years ago, when the government decided the loss of human life in the trials outweighed any gains they might make in future military exploits. The program disbanded. But one scientist wouldn't let it be the end—in fact, he continued his own illegal experiments for years." The corner of W's mouth twitched, and he turned away from the desk, fingers drumming on the paper-strewn surface, tapping out a restless beat. "He became obsessed with perfecting the gene serum on his own. Until he finally snapped— had the brilliant idea to use his own city as a test tube. Ten years ago, he dumped every last drop of his latest serum into the Orion City reservoir." The long, taut tendons on the back of his hand jerked. His fingers stilled. "That next day, four hundred people died. The Center for Disease Control called it a freak virus."

"I remember," Courtney breathed. The memory thumped through her, chills tightening her muscles. "I was eleven. My Dad called it a plague."

"They thought it was, at first. Then the real nightmare began." Her stomach knotted. "Freak Week."

W nodded. "Everyone who died that first day was over thirty years old. When the serum hit their system, their genes couldn't support the mutation. The ones who survived either resisted the Change or mutated. The rest is history."

"History?"

"Quarantine. The first Changer was triggered, and started a chain reaction. After that first wave, the worst one—three thousand deaths in a day was a major trigger for most—the next few out- breaks were smaller. But Changers kept appearing across the city. And they'll continue to do so." Rapping his knuckles on the desk, W looked down at the mess of papers and sighed. He took his hand back. "It's a simple pattern. First comes the spark: a death in the family, a car accident, a divorce. Then one unlucky theriomutant Changes, and all the fear and widespread panic that follows sparks more dormant Changers."

"You're saying everyone else still has the ability to Change?"

"Not everyone. Anyone old enough to have had the serum in their system ten years ago has the potential. The serum didn't im- pact everyone's genes the same way. Some adopted it, started to mutate, while others passed the serum straight out of their system unchanged. Of everyone that's left, there's no way to tell who's a potential Changer and who is not. They're scattered all over this city. Balloons waiting to pop."

Courtney struggled to swallow that. There was so much more she wanted to ask. How he knew all of this, why he would create a drug to trigger more unstable Changers. "I still don't understand," she finally said. "Where does AITO fit into all this? You said the government shut down the program that made the serum."

"They did. But some of the scientists went underground. They control the new program called AITO now—not the CDC or the state, but a rogue branch of the military. They took over after the Wall went up, even got the government Outside convinced AITO answers to them. It's the perfect setup. They're the only way in or out of this city, and the Director has sole communication with the Outside. They can spin whatever stories they want, and since everyone's too scared to come in and see for themselves all the horrors these brave heroes are 'risking their lives' to fight, they can keep us here indefinitely: a concrete cage of human guinea pigs with no pesky supervision or ethics to get in the way. It's genius, really."

Courtney looked back at the papers on W's desk. Huge blueprints, maps, floor plans spread out from corner to corner. Lines scrawled across the printed shapes like diagrams for a football play.

"So they're the enemy," she said. "This whole time… the cops, the media, everybody thinks you're just the Whistler. This larger-than-life killer. A kingpin of the underworld. But all those victims, those scientists… they were AITO."

He watched her. The light drifting in from the window shadowed his gaunt cheekbones, painting his gray eyes a clear, piercing gold. In a split second, Courtney saw him for the first time. His ragged long coat. The tendons standing out on the backs of his hands where they splayed on the papers. He'd always struck her as someone burning with energy. A lighter, eager to set any nearby scraps of paper on fire. But *he* was the scrap of paper. Fighting to stay lit. To keep from burning out and crumbling into ashes. Fighting to light those around him just hot enough so they could burn on without him, should he finally go out.

But why was he still fighting? In all this time since Quarantine, surely his extraordinary Change ability could have given him an edge against AITO. Red had mentioned only little attacks here and there. Tiny raids against AITO facilities under the radar.

"You've had ten years to strike," she said. "Why haven't you made a run on AITO already?"

He shook his head. "I can't give myself away too early. This city is tiny. I can blend in, become anyone, but my followers can't. I'm a shark in a fishbowl. There's not enough room to fight if they send the entire force after me and mine. They've got connections in the police. If I were discovered too early, I wouldn't gain enough momentum to topple them. I need more power." A shadow flickered through his jaw, a muscle clamped tight over bones. "I need people in every nook and cranny of this city, blending in, ready to strike when the time comes. People who can keep their minds on the tightrope of sanity. I can't just take any Changer. If you try to use the Change as a weapon, it turns into a gun with two barrels. One facing the enemy, the other facing yourself. It's hard to build an army when half your troops are shooting themselves in the head."

Courtney thought of Reggie. And Daisy, the girl who talked to herself. The hysterical laughter she'd heard behind the door in the hall.

"I kept my mind," she surprised herself by saying. "I could be one of those people."

He smiled. A softer one than this normal smirk. "You could, perhaps. One day."

She studied the papers on the desk. "Or today. You're planning something. Let me help."

W laughed, a short puff of air through his nose. "No."

"Why not? You brought me here to be part of this, right? I could be useful."

He walked around the table. "Useful?"

"Yes. I'm a Changer, too. I'm one of you."

He neared, until he stood an arm's length away. "One of us, huh?"

"You know I—"

He moved so fast she blinked and saw nothing but the hem of his coat flipping out of view. Her shoulder slammed into something hard. She stumbled. A loose grip around her neck, cold steel under her chin, kept her from going anywhere.

W's breath slid past her cheek. "One of *us* would've seen that coming a mile away. And one of us would've had the skills to defend herself."

Anger spiked instead of fear. She turned against the knife so he'd be forced to move it away or cut her. As she'd gambled, he edged it away enough for her to turn and glare up at him.

"Then teach me."

This close, the knife against her jaw, his fingertips beneath her chin, it all felt reminiscent of that first night in the alley. She remembered the raw fear she'd felt then. The young barista who'd cowered against the dumpster felt like a different woman. Now, her blood hummed with anticipation, her mind sharp and ready to fight.

She saw the flicker in W's gray eyes. Perhaps he was also remembering. Or maybe he threatened so many people at knifepoint they all blurred together. For a second, her pulse hammered for an entirely different reason when he didn't inch back from the shared air between their lips. Her focus snagged on the featherlight glide of his fingers against her jaw.

He lowered the knife. Mirroring that night in the alley, he flipped it around by the hilt and placed it in her hand.

"Alright," he murmured.

And, exactly like that night, Courtney felt the cold too keenly when he left her space, her heart thumping against her ribs with only the ghost of a touch lingering beneath her chin.

5. THE CHANGE

"**A**ND YOU'RE *DEAD*. Dead, dead, a hundred times dead. If this were real, I'd have just shot you in the back."

Courtney doubled, chest heaving, and planted her palms on her knees. "Can we take a breather?" she called up to Strings.

"Yeah, when you're *dead*."

"You can't seriously still have this much energy."

"No rest for the wicked," Strings barked down. "The point is to fight the Change when you're tuckered out beyond belief. When you're at your weakest, that's when it's hardest to control, and you *need* to know how to control it before it controls you."

"It's hard to focus with you shooting paintballs at me every— *ow*!" Bright orange splattered over her arm.

"That's nothing, you wuss. Compared to the Change, these

should feel like butterflies bouncing off you."

"They definitely do not feel like—*gah!*"

Courtney dove sideways under the stinging hail of paint-filled pseudo-bullets sprayed from the rafter Strings perched on. The basement floor of the Dugout echoed with a dozen thumping *splats*. Empty of all trainees this early in the morning except herself, Strings, and another trainer she'd met this week named Des. The bullet-and-soot-scarred walls stared back at her as if judging their newest recruit. She was probably the lamest fighter they'd seen yet.

"C'mon, W won't ever let you go on a raid with us if you can't even handle a little bit of paintball action."

A quieter voice rumbled from the corner. "Remember, you're not trying to find a way out or defend yourself. The point of this exercise is to undergo stress, and handle the Change it triggers."

"I've never handled it," Courtney panted in Des' direction, tripping as she dodged another round of colorful zings. "I've fought it."

"You won't be any good in a *fight* if you fight it," Strings said.

"The Change is not something to fear." Des' soft voice, at odds with his looming bulk in the corner of the room, distracted her for a second. "The Change protects you. And, if used correctly, it can protect others."

Phlat. Flinching, Courtney dropped to one knee and raised her hand over her head, muscles shaking as fresh green paint ran down her forearm.

"Perhaps a break is due, Strings," Des called. "You remember how this was for you, when you were new."

"*Hrpmh,*" came the reply from the rafters.

Lumbering footsteps approached as Courtney snatched a moment to catch her breath. Her every muscle quaked. Bones squirming, blood simmering. She wasn't scared, not really—it was just paint that *hurt*—but the fear of the Change growling under her skin was very real.

"It would not be so hard if you did not fight it," Des said.

A water bottle appeared in her peripherals, dwarfed in the enormous hand that held it out. She wiped a bead of sweat off her nose and took it, offering him a shaky smile, which he returned with a twitch of his lips.

Courtney found Des' shyness endearing, with his gentle, halting words in an accent she couldn't place, and his huge frame hunched forward a little as if he didn't like towering over anybody. The Dugout's largest member never went on jobs except to drive the getaway van, and despite the rough-and-tumble culture here, Courtney had never heard him raise his voice against anyone, let alone a hand. He looked somewhere around her father's age, but the youngest members of the Dugout liked him best. He didn't look down on the newbies like most of the veterans did. In fact, from what Courtney could tell, he seemed to enjoy taking new-bloods under his wing. With arms the circumference of her head, and close-cropped black hair that hinted tattoos shadowing the dark scalp beneath, Des' meekness fit him strangely, pulling people in at the same time his fierce appearance kept troublemakers in line.

Courtney took a long drag from the water bottle, and coughed. "Thank you."

"It was not easy for me to first control my shift," Des told her.

"Really?" When she tipped her head back to meet his gaze, his dark eyes shied away. "What is your shift?"

"You'll never see it." Strings laughed from above. "Des has the best shift of the Loons, maybe except W's, but he never shows."

"Why not?"

The floorboards creaked under Des' shifting weight. "I have more to offer than my strength. W accepted my terms when I joined."

"Yeah, yeah, but it's badass anyway," Strings said. "Just the fact that they *could* have a Kodiak grizzly on their hands is enough to keep people from messing with Des. Even Torch."

"A bear?"

"Not just any bear. The biggest, baddest—"

"That's enough, Strings." Des fidgeted. "It's not the image I want to carry. I am a protector. A defender, not destroyer. When I learned to control the beast, I found a deeper strength to give to the cause."

Courtney gripped the water bottle. "How did you learn to control it?"

"I have two little girls." His lips twitched again, into the start of a smile, then sobered. "My first Change scared them to death. Their mother wouldn't let me back home for weeks. It took twice as long before I was ready to risk staying there again." He lowered his eyes, the thick line of his brows tightening. "Now, I see their faces in my mind when I shift, and find my tether. Much like Strings, and her music—I have something to hold onto, stronger than the Change, to force my bones to realign." His eyes softened, and Courtney thought of her own tether she'd found in her little brother. Where would the Change have taken her without Michael? Rescuing her from that disturbing line of thought, Des lifted his chin and continued: "I'm here for them; to make this city into something I'm not afraid for them to live in. When I met W, I knew he understood something of this. Once he saw what I could do, he carved a place for me here to utilize my true skill, beyond the Change."

"Your true skill?"

Strings whistled. "That's right, you haven't seen Des' real superpower."

Des scratched the back of his buzzed head. His massive bicep bulged. "I am the driver, yes, but more than that. No AITO agent or law officer could follow me through these streets. I can turn an eight-thousand-pound van on a dime, navigate icy pavement at high speeds, and outmaneuver any tail. In the most high-risk raids, we've never been caught. That's why W wants me on every job. Not for my shift. For my control."

Courtney rubbed a stripe of paint off her welted forearm. "I want that control."

"You won't get it by running away from your Change," a voice echoed across the training floor.

They both looked up to see a small figure leaning on the doorless entry to the stairwell. Skinny limbs and Converse shoes, glasses pushed firmly up his freckled nose, the young man called Books eyed them with a narrow gaze. His tousled brown hair shifted in the draft from the stairwell—why nobody boarded the broken windows in this chilly building was beyond her.

"Join the party, Four-Eyes," Strings sang. "Want a turn shooting the noob? You're our crackshot."

"Not if she's as bad at dodging as she looks." Books' blue eyes ran over the paint-splattered nylon jumpsuit Courtney wore—an outfit of Strings' own design, created to stretch and morph with the Change, moving with her instead of against her. Supposedly. Courtney hadn't Changed in the Dugout yet, but she liked the idea of not ripping through her borrowed clothes and exposing herself in front of her new... friends.

Strings hopped down from the rafters with a neat little *thump*, shouldering the paintball gun with a sigh. She tugged at the collar of her own jumpsuit. It clung to her figure tighter than Courtney's—stretched to its limit with her human form so it could shrink down to a manageable size when she shifted smaller.

Courtney didn't miss the way Books' eyes flickered to her, then quickly away, the tops of his freckled cheeks dawning a faint rose hue.

"Control is not learned overnight," Des said. "Perhaps you could give her a few pointers, Books."

Books studied Courtney in a way that made her feel like something in a petri dish. She struggled not to fidget.

"It took me years to stop shifting," he finally said. "I'm like Des; W knows what I bring to the table. My brain's more useful to the cause than my Change."

Strings snorted. "He wishes he were like Des. More like the opposite; wanna tell her about *your* shift?"

Books stiffened, arms crossing over his chest. "The specifics aren't important."

"He's a mouse!" Meeting his scowl, Strings' grin looked more like a Cheshire cat's than any of W's. "Perfect fit for someone with a computer for a brain. Really, Books, you'd be *so* useful; you could fit in the smallest spaces, spy on people, provide entertainment when we get bored."

"Yeah, and give you something to chase besides strings. No thanks."

Her smile dropped. "That was *one* time. And Boss earned himself a wicked scar for that."

"*Would* have earned a wicked scar, if he didn't heal like he does."

"Whatever. He knows not to do it again."

Books grinned. "I wouldn't put it past him. He'll get you when you least expect it."

"Then I'll go for his eye next time, see how he heals *that*."

"A smart person would just throw out all the yarn in the Dugout."

Courtney cleared her throat. They both looked up like they'd forgotten she was there. "How did you stop shifting?" she asked.

"It was a process." Books pushed the glasses up his nose. "First I had to learn not to fear it. The Change is painful for anybody, but I hated turning into something small enough to get stepped on. Once I realized fighting it only made it harder to control, I let my shift go. The more I shifted on purpose, the less painful it got, and the more in control I felt. I just had to remember I was still me, inside there, a rational being with logic and reasoning higher than the animal I was forced to become. The instincts are overwhelming at first. But you can fight them by *not* fighting them. It's somewhat like swimming. You can dog-paddle, tread water, do whatever you want to stay afloat so long as you're not fighting the water itself. You start fighting the water—you sink and drown. You keep your cool, move with it, and your head stays above the surface."

Move with it.

Let the shift go...

Courtney swallowed. She felt it, ever present, drumming in the marrow of her bones. "There's... no way to just *not* Change?"

Books regarded her with a flatness in his blue eyes. "If you want to go insane, there's two ways: fight the Change until it fights you back and takes over, or stop fighting and let your head go under, totally, and end up like Torch who lost his anchor. He jumped overboard and quit swimming, and now even W who hates the c-word calls him crazy." That firm, clinical gaze bored straight through her. "You either control the Change, or it controls you. There is no in-between."

The corrugated plastic of the bottle crinkled in her hand. Courtney tried to relax her grip. "So, if I fight it, I go crazy... but if I don't fight, I go crazy too?"

Strings waved an irritated hand in Books' direction. "He's

great at analyzing, bad at explaining. Look, all you gotta do is face it. Monsters look bigger in the dark. But once you face it down, and realize it's not as big and bad as it seems, it's actually kinda fun. Your shift's a wolf, right? You can do loads with that. But first you gotta accept it. You're Changed, right down to your DNA, and there's no going back. So accept it, move forward, and use what you got. You don't have to be like Books and Des—you can be like me."

"Like you?"

"W might let you shadow me or Red on the next raid. But only if you can control your shift; otherwise you'll get in the way or get yourself killed." Twirling the gun off her shoulder, she popped a paintball round straight into the floor at Courtney's feet.

Movement came before thought. Color splattered the wood beneath Courtney's bare toes—a half second before she dropped back to the balls of her feet, sliding in the slick bright green.

"See?" said Strings. "You're already using some instincts. Not quite as fast as a cat's reflex, but that was something. You dodged that because you got out of your head. The Change isn't much different."

Her heart thumped, too fast for the small jump she'd just completed. Lifting the water bottle, Courtney pressed it to shaking lips.

"Maybe a real break," Des said softly. "Let this sink in."

Strings swung the gun back onto her shoulder. "Fine. But we're back at this right after dinner."

Courtney wiped her mouth, took a deep breath and stilled her fingers. "I could keep going."

"No, Des is right," Strings said. "Your body's overloaded from fighting the Change all day. I can see you shaking from here. Go take a nap, do some yoga, I'll give you the room to yourself this afternoon. And shower before you ruin my suit, that was hard to make, you know."

Reaching up to rub an itchy spot of paint at her temple, Court-ney sighed. "A shower sounds nice."

Twenty minutes later, Courtney stood alone in her room with drooping eyelids and changed priorities, too exhausted to peel off the suit and scrub the colors from her hair. She stared at the bed and debated flopping down onto it, paint and all, and sleeping until din-ner.

Strings was right. Fatigue made the Change harder to fight. Up here, in her quiet room, it pulled at her bones with a vengeance, a pounding ache demanding relief.

Don't fight it, Books had said.

She closed her eyes and swallowed against the nervous coil of her stomach.

The more he Changed, the easier it got.

I'll still be me.

I will.

It happened slower than the other times. Not ripping through like a triggered nerve, but a rolling wave that twisted and groaned. She tried to stay on her feet, but her hands hit the side of the bed in the transition to all fours, and her ribs buckled in, tugging her down. She hit the wooden floorboards with gritted teeth that were no longer her own.

The smells hit her first. Then the sounds. Warm, doughy aroma packed with citrus and dairy drifted up from below—*pizza*, the hu-man edge of her mind supplied the name. Voices swam up after the scent. Rough and light, deep and tinkling, different kinds of throats made different kinds of sounds that strung together into syllables she knew she should understand, but no longer did.

The knotting, cramping pain in her limbs subsided. Now it was just the voices, the smells, and the frightening lack of color squeezing in all around.

More scents invaded. Cold brick, damp wood. Mildew. Earth. Sharp metal, tangy and *wrong*—instinct named that *blood*. Old blood, stale blood... new blood. Somewhere downstairs, near the door, a small bit freshly spilt. Angry shouts, laughter. A thudding punch. More whoops. A scuffle, then hands clapping together— and the tussle broke up. The smells of human food grew stronger. The dry scrape of a cardboard box opening, and her mouth watered as the aroma swept up the stairs. All voices died away with the sounds of happy chewing.

A whine built up in her own throat. Gravelly, scratching, foreign. Closing her eyes, she hunched close to the floor and tucked her head between her... paws. A swishing, fluffy tail curled itself around her haunches—freed through the slit in the spine of her suit. The nylon pressed in close around her, a grounding, light pressure. She lay there, breathing for a moment.

Come back.

It wasn't a thought, not with words anyway. But a desperate, pressing pull inside her flesh; a human mind beating at the door, begging to be let back in.

Bzzzzzz.

The rattle made her jump. Something shuddered on the bed beside her, buzzing against the mattress. Shrinking backwards, she lifted her eyes to see over the edge. A tiny square of light glowed like an angry bee atop the blanket. *Bzzzzzz.* It vibrated throughout the whole bed frame, sending tremors through the floor into the pads of her feet.

Come back.

A picture filled her head. Warm brown eyes, round freckled cheeks, copper hair tousled and sticking up in all directions over a cheeky smile.

An urgency gripped her bones. They shifted.

Pain squeezed the air from her lungs, but her limbs rearranged with a speed that startled her. It was over in a moment. She stood, panting, braced on one knee with a shaking grip on the side of the bed. Her knuckles were white, but the nylon hugged her, snug and loose in all the proper places. No exposure, no torn clothing. Colors returned to the world, smells muted.

The phone continued to buzz.

A tiny picture filled the caller ID. A round, freckled face, dimpled smile, copper-blond hair tousled over chocolate brown eyes. *Michael.*

Pitching forward, she snatched it before her knees gave out and she thumped shoulder-first onto the bed.

"Corny?" came the blessed voice, as soon as she answered. "I saw your voicemail."

"Mikey," she rasped.

"Are you okay?"

She coughed. Cleared her throat. "Yeah. Sorry."

"You said…" He halted. "It's not like before, right?"

She knew what he meant. When she'd left, that first time—the night she'd run out into the street after their father's disappearance, broken and disoriented, and felt the Change first invade her bones. W had taken her in and not let her return for days, until she could get it under control. To Michael, and everyone else, it had looked like she'd abandoned him.

Her throat squeezed. She had to clear it again. "It's not. I promise."

The other end tingled with silence for a moment. Courtney

fought the urge to fill the void. She could hear him thinking.

"Your message was weird," he said at last. "I didn't want to call you back at first, because I thought I'd yell at you."

I'm sorry, she wanted to say, but she bit it down.

"But now I think I get it." Michael's voice quieted. "You're a Changer, aren't you?"

Words left. Now it was her turn to fill the phone with her breath.

"I figured out why you left," he said. "That first time. You'd never just leave like that for any other reason. It makes sense. It's just like T.K. Wang's comics—all the superheroes had something bad happen to them right before they got their powers. Even the Orion Giant, the Bird-Man, all the best vigilantes. They couldn't Change without some kind of trigger."

Courtney stared at the ceiling, the phone shaking against her ear.

"Maybe… Maybe Dad was your origin story."

A hot trail burned down her cheek, followed by another. She dug her palm against her eye. *He thinks I'm a superhero.* "Michael…"

"I'm not mad. Not this time." He paused. "It's actually pretty cool. You going off to fight crime and stuff. I wish I could go with you."

"I don't know if what I'm doing is right," Courtney whispered. "Don't copy me. Okay? I'm… still trying to figure out what to do next."

"I know," Michael said. "Superheroes never know what to do next when they start."

"Michael, I'm not—"

"Don't worry, I won't give your secret identity away, right? I won't tell Jasper, I won't even tell Dina. We got to keep them safe from the bad guys. And AITO can't find out."

Courtney sat up abruptly. "What do you know about AITO?"

"T.K. Wang says they're the bad guys. That's why his books are banned, and why he has to write his comics under a secret identity too."

She took a shuddery breath. "Michael?"

"Yeah?"

Her tongue stuck behind her teeth, filled up and weighed down with all the things she couldn't say. "Stay smart. Keep those books out of sight, okay?"

"Duh. I'm not an amateur." A beat of silence. "Hey… Corny?"

"Yeah?"

"Does it hurt? The Change, I mean."

The vulnerable, trusting note in his voice made her search for a real answer. "It gets easier."

Lying on her bed, staring at the boards in the ceiling, Courtney felt the tear running down the side of her face dry. She licked her lips. "I'm not a hero, Mike. If you could see where I am right now, I'm worried you'd be disappointed. This crowd… we're pretty far from your comic-books' good guys." She inhaled. "But I'm doing something. I'm not just surviving anymore. I joined something bigger than myself, a group that's making a change. I don't know if it's the right one, yet, but…" Gripping the phone, she chased the words. "I need to do something. We need to make a change. If we don't, the change will happen *to* us, and it won't be pretty."

The other end of the phone hummed. "I don't believe you."

"What?"

"Heroes never think they're heroes. So, you can't tell me you aren't one. Not yet."

A dry laugh tickled its way up her throat. "When can I make that call?"

"I don't know." He inhaled, as if snatching a conclusion out of the air. "When you can't look at yourself in the mirror. Remember? You told me—you wanted to look in the mirror and see someone who keeps fighting. So... once you stop fighting, I guess, you can make the call."

Courtney closed her eyes. She saw Strings' face, then Books'. Des' and Red's.

W's.

"You're pretty wise, little brother," she managed at last. "I might start calling you for advice from now on."

A snort. "Don't tell Dina."

Something sharp lanced her ribs. "She's a good advice giver too."

"But not a good secret keeper."

"She's better at keeping secrets than you know."

"Yeah, well, I've got dibs on the sidekick spot. She can be number two. Alfred or something. I'm Robin."

A smile eased across her lips. Courtney opened her eyes. "I thought you just read T.K. Wang's comics?"

"I'm a well-read man." Beyond the scope of the phone, someone called Michael's name. "Oh. Gotta go. Joey's mom has dinner. Call ya later?"

Reaching up to dry the corner of her eye, which had started to fill again, Courtney put a smile in her voice. "Definitely. Call later."

"Bye!"

The click of the phone left her listening to the quiet for a minute. Then, the sound of someone calling her own name from below—a high, throaty holler that could only come from her roommate's vocal chords—relieved a little of the ache in her chest.

She swung her legs off the bed and dropped the phone back to the mattress.

Checking her nylon suit—which fit her so perfectly it needed no adjusting even after the Change—she opened the door to the warm mix of fast-food aroma and rowdy laughter. The happy sounds drove away the ache in her chest with surprising speed. Fighting a grin as Strings bellowed her unofficial nickname again—*C!*—she headed down the stairs.

◆ ◆ ◆

"*Ow!*" Courtney coughed, pressing a hand to the throbbing corner of her chin where Red's knuckles had just collided.

"Hey, if you don't want me to hit you, *dodge*." Red bounced on her toes, brown eyes bright, looking like she was having just a little too much fun beating the snot out of her inexperienced sparring partner. "Or better yet, hit me *back*. That'll save you a few bruises."

"I'm trying," Courtney panted, ducking under the next swing. But it was a feint. Red's other fist thumped the air out of her diaphragm in a brutal *whoosh*, sending her tripping back to land hard on her rear. She sat there wheezing a moment on the cold concrete. Above her, the training room's lights streaked and blurred. The splintered ceiling beams swam back into focus, hung with a few stray cables that almost looked chewed. At least the basement level was empty again, this late in the evening; nobody was around to watch her pitiful first hand-to-hand lesson.

It was her second week. Already, she'd been punched, kicked, pinned to the floor, and almost knocked out more times than she could count. She *had* been the one to ask for training. But W hadn't been kidding when he'd said this team wouldn't go easy on her.

Red waited, fiddling with the padded strips she'd wrapped around her knuckles for this exercise. "Y'know, you're not half bad at this."

Courtney snatched back enough breath to cough out a painful laugh. "You've knocked me on my ass eight times, and I haven't landed a single hit on you."

"But you keep getting up. That's more than I can say for half the newbies I've trained."

Scrubbing a hand under her nose, Courtney struggled to her feet. She dragged in a rasping lungful of air. "How many people have you trained?"

"Eh, I've lost count. Half of 'em quit as soon as they learned how to control their Change. That's W's bare minimum for turning anybody loose." She rolled her shoulders, and tugged one arm across her chest to stretch. She'd forgone the standard nylon Loons uniform, in favor of a leather jacket peppered with pins and neon studs, short denim shorts and bright red kicks. The thick leather brace on her forearm remained. "You never got in fist fights as a kid? Seems like you can at least take a hit."

"No."

"Huh. Well, then you're stubborn as hell. I like that. Not one to stay down when you get pushed."

Courtney snagged the opportunity to stretch her own sore arms, hoping to delay the next few rounds of punches for at least a short breather. Her own nylon suit stuck to her like a second layer of skin, sweaty and tight. She wondered how Red could workout in her leather and denim. "How long have you been on the team?"

"Huh. Good question." Red poked a tongue against the inside of her cheek, nodding like she was counting in her head. "I joined the Loons when I was twelve, so I guess… seven years ago now."

Courtney blinked. "You were twelve?"

"Yeah. W caught me digging through some dumpsters, out be-hind the old digs the Loons used before the Dugout. I was a lynx back then half the time, so I was a little feral. He was impressed I could already control my Change. Took me in, gave me a roof to sleep under."

"Did your... parents kick you out when you Changed?" Courtney remembered Strings' story.

The corner of Red's mouth quirked, but there was no humor in it. "They didn't really get the chance. It sorta... hit them as hard as it hit me." When Courtney frowned, she sighed. "I killed them. The day I Changed, I ripped their throats out."

Horror rolled through her, cold and impossible to conceal. Red took her reaction in stride, pursing her lips and waiting for Courtney to get her tongue back.

"I'm... sorry," she finally whispered. "How old were you?"

"Ten."

"So you were on the streets for two years?"

"More or less. I couch-surfed a few times, but nothing really stuck. I was scared of putting anyone else in danger." She shrugged. "It's okay. They weren't all that great, anyway. My parents didn't run with the best crowd, so I got exposed to a lot of shitty stuff as a kid, y'know, the kinda stuff that makes a girl in Westside grow up real fast. Living on my own wasn't as tough as it might've been if I'd had a cushier childhood."

Courtney fumbled for words. There weren't many. "I'm sorry," she said again.

"Didn't tell ya for pity points. I'm just saying, I know a bit of what it's like to pop back up after you get knocked down a *hell* of a lot of times. So keep that spark. It might turn you into somethin' scary one day."

It was obvious *scary* was supposed to be a compliment. Courtney picked at the wrappings around her own knuckles, shaking her head with a forced smile. "I don't think I'll ever get to your level of scary."

"I dunno." Popping a joint in her neck, Red grinned. This time the expression hit her eyes. "Sometimes it's the soft ones that surprise you."

She lunged forward with an abrupt swipe of a fist, which Courtney surprised herself by ducking, her own fist snapping out. It sailed over Red's head close enough to feel the tickle of wind across her knuckles where Red's cheek had just been.

Red righted herself with a laugh. "See? You're learning."

6. MARGO

ANG. BANG. BANG.

Courtney put the gun down and pulled the plugs from her ears. The air felt too quiet.

The basement level of the Dugout swallowed all sound. Buried beneath cracked asphalt and four stories of crumbling bricks, someone could set off a bomb down here and go unheard. The scorch marks on the walls made Courtney wonder if the Torch had tried it. A short wall divided the room, stacked with boxes of ammo and extra guns, all lying around in hazardous, disorganized piles.

She rubbed the blisters on her hands. One week. W had given her one week to learn how to handle a weapon. The whole team was prepping for a raid on one of the AITO facilities. She didn't know what they were stealing, but her blood pumped a little faster when she thought of finally joining the fight against the hidden terrorists in her city.

Courtney couldn't believe how much time had passed. It felt like she'd left her apartment years ago, not barely a month. Yet, at the same time, she couldn't believe she'd been here a month already. The nights and days blurred together in this place. No alarm to wake up to, just the burning adrenaline of another day. Another chance to prove herself. Training with Strings, learning to control the Change at will. Basic knife defense with Red, peppered with sessions of hand-to-hand. Guns with Deadeye. She'd thought she'd have turned tail and run by now. She'd surprised herself—and everyone else—when she hadn't.

"So?" She nodded to the opposite wall. "How did I do?"

W regarded her work. Someone had painted a bunch of life-size black silhouettes on the far wall. Little flecks of white plaster showed through the paint, peppered with hundreds of bullet holes. Her own targets – pizza boxes taped atop the silhouettes so she could see where her hits landed—sported several tiny holes.

"D plus," W said. "Maybe a C minus."

"What? But I hit all of them."

"Not in any vital places."

"A bullet to the knee would still slow down a bad guy. I'm not trying to kill anyone."

"That's the problem." W shook his head and handed her a knife. "Show me what else you've learned."

Courtney grimaced down at the switchblade. In the weeks of Red's brutal crash course, the only things she'd earned were several shallow cuts and the knowledge that she didn't have what it took to slice someone open.

"I can't do knives," she said.

"Anyone can use a knife. That's what makes them deadlier

than guns."

"No. I mean… I'm not a killer, W." She held it out. "Red is your knives woman. Deadeye can shoot a dime out of the air. Strings doesn't use a weapon, but she still goes on every job. I don't have to kill to be useful. Give me a tranq."

He raised an eyebrow. "A tranq?"

"Yes. Even if I hit people in the knees, I can knock them out. I could tranquilize anyone you guys might kill."

A thoughtful smirk started on his lips. "You'd have to hit 'em before we do."

"Is that a yes?"

He pressed her fingers back over the knife she still held. "You'd still need to defend yourself if someone got too close."

"I'll stick close to Red."

"That's not good enough."

"I'll be fine. Your team is small, an extra hand could—"

He pulled her in, hand tightening over hers. "I don't waste people." The grip around her wrist bruised. "You're not going until you can prove to me you're not a liability. Got it?"

She blinked. Without meaning to, she nodded. His pale eyes studied hers a moment longer. He let her go.

"I didn't bring you here to die in the first month." He jerked his chin at the wall. "Get some more practice."

Courtney fiddled with the knife in her hand as she watched him go. Irritation coiled inside her. Setting the knife down, she jammed the plugs back in her ears and picked up the gun again.

She was irritated until dinnertime. Once she finished practicing at the gun range, she went up to prowl around the common room to see if Des had brought the pizza yet.

Des, the gentle giant. *He* wasn't a killer, either. Honestly, most people around here forgot he was even a Changer. Now that she thought about it, several people on W's team weren't killers. Strings, the little feline acrobat who climbed buildings and fire escapes to scout out enemy territory. Books, the scrawny kid-genius who could read people and rooms in all ways but social. He could tell W where weapons were hidden from a glance, and hack security systems with his eyes closed. But he wasn't physically threatening at all.

Why did W care so much that *she* learned to kill?

She plopped down next to Red on the sofa, and the other girl smirked at the look on her face.

"Lighten up. If you don't make this one, you'll be on the next op."

"I don't think it's a matter of making it," Courtney said. "You could throw a knife between a man's eyes. Even if I had the skill, I couldn't do that."

"So what? You've got other skills. You think outside the box. Did you tell him about your tranq idea?"

"Yeah. He still thinks the raid is too dangerous for me."

Red eyed her. Something like curiosity sparked behind her gaze.

Deadeye walked up. He slid into the space between Red and the armrest of the couch. The glance he gave Courtney was marginally less cool than the ones he'd given her when she'd first arrived. Perhaps her quick improvement at the shooting range had boosted his ego as a teacher.

"Gonna steal her for a minute," he said, pressing his face into Red's neck. "If you don't mind."

Courtney took the hint. She left them on the couch and headed for the stairwell. She considered heading to her room to see if Strings was around, maybe ask her for another training session. But she heard raspy violin notes when she reached the second floor. Deciding not to interrupt, she continued up to the third floor.

Her confidence had grown in the week since she'd arrived. She hadn't explored the entire complex yet, but she knew roughly where everyone lived. The fourth floor housed the scariest residents, she'd quickly figured out: Torch, Cassandra, and a few others she'd been fortunate enough not to meet. The second and third floors housed the rest of the Loons. Most of the newer recruits bunked on second. Some people, like Des, didn't live here at the Dugout at all. Apparently W got a lot of his hired muscle from outside his core team. People who were more... disposable. He didn't waste his *own* people, it looked like.

That thought made her insides squirm.

She heard a noise and stopped to listen at the entrance to the third floor. A soft tune, unlike anything she'd heard in the Dugout before. It drifted out into the hall from an open door. She stepped closer. Someone was humming.

She peeked into the room. Margo sat in the middle of the floor, surrounded by stacks of empty pizza boxes. Towers four boxes tall stood end to end. On top of that wall, more pizza boxes lay on their sides, opened into upside-down V's. Margo looked up. Her arms held two more pizza boxes, which she looked to be in the middle of flattening into cardboard shapes.

"Is that a castle?" Courtney asked the first thing to pop into her mind.

Margo looked down at the greasy towers. She nodded.

Encouraged, Courtney edged into the room. She sat down some feet away from Margo's fortress. "I used to build castles when I was your age. Out of sofa cushions and pillows."

Margo watched her for a moment, then continued flattening the pizza boxes. Courtney picked up a box from the ground. Margo's eyes flickered up to watch her again.

"My brother and I always tried to build the tallest tower." Courtney folded the box into a semi-sturdy cube and turned it on its side on the floor. She grabbed another box. Fashioning it in the same way, she placed it on top of the first. "Could I build a tower for your castle?"

Margo studied the two boxes she'd stacked together. Courtney wasn't sure if she understood the request, or if she felt offended by her presumption to join. But she felt an unexpected rush of joy when the little girl nodded again.

They worked in silent tandem. Courtney's tower grew to five leaning pizza boxes. She tore a lopsided flag shape out of the final box lid. Placing it on top, she sat back on her heels and glanced sideways at Margo.

The little girl stared at her creation. Then she stood. Courtney held very still when she neared, remembering how cautious W always was with Margo. Margo squinted at the flag. She reached up, straightened it, and sat back down. Her gaze slid to Courtney's.

She laughed.

Courtney blinked. It wasn't really a laugh, more of a short burst of sound from the child's chest, almost cough-like. But the way her mouth quirked up at the corners put a warmth in Courtney's chest. She smiled back.

"Margo doesn't usually like strangers," said a woman's cool, silky voice.

Courtney glanced up. Cassandra stood in the doorway, dark hair tumbling loose over one bare shoulder, a small black dress wrapped around her curves like a satin glove. Knee-high boots, a thick black belt with a pistol holstered at her hip. Somehow the outfit managed to look practical and seductive at the same time.

"Downstairs, doll," she said to Margo. "It's dinnertime."

The smile vanished from Margo's eyes. She stood, stepped over the cardboard wall and scurried past Cassandra out the door. Courtney stood too. She started to follow, then stopped when she realized Cassandra had blocked her path.

"But you're not a stranger, are you?" She spoke like they were in the middle of a conversation, which Courtney was rudely trying to leave.

"I've met Margo before," Courtney replied. Her tone sounded neutral enough to her own ears. But Cassandra's sienna eyes sparked like she'd just thrown out a provocation.

"Oh," said the red smile. "Then you know who she is."

Courtney glanced past her to the hallway. "She's a street kid, who W's taking care of for some reason."

Cassandra's smile grew. "That would be charitable, wouldn't it?"

"Did you want to talk to me for some reason?"

Her own boldness surprised her. Cassandra radiated danger, from the little black dress that split over a knife sheathed at her thigh to the hard, dark light behind her eyes. Courtney realized the woman was older than herself by at least ten years. Maybe fifteen. Her age only sharpened her beauty. She felt self-conscious under that glittering stare.

"We haven't officially been introduced," Cassandra said. "Of course, I know who you are. And you know who I am. But I'd be a poor host if I tossed the formality."

She stuck out a hand. Courtney stared at the offering. Adrenaline coiling in her belly, she took it. Cassandra's long fingers squeezed.

"I never thought he'd actually bring you. Seems a little cruel, given your…" She gestured up and down. A melodic laugh left her lips. Courtney pulled her hand away.

"I'm not sure I know what you mean."

Her smile turned sympathetic, a wry twist of pity as she cocked her head, eyes hooded. "You're in love with him."

Courtney laughed. The jerk in her chest hurt, involuntary and rough, less like a laugh than a spasm.

"It's alright," Cassandra said before she could protest. "A little sad, but understandable. You got caught up in the thrill of it all. The speed of our world. It's perfectly normal to hate your little life. But to follow him all the way out here… *Honey.*"

She patted Courtney's shoulder. Courtney stepped back.

"I'm not in love," she snapped. "I followed him because I…"

The words got stuck in a memory. The steady weight of his arms around her on a pitch-dark night, her hot tears soaking into his shirt. Raw fear and grief twisting her bones, threatening to splinter them. Holding onto him had kept the Change from ripping her apart. Another memory barged in. Her cheek on his shoulder, his chin on her hair as they danced to the radio in her kitchen.

Her throat tightened. Surely that hadn't just been his delirium. Surely he'd felt *something* too.

The cold kiss in the doorway. The crush of rejection as he'd turned away.

Cassandra's smile lost its edge. She sighed. Courtney felt the air around them change, her own open hostility melting into a kind of resignation. The corner of those red lips lifted, a sad tilt more unnerving than any sneer.

"You and I are not enemies." She leaned back against the door jamb. "I envy you, actually. You're right on the edge of this. Toes in the water. You can still run away."

"I'm not running."

Her eyes gleamed. Pitying. "Do you even know his real name?"

Courtney hesitated.

Cassandra closed her eyes. Her voice softened. "I can tell you the whole story of James Wilder. How he ran away from his abusive scumbag of a father at eleven. How he became the most feared mobster on the streets by the age of seventeen. How he returned after his sister's death, murdered his father, drove his own mother insane."

Courtney's stomach turned. "I don't want to hear any more."

"But you need to. I can see it in your eyes. You don't know him, but you want to and you're terrified to. Do you want to know how he did it? How he pushed me out of my own criminal empire, transformed the streets of Orion City into a network of people who fear him? Can't touch him?"

"No," Courtney whispered. They both heard the hollowness in the sound.

"Ask me anything." Cassandra leaned in, and Courtney caught the faint whiff of sulfur on her hair. Or was that gasoline? Gunpowder? "I can set you free. You can run before it's too late."

Courtney studied that gleam in her eye. She pressed her lips together.

"You've got a soft spot for Margo," Cassandra pressed. "Want to know the real reason he keeps her around? It's not out of the goodness of his heart."

Courtney's eyes slid to the cardboard castle on the floor. That awful spark of curiosity flickered. Cassandra's smooth voice fanned it like a dry wind.

"Her parents were AITO scientists. James killed them to gain access to their compound. He found Margo later when he raided their apartment for files on AITO's victims."

Courtney sucked in a breath. "He just... kept her?"

Cassandra nodded. "She was too little then to know much. Torch wanted to use her as bait to force her parents' colleagues to give up more valuable intel. But James knew AITO members aren't that soft-bellied. He took Margo in as his own. Forced to live with her parents' killer." Her vivid eyes traced Courtney's face, empty of the malice they'd held earlier. At least, they looked empty. "Still see him in that rosy light?"

Courtney's voice left her in a hollow rush. "I never saw him in a rosy light."

The two of them stared at each other. Only after the floor started to feel uneven under Courtney's feet did Cassandra step aside, freeing the doorway.

"Think about it," she said. "I'm just two flights up—the room next to W's—if the questions wake you in the middle of the night."

Courtney slid past her. "Thanks for... the official introduction."

The words fell out flat on the floor between them. Cassandra's lips gave the faintest shimmer of a smile. Slipping out into the hall, Courtney forced her feet to move calmly, casually, toward the stairwell.

They carried her back downstairs.

Thoughts flitted through her mind like signs past a bus window. Blurred, too fast to catch and interpret, colors and edges and lines tangled together. She hit the second floor and paused at the entrance to the hallway. The faint song of a violin trickled out to meet her.

What could she do? Pack her things and leave? She'd known W had his secrets, understood from the get-go that his alias as the Whistler had an ugly, shadowed history. He killed. He lied. The faintest echo of his trademark tune put fear on the wind, cleared any street. Even if he wasn't all the media blackened him to be, his reputation hadn't grown from nothing. So what if he was trying to free the Changers? So what if AITO was the real monster behind it all? W might be going after a bigger devil, but his methods made him no less of a villain.

It didn't matter if she was—if she had *feelings* for him. None of it mattered. He was a shadow. The longer she stayed with him, the darker she'd become.

She'd almost made up her mind to knock on Strings' door, grab her few possessions and wave a hasty goodbye, when the next thought crashed into her.

If she left, nothing would change. There would be no one there to stop him from continuing to kill. From orphaning more children like Margo. Torch would continue to burn, Deadeye and Red would continue to use lethal force, and W would plan it all, watching the death toll mount until he reached his goal. No. Leaving wouldn't solve anything.

But if she stayed…

The thought twisted her insides, crystallized into something sharp and metallic. She could make a difference. Stupid feelings or not, she was here for a reason. She could put a dent in the fight against AITO… but do it in the right way. She was on the inside now. She could reign in W's growing body count, stop him from killing. Learn to hit with vicious accuracy, all while using a tranq gun. She'd seen the flicker of interest in W's eyes when she'd suggested the tranquilizers. For some reason or another, her voice held some sway over this unstoppable force. She wasn't quite an immovable object—but she had some small amount of power here. Perhaps *only* here: on the inside of this renegade team, self-named the Loons. If she retreated back home to her little apartment to while away her hours making coffee, she'd lose this chance. And probably go insane, unable to fit back into the too-small shell of her old life. No. She couldn't give it up. This tiny chance to save her city, to change what could be without her. Her heart beat a little harder. What could be… *without* her. For the first time, she felt bigger than a dropout barista struggling to pay rent on Westside.

She was in the right place. At the right time.

And just maybe… she was the right person.

Her feet began to move again. She bypassed the second floor, then the first, until she hit the basement. The smell of greasy food drifted down the stairs from above, triggering a growl in her stomach. She grit her teeth and kept on going.

She practiced shooting through dinner. Then for hours more. At least, it felt like hours. With no windows or way to tell the time, all she had to measure her progress by was the tattered state of her cardboard targets and her growing exhaustion. Her fingers trembled. The muscles in her hands numbed, throbbed, then numbed again. The blisters on her thumb burned from straining against the kickback. Her shots didn't quite improve to an "A." Or even a "B," if W were there to judge. Her poor pizza boxes no longer looked remotely square. They hung mangled by threads of duct tape, revealing the millions of old scars in the wall. But she could still vaguely tell where her bullets landed. She hit the knees of the targets, the thighs, the sides of their chests. Nowhere a tranq needle might puncture something important, but high enough to drop a living target into a stupor. Hopefully.

She only set down the pistol when it hurt too much to shoot straight. Then, after shaking out her hands and rubbing the blood back into her fingers, she eyed the punching bags in the corner of the training room Red had told her to practice on. Maybe beating up the other side of her hands would give her something else to focus on. Crossing the room, she reached for the hand-wraps Red had left for her training sessions from the little stand behind the bags. A deep, slicing ache rippled through her. Up from her sternum, radiating all the way out through her fingers. She stopped, hand frozen mid-air.

The Change was always closer to the surface in exhaustion. Pausing a moment, Courtney withdrew her hand and stood there, quiet, eyes falling closed. She drew in a slow, even breath. It pressed deeper, edging in against her control: a fierce, silent demand.

It is *in my control.*

She let go. The odd release thundered through her, gentler than before, but still an earthquake of muscle and bone and blood rearranging within her skin. She sucked down a choked gulp of air, eyes squeezed shut, teeth gritted. When she met the concrete on all fours, the blast of smells assaulting her nose was dizzying. She waited, breathing until her pulse slowed, her aching bones stopped shaking.

It was faster this time. Her body didn't cling to the pain as long, or freeze in the shock of the Change like it once did. Her head cleared. Her eyes opened. Slowly, the world came back into crystal, calm focus.

She crouched there for an immeasurable moment, studying the dulled colors, the cacophony of scents, the distant pitch of voices and noises above. Her heart thumped back to a regular, sturdy beat.

Waiting. The fuzzy edges of her brain knew that was important, though it couldn't name why. She didn't know how much time passed before the Change shuddered through her again, pulling and twisting and shifting. Cold concrete met the bare skin of her palms, firm beneath her nylon-clad knees, and she saw the ends of own hair—vibrant copper again—hanging down to frame her vision.

Climbing back onto shaky feet, Courtney gripped the wobbling punching bag with both hands while she blinked for a few seconds. The leather creaked beneath her grip.

Okay. That wasn't so bad. It hurt, like always, but that was unavoidable. She'd pulled herself back on her own. At least—she'd come back to herself, maybe not as fast as she'd wanted, but she'd still managed to get back on her two human feet within a decent span of time. She could still hear the faint buzz of dinner going on upstairs.

Letting go of the punching bag, Courtney straightened the twisted sleeve around one elbow and bit her lip. She should probably try practicing that again. But the vulnerable, disoriented state of mind the Change left her in wasn't a feeling she welcomed. The prickle of anxiety that had driven her down here in the first place resurfaced—her careful, compartmentalized control fractured in the wake of the Change.

She could work on it more later. She could only run herself so ragged, tonight, and bruises on her skin were easier to deal with than emotions she couldn't name.

Moving for the table again, she picked up the long, leather strips and wound them around her knuckles.

The punching bag shuddered under each blow. Red had taught her how to catch it, to strike it at the right angles so it didn't swing back and knock her flat. Although it was good practice to dodge, when she did hit it wrong.

She didn't hear the door open. Muscles burning, heartbeat loud in her ears, she only realized she wasn't alone when a shadow approached from her right. Tall, slow, with gliding steps.

Her heart tugged. She knew who it was without turning her

head. The faint scent of peppermint, the almost-silent footfalls. How was it possible to know someone so well, down to the very rhythm of their walk, and yet not know them at all?

"You missed dinner," W said.

She continued slamming her fists into the bag. He watched her, silent for a moment, while she attacked the leather sack with renewed vigor.

"What are you doing?" he asked.

Courtney wiped a bead of sweat from her temple. "You told me to get some practice."

He sighed. "You can relax. You're not going on this job."

Courtney adjusted the wrappings around her fist. She didn't look at him.

"It takes time to build strength, develop instincts and a good shooting eye." W reached up to rest a hand at the top of the bag, stilling its shuddering swing. "There will be other raids."

"That's the problem." The words jerked out, echoing his from earlier. "How many raids will there be, James? How many more orphans will you make before this is all over?"

She looked up just in time to see him blink. Either at the sound of his real name, or her harsh accusation. Stepping back, she dropped her still-clenched fists to her sides and filled her lungs. Courage usually grew from anger when she spoke this freely to him, but now she pulled it from somewhere else. Some place deeper, a hollow in her chest that didn't burn hot and dark, but sure and cool. A determination grounded her. Her words were going to count. Immovable object or not, if she had any influence here at all, it was with this force. This force she needed to understand.

"I know about Margo. I know you murdered her parents."

For the first time, his carefully blank expression cracked. He looked away from her.

"Killing is a part of what I do. You knew that from the beginning."

"From the beginning," she repeated. "I've been trying to piece together who and what you are, and everything is a contradiction. How you act around Margo. Then how you act around Torch, Deadeye, the rest of the team. How you act around me…" She swallowed. "How you act around Cassandra."

W's eyes flickered to the ceiling. "She's been talking to you, has she?"

"She shouldn't have to be the one to tell me who you are. I don't trust her to tell the truth, anyway."

"But you'd trust me to?"

"You said you've never lied to me."

His gaze fell back to her. Those eyes looked different than she'd ever seen them. The mask had dropped away, and they rippled, burning with something barely contained.

"It's not a pretty story."

Courtney met his stare dead on. "I wouldn't believe you if it was."

The height seemed to leak from his shoulders. He chuckled, lowered his head, and moved away, taking a few steps toward the wall beside the punching bags. He slid down to sit against it, elbows on his knees, facing her. "What more could you want to know about a murdering psychopath who orphans children?"

His voice started out light, but flattened by the end of the question. Like the words stripped away even his talent for nonchalance.

Courtney loosened the strips around her knuckles, unwrapped her aching hands, and returned the leather padding to the stand. She sat down beside him. "All of it," she said. "Margo, your father, Jessica. Why a mobster who owned the streets would turn his sights on an enemy like AITO. The whole ugly truth."

His smile was thin as he tipped his head back against the wall. "That's a lot of ugly. You might run before I finish answering the first question."

"I'm not going anywhere." Courtney pulled her knees to her chest, closing her arms around them. "I threw my cards on the table when I followed you here. It'd be nice if you trusted me enough to do the same."

"Hmm," he murmured. "You did, didn't you."

Why did she have to bring it up? Now they were both thinking about it—that embarrassing kiss in her apartment. No way to pretend it had never happened. She couldn't look at him, but she felt the air change slightly between their bodies. She picked at a loose thread on her knee.

"I had a sister," he finally said. "Jessica. She was five—Margo's age—when my father killed her."

Courtney heard her own blood rushing in her ears in the silence that followed.

"It was my fault," he went on. "He used to concentrate his experiments on me. Selfish brat that I was at eleven, I didn't think past my own skin when I ran away. I was his prototype—his proof that human beings could survive and thrive after theriomutation. When I left, he turned his attention to Jessica. He was more ruthless, more reckless as he tried to duplicate his first success. Her blood couldn't take it—her *body* couldn't take it. She died before I learned what he was doing."

Courtney fought against the lump in her throat. She imagined losing Michael. Remembered the flickers of violence she'd seen in her own father before he'd conquered his drinking problem. "You were just a kid. You couldn't have stopped him."

"I could've diverted his attention if I'd stayed." W paused. "She'd be about Red's age now, if I had."

"Or maybe not," Courtney whispered. "Maybe your father would've killed you, and then moved on to her."

W shrugged. "Maybe. But he always talked about my DNA like a living miracle. It endured every mutation, only growing stronger. If I'd stayed, he might've found the element he was looking for. Might've finally perfected his serum. The government might never have shut down his program, he might never have snapped and turned Orion City into his last experiment."

The realization jerked through her like the kickback of a pistol. "*He* was the one who infected the reservoir? Who created the Changers?"

W nodded. "I tracked him down too late. When I finally scraped up the courage to confront him, he told me his plan. His mind was so far gone, he thought we were in it together, thought I'd figure myself a hero for contributing my genes to history. I acted without thinking. Six years on the streets had taught me how to kill." W lifted a hand, palm up, and studied the lines of his fingers. "I thought I'd prevented him creating others like me. I didn't know he'd already done it."

Courtney watched the hand close into a fist. She searched for the horror within herself, any trace of a normal response to such a story. But she felt only grief.

"I'm sorry," she whispered.

W blew out a breath, blinking as if coming back to himself. "It's ancient history."

"You said once the Changers were your responsibility. I guess now I understand."

He shook his head. "If you understood, I wouldn't like you half as much as I do."

Something warm skittered through her. She pressed it down.

"It's not so hard to comprehend. You're not fighting AITO for revenge, or creating Changers from some twisted desire to finish what your father started. You're fighting to make things right."

He stared at her. "The way you phrase things makes me sound almost pardonable."

"Well…" Her eyes slid away from the intensity of his. "Not all of it. There's still a little girl upstairs with no parents to go home to."

"Ah," W said. "That's not a pretty story, either."

"Tell me why."

"Why I killed them? They were AITO. Easier targets than the other scientists. They tried to have it both ways: live a normal life, raise a family on the outside of that concrete fortress."

"I meant… why you kept her."

He hesitated. "I didn't know anyone else was in the apartment. It was a fast job. Clean. They were both in the living room. Amanda and Tyson…" He closed his eyes. "I cleared out all their files, every last scrap of research from the back office, and was passing back through the living room on my way out when I heard the static. That's when I saw the baby monitor on the table."

Courtney exhaled. The air felt crushed coming from her lungs. "She heard?"

"Undoubtedly. Amanda screamed. I'd gotten Tyson first."

A sound leaked out of her throat. W opened his eyes. He looked down at his hands again, long white fingers curling open in the light. Like giant pale spiders. Death lay between those fingers.

Courtney wondered how many times they'd been stained scarlet.

"It shook me," he whispered. "Seeing her there. Huddled on the floor next to that tiny bed. I didn't know what to do. She didn't make a sound. Just looked up at me with these huge brown eyes."

The white outline of his fingers trembled. "Killing her wouldn't be like killing my father. It wouldn't be like killing an AITO scientist. Someone cold-blooded, more computer than human. It wouldn't be like killing someone on the streets. My knife against theirs, kill or be killed. No. Killing her would be... something else. Something darker than any place I realized I ever wanted to go."

He went quiet, so long that she worried he wouldn't continue the story. But he spoke again, his voice barely audible. "I look at her every day and wonder when she'll be old enough to understand. Who I am, what I did. All I took from her. But she sticks to me like *I'm* her parent. It's sick."

She touched his arm. The move surprised her—and him, his muscles going stiff beneath her hand. "You have a conscience," she whispered.

He laughed hoarsely. "That's punishment in and of itself. I couldn't take her to CPS—this godforsaken city doesn't have one. Without me, she'd be dead or on the streets. I couldn't leave her." He shook his head. "But *without* me, she'd probably be in kindergarten somewhere, playing and talking like a normal child. Not a kid surrounded by freaks and violence. What sort of role models are we?"

Quiet settled between them. Courtney realized how unused to silence she'd become in these past days. The Dugout buzzed with constant noise. Shouts over a game of cards. The intermittent knock of boots on the ground as the trio practiced kickboxing. Red's pitchy laughter, and occasional holler when a scuffle went too far. Down here, the silence hung on the air like a foreign scent, uncomfortable and refusing to be ignored.

Freaks and violence. Oddly enough, she felt more unnerved by the absence of it all. She imagined a red light blinking somewhere, signaling the time for a checkup on her mental health.

"You can run," W said at last. "No one will come after you. We'll set up camp somewhere else, so you won't be liable for knowing our location."

"What?" Courtney blinked. "You think I'm going to run?"

He watched her as if she were a wild creature: unpredictable, potentially dangerous. It was the same look he'd given her in the doorway to her apartment. The one that lit her blood on fire.

"I'm not running," she repeated firmly, almost harshly, the same promise she'd given Cassandra. "I knew what you were before. But now I know something else. You told me once I was driven by a moral code. So are you. You said a city like this should've destroyed someone like me. But *you*... all those skeletons should've destroyed you, turned you into something without a conscience. Someone who wouldn't have spared the daughter of his enemies. Who wouldn't devote his life to freeing Changers from the hell you had to go through. You *aren't* that someone, W. You're... I don't know what you are, but you're not someone that scares me. Not anymore."

He stared at her with a look of such unmasked shock, the seriousness inside her cracked, and she almost giggled. An incredulous laugh trickled up from his chest instead. "You never cease to surprise me."

She found herself smiling at him. A real smile, free of fear and suspicion and doubt. His pale eyes latched onto it. Rested there a beat too long.

She cleared her throat. The heat from earlier found her cheeks again, and she stood up, returning to her abandoned punching bag. "Well, I hope to surprise you again on the raid tomorrow. I've still got till sunup before my week of practice is gone. Now if you don't mind, I was making real progress before you distracted me..."

She reached for the leather hand-wraps again, resting on the stand beside the wall.

His hand stopped her. He stood in one fluid motion, fingers trapping hers to the stand.

"C…" There it was. The edge that had been missing from his voice. "I believe we had this conversation."

Courtney attempted to tug her hand free, but it may as well have been nailed down. "I told you I'm not running away. I'm already part of this fight." She waved over toward the gun range, across the training room. "Even if I'm not good enough to punch anybody, look at my targets. I hit almost every man. If those were tranqs, every guy would be down. I can help. No one would have to die."

"That's not the point. *They're* not shooting tranqs. And I don't waste—"

"I know," she cut him off, voice rising. "You don't waste people. But you need every person on your team you can get. I promise, W, I won't get in the way, I'll—"

"This isn't a negotiation."

"But that's—"

His grip switched to her arms, shaking her a little. "You. Are. not. Going. End of discussion. If you fight me on this, I'll have Red lock you in the basement until the team gets back. I mean it. Some people are replaceable. Others—" The word caught on itself. "Others are not."

Their faces were inches apart. Any argument left on her tongue evaporated, the air in her chest squeezing. She forced herself to swallow.

"Why do you care if I go or not?" she whispered. "I'm the most replaceable member on your team. Just let me fight. So long as I hit the bad guys… I'll do my best not to be a waste."

The look on his face almost burned her. "You are the furthest thing from replaceable."

"Don't." She shut her eyes, blocking out those gray ones. So close, *too* close. "You saw my cards, don't play with me. I'm just a fool who followed somebody into a lion's den. I know it's one-sided, but I'm somehow ridiculous enough to stay even though—"

He kissed her. Shock ripped through her body, so electric her eyes flew open. She gasped—but he stole it, lips crushing hers. The force took her almost off her feet, his grip on her arms digging in, lifting her from her toes. She reached for him to steady herself. Her eyes fell closed.

He didn't let her go until she pushed her hands to his chest, begging oxygen. He pulled back, but kept their lips an inch apart. His breath tickled her cheek.

"That would be my fault," he murmured.

It took a minute to remember she had lungs. "What would?"

"If you thought this was one-sided."

The raggedness in his voice launched a shiver down her spine. Courtney tried to think, to push through the thoughts muddling in her mind. She was hyper-aware that his hands had left her arms, one threaded through the hair behind her ear, the other at her waist. Her own still rested on his chest.

"But—Cassandra," she blurted out. "She's been with you since... I mean, I thought you two were..."

He smoothed the hair back from her temple. "*Were.* In a different time, a different place. Cassandra is a woman from my past." The pale gleam of his irises darkened. "Who would very much like to keep me there."

"I don't understand. Why didn't you say something? Give some sort of sign, or..." Courtney trailed off, lost in the sensation of his fingertips against her hair. "That kiss in my apartment," she struggled out. "You made me feel like I was out of my mind, imagining anything between us."

The hand in her hair stilled. His eyes slid away, shuttered just fast enough that she got the distinct impression he was worried she might read them. W, worried *she* might read *him*.

And then, suddenly, she could. The realization threw a sharp light over everything, and she saw it all as if for the first time. The things he'd said, before and after she'd learned he was the Whistler. Testing her out. Feeling to see if she would spook, run away as soon as the shadows got too dark. *You don't belong in my world…*

"You thought I would run," she whispered. "You believed one day I'd see you for what you were, and it would be too much. You never imagined I would stay."

He kept his eyes down, but the flash of vulnerability she glimpsed in them stunned her. Boldness swelled. She slid her hands up from his chest to his jaw, tilting his face toward her. She held him there until he met her eyes.

"Do you see me running?" she whispered.

She felt the muscles in his neck tense as he swallowed. His eyes ticked between hers, reading her sincerity. Doubting it. Craving it. Picking it apart. She could see it all, finally, right there on his face. He'd never let her get this close.

"I don't care about what you were," she whispered. "I care about who you're going to be."

The light changed in his gray eyes. From wariness to confusion to stunned disbelief. Stretching up on her toes, Courtney pulled him back down.

He returned the kiss. Gripping her like a man who wasn't quite sure she was real.

7. DEADEYE

"WELL, WOULD YA look at that," Red drawled, leaning back against the gun range wall and popping bright red bubble gum between her teeth. "Somebody's got luck on her side. You get two more days."

Wiping a bead of sweat from above her eye, Courtney switched the gun to her other hand. Blisters stung the curve of skin between thumb and knuckle, rubbed raw from gripping through the kickback. All this back-to-back training hadn't given her fatigued fingers any time to toughen up.

"Two days?" She tugged one foam earplug free, glancing between Red and Deadeye, her trainer, who stood a few paces away with folded arms.

"They postponed the raid." Deadeye's voice always put Courtney a little on edge. The low, gravelly bass carried a dark note of disdain that never seemed to fade—at least when directed at her. "Friday is the earliest the weather clears. The ice on the roads is too thick for even Des to navigate a quick getaway."

"Which gives you one more chance." Red said. "Boss gave you the green light to tag along, *if* your defense skills are up to par."

Bang. Snap.

Down the gun range, a dozen other Dugout members honed their skills against the cardboard silhouettes on the far wall. Half new recruits, half old members blowing off steam: their skill contrasts were apparent inside the spray of bullet holes in each target. The newbies clipped and peppered; the more seasoned members hit the center of mass every time.

Courtney's own bullets hit her flat dummy every other shot. Its chest area was embarrassingly clean.

At least its face was, too.

...to Deadeye's disapproval.

When she'd told them she'd be shooting tranqs, the cold glint behind her trainer's uncovered golden eye had grown cooler. And here she'd thought he'd been warming up to her.

"Let's hope you stay lucky." Red clicked her gum, and grinned. "If the weatherman's any more reliable than the rest of these fake-ass reporters, you get two more days. Two days to shape up until we ship out. Otherwise Strings is babysitting you."

"Strings isn't going?"

"We already got a scout on this mission. Deadeye's the better option for this kind of job anyway."

"Why?"

Red shrugged, blowing a bubble in her boyfriend's direction with a sly, deliberate pop. "You'll see."

Catching her gaze, Courtney's trainer glared at her with his single eye, as if daring her to question him. That golden stare pierced. Courtney did her best not to stare back.

"You'll be my shadow." Red saved her from scraping up a reply. "If your luck's as good as your aim by Friday. You won't be Changing on this job—first time's always a dummy run for new recruits, making sure they can stick to their lead and follow directions. We don't need some untried Changer going loony on us and throwing the whole op sideways."

Courtney fidgeted with the grip of the gun. "Makes sense."

"Our target's Pierce & Bailey's," Red continued, referencing the tallest building in Orion City. "The law office is actually a front for an AITO storage facility. That sixteen-story roof is where they chopper in their supplies. According to W's source, they just got a huge drop of medical equipment and weapons stock. We'll have to clean them out. Last thing the White Coats need is more weapons."

Hands itching for movement, Courtney unclicked her pistol's magazine and reached for the box of bullets on the gun range wall. It didn't need a reload quite yet, but she busied herself pressing the bullets into the clip anyway.

"You're scared," Deadeye grunted. "Not too late to stay behind."

"I want to go."

"Tranqs shoot slower." Colder, sharper. "If you're too squeamish to be of real help to us, you may as well stay back with the cat and the mouse. I don't take deadweight along."

So Books wasn't going either? "I won't be deadweight."

"Oh?" His single syllable prickled her spine. Courtney looked up to see Deadeye pushing off from where he leaned against the range wall, the thin slant of his mouth curling at the end. "We'll see."

Swallowing, Courtney clicked the magazine back into place. She switched the safety off, lifted the gun, and pinned the dummy in her sights.

Bang.

Bang, bang.

"What'd you say W gave you, a C minus?" Red whistled at the three crisp new holes in Courtney's target. "I'd say you're up to a B minus now at least."

"F," said Deadeye. "She's shooting for the legs."

"A smaller target, but she's still hitting them."

"You can live without a leg. You can't live without a face."

"But these will be tranqs," Courtney said. "W gave me permission to swap out real bullets. A hit to the leg will still—"

"*W* isn't going on this job," Deadeye snapped. "He can hand out pity letter grades to anybody he wants on the range, but this is a pass/fail op. You get someone killed because you're avoiding headshots, you're deadweight." She flinched back when he loomed forward. "*Dead* weight if you drag us down with you."

"He's got a point." Red pursed her lips. "You might be a night-and-day better shot than you were last week, but if you're avoiding headshots and missing center of mass just to make sure you're not killing the enemy, that's a liability." She chewed thoughtfully, then snapped her fingers. "I know! You need a pop quiz. A test to see if you can hit under pressure. Babe, where's that ribbon we used last time?"

Deadeye narrowed his eye. "You couldn't hit it."

"I could at *close* range. But hey, she's W's little protegé isn't she? Maybe her luck'll hold."

The spark of mischief under Red's voice made Courtney turn. "Ribbon?"

"This." From the pocket of his leather jacket, Deadeye pulled out a thick scarlet ribbon the length of his forearm. A small tear hung frayed silk near the top, and a second slice halfway through the width of it fluttered a few inches from the bottom. "Moving target practice."

"Moving," Courtney repeated, wary.

"All your targets will be moving on the job," said Red. "If you're serious about going, show Deadeye you're not deadweight. Hit it… without hitting *him*."

Courtney stiffened, at the same moment Deadeye's smirk vanished in a blur of shadow and feathers. The jacket dropped to a crumpled leather heap; above, an owl fluttered to a perch on the range wall. The great horned head turned to fix her with a golden stare—one eye clouded—and a nearly five-foot wingspan spread wide enough to brush her arm. She stepped back.

Red let out a low whistle, and held up a hand. Wickedly long talons picked up the ribbon with razor delicacy, and the owl relocated with one powerful flap onto the leather brace Red wore on her forearm. She didn't wince as the talons dug into the material. Deadeye's nylon jumpsuit hung loosely around the owl's enormous body—twin slashes cut for wings and claws.

"Seriously, don't hit him." Red pressed a kiss to the side of the owl's feathered head while he locked Courtney in his unblinking stare. "These claws can dig in five hundred pounds of pressure per square inch, so he won't be happy if you chip one." She winked. "Avoid the money-makers, hit the target, and you ace this test."

"Wait." Courtney inhaled. "I'm supposed to try to hit that thing while he's moving?"

"You catch on quick."

Red dropped her arm with a jerk, and the owl took flight. Courtney skittered back as he swiped over her head. Her hair fluttered.

"But—" She couldn't blurt out much more than that before he looped back around, scarlet ribbon swinging from his taloned grip.

She lifted the gun with shaking fingers—then, horrified, pulled it back. "I'm not going to shoot live bullets at your boyfriend."

Red smirked. "And here I thought you'd totally do it for a second. Here." Plucking away Courtney's gun, she pressed the grip of a larger pistol into her palm. "Try this on for size."

The weight of this one felt different. Hollower. Looking down, Courtney recognized the dark green band of a modified tranq barrel. She squeezed her lips together.

I can't hit him.

The owl's graceful soar stole the attention of the rest of the training range. Gunshots ceased; conversations dimmed. People paused to watch Deadeye's silent arc up through the ceiling beams, around the crumbling support pillars at the far end of the room and circling back, wings barely dipping as they carried him down again. His one-eyed stare held only Courtney, horned head twisting in an unnatural swivel as he glided by.

Red snorted. "You just gonna gawk?"

The sights shook in her grip as she tried to pin him down.

"Any day now," someone whooped from across the room, followed by snickers.

The trigger sweated under her finger. Deadeye's silhouette flickered in and out of her sights. If she hit him, at this height, even with a tranq, would the fall kill him? Despite the chill in the basement, the back of her neck felt hot as everyone's eyes gripped her.

"Stop hazing the new girl." A new voice slid from the stairway. "Nobody could hit that."

Courtney had never been happier to hear Books' dry monotone.

Red turned, blew an enormous bubble, and popped it with a smack. "I could."

"You couldn't," Books returned.

"Wanna bet?"

Glasses glinting under the fluorescents, Books folded his arms and leaned against the doorjamb the way he had when he'd peeked in on Courtney's first training session with Strings. "First pick of the loot after the job."

"Ha! You're on."

Red reached up, removed her gum and stuck it on the range wall. With a shameless flip of her braids, she planted a boot on the wall and unsheathed a knife at her thigh.

Books' gaze flickered to the gum on the wall, squished between the bricks just below the ammo refills, then back up to Red with an unimpressed twitch of his eyebrow. She shot him a bright grin full of teeth. Then in one fluid motion, she turned and hurled the knife straight across the training range at her boyfriend.

The blade sang. It hit the wall an inch below the owl gliding past and screeched down the bricks, dropping with a clatter. Deadeye didn't flinch. Soaring on steady wings, he drifted on, circling the end of the room to loop back around. The ribbon flickered from the ends of his talons, bright and untouched.

"C'mon, Red!" a throaty voice yelled across the room. One of the brawlers from the trio Courtney always saw sparring upstairs. The one with the ponytail—she didn't know his name.

"Yeah," shouted his friend, a short woman covered in scars. "That the best Blade Beauty's got?"

Red growled, the edge of her smirk dimming as she pulled out a second knife: a wide, wicked looking thing with a heavy base. Curling her arm back behind her head, she snapped it forward and released with a quick breath. The knife hissed through the air.

KLANF.

It scraped down the wall and smacked the concrete.

Courtney dug her fingernails into the grip of her gun, watching

Deadeye dip and glide with practiced ease, avoiding the beams and pillars scattered throughout the enormous training range. He swung back around with almost mocking grace, tucking one talon up closer to his nylon-wrapped ribcage—as if daring Red to take sharper aim.

Red did. With a determined glint in her eye that made Courtney step back, she threw knife after knife. They dropped and clacked one by one off the walls and ceiling. One unlucky trainee dove out of the way when Deadeye's path drew the knives too close to the populated end of the gun range; a knife arced down and stuck straight up from a crack in the concrete inches from where he'd just stood.

Huffing, Red fiddled with her empty case of knife sheaths at her hip. One dark cheek twitched, and then both filled up with air and blew back out in a sharp, amused chuff. "Alright, Four Eyes." She spun on her heel, lifted the corner of the knife-belt like a skirt and dipped her knees in a goofy curtsy. "You get first pick-through of Friday's goodies. Nobody could hit that."

"W could," Books said.

Red rolled her eyes. "Nobody *besides* W."

Courtney's memory flickered, planting an image she'd tried to forget back in her mind's eye. The Whistler, dressed in the face of a dead man, lifting a gun and putting a point-blank bullet into a man's head—leaving a precise hole in the mirrored spot the thug had kicked her.

Her forehead throbbed. Shuddering, she gripped her own tranq-filled gun and diverted her attention back to the owl fluttering to a perch on one of the support beams stretched across the wide ceiling.

In one smooth contortion, he Changed. Feathers traded out for sinewed bare arms, beak for angled human features, and Deadeye glared down at her. He perched on the support beam, nylon suit stretched back to normal capacity—bony bare feet gripping the wooden edge with Strings' acrobatic precarity.

The eyepatch was gone. Lost somewhere in the transition. A cloudy dead eye stared down at her with the same ferocity of the golden one, freezing her in place.

Was this how mice felt under an owl's gaze?

"The moving target is no hazing," he growled. "It's life and death. There is no *B minus* on a job. You hit them first, or you die. Dodge a bullet or take one, no in between." That single eye narrowed, burning gold. "Your inability to make a fatal shot isn't precision. It's not caution. It's soft, and AITO crushes soft."

"She'll be shooting tranqs," Red called up. "Her shots don't need to be fatal, they just need to land."

Courtney started, "I've been improving—"

"You couldn't even *fire* at me."

"But that ribbon was—"

"I don't care if the ribbon was impossible to hit. The fact was you didn't shoot. And that's deadweight if I ever saw it."

Courtney grit her teeth and squeezed the gun, but had no words to fire back at those mismatched eyes. He was right. She hadn't pulled the trigger. If Books hadn't walked in, she would've stared down the barrel for minutes more, maybe longer, before Deadeye and Red ended the exercise.

"She's got till Friday," Red said.

"And I've got final say on whether she goes." Deadeye's scowl swung to Red. "You want to risk an op this big for a pet project?"

Red held up a fingerless gloved hand. "No skin off my nose." She tipped her head. "But I liked her tranq idea. She's innovative. We could use that kind of new-blood thinking."

"New-blood thinking and new-blood *doing* are two separate

things."

"I'm saying give her a chance."

Courtney held her ground as that dual-toned stare scraped back over her. If she looked hard enough, she could see the lines around Deadeye's clouded pupil from this distance, the downward slash of his scar matching the odd dark scratches across his iris.

"Fine," Deadeye said. "You can go if you hit me with a tranq."

Her spine tensed. "What?"

"Hit me. Before I hit you."

He gave her no time to respond. Within the space of a blink, he was wings and feathers and talons again, barreling down at her with all the speed of a diving bird of prey.

Courtney skittered back. Boots scritching on the floor, she almost lost her balance lunging away from the talons that scraped her hair. Not fast enough. The tearing sound hit her senses a second before the pain—either the nylon suit or her skin opening, she couldn't tell—until the fiery sting up her arm made it clear it was both.

With a hoarse cry, she dropped to a crouch, raising her arms above her head.

The hard *whap* of wings above kicked her instincts into panic. As they closed back in, she raised the gun, fired off a wild shot.

Red's laugh rang out. "Come on, babe, give her a break!"

Courtney tried to right her stance, stumble back in the safety of Red's direction, but Deadeye's shadow swarmed in again. The talons scraped down a new tear on her opposite forearm. Hot and smarting.

She yelled, firing off another blind shot.

Open your eyes! Instinct screamed. *Hit him!*

She did—at least, she opened her eyes and squeezed the trigger.

But Deadeye didn't go down under her fire.

The gunshot cracked across the room, deafening in the pause that had swallowed the range as everyone watched the newbie get attacked by the Dugout's fiercest marksman.

Deadeye's owl form jerked back in a flurry of feathers, and raced back up to the ceiling to scramble onto a perch. He Changed on the beam and almost fell off. Bare hands and feet clinging to the scratched-up wood, chest heaving, eyes wide. His hair hung over his clouded eye.

"What the hell," he rasped.

Courtney turned to see where he was staring—and caught W's tall, imposing silhouette in the center of the room, gun cocked, eyes dead-locked on his target.

Had he been there the whole time? Wearing someone else's inconspicuous face? Blending in with the new recruits, a shadow in the background...

Red took a step back. Shooting a furtive glance up toward Deadeye, she made no other move. The rest of the gun range stood equally still, eyes dancing between their raid leader and W. A few murmured amongst themselves. A smirk, a twinkling exchange of glances. Silent bets placed.

Slowing the quick, birdlike heave of his chest, Deadeye settled lower on the beam and glared at W. "You clipped a wing."

"Did I hit ya?" Dry, light. W's voice sounded out of place— too chipper, like it had back when Courtney had first met him. The hidden edge of a blade.

Deadeye looked down and checked his hands, turning each one over and wiggling his long fingers. Scowl deepening, he sat back and pointed to the ground. Three large feathers lay on the concrete, torn and bent.

"Those don't grow back overnight, you know."

"Feathers don't bleed." The blade sharpened behind W's smile. "She does. Watch yourself."

"We have a job on Friday," Deadeye shot back. "You really want me flying crooked?"

Off-kilter grin tipping further, W twirled the gun by the handle. His silver tooth flashed. Courtney's memory snapped back to that day in the cafe, when he'd done that very thing wearing a stranger's face. She'd flinched then.

She didn't now.

"I'll clip the other side so you're even," W said. "Why don't you take another lap around the room?"

Fear flickered behind Deadeye's stern face. His eyes dropped. "I'm good."

"No, really." The lightness seared, a bright toothy threat. "Show us that little trick with the ribbon again. I'd love to put everyone's little theory to the test. Get some practice flying straight with a few inches less wing."

Deadeye's throat bobbed. Holding W's gaze for a minute longer, he ducked his head and exhaled. Shoulders bent and curved, skeleton rearranged. The great horned owl reappeared, picked up the ribbon with ginger talons, and took flight.

Nobody spoke. Or moved.

Smile gone, W lifted the gun again with lazy grace, pale eyes fixed on the owl's path across the room.

The muzzle flashed.

Now Courtney flinched. Without her earplugs, every shot vibrated her skull.

Bang. Bang. Bang.

The owl flinched, too. Gliding down to land on Red's outstretched leather-clad arm, he hunched himself into a tight ball of feathers, huge eyes flickering, talons digging in. His chest rose and fell in little jerks.

Red reached over and slid the ribbon from Deadeye's grip.

"Damn," she whistled.

Three holes punched a perfect straight line up the ribbon, the highest an inch from the crinkled silk where Deadeye's talons had gripped.

Someone hooted from the back of the room. Claps broke out, then a few rounds of *I-told-you-so*'s traded between the older Loons as applause built among the new recruits.

Slipping the gun back into his coat, W strode in the direction of the stairwell. He cracked his trademark silver grin as he passed, dropping a flat-handed pat to the top of Deadeye's head. The feathered horns flattened over irritated owl eyes.

"Books, you're our next-best shot," W announced. "Why don't you swap out C's teacher for a spell?"

Leaving a disgruntled raptor in his wake, W ignored the stares following him as he nodded Books out of his way and climbed the steps, whistling a cheery tune.

The four-note melody faded onto the second floor.

Conversations bounced back, followed quickly by the sharp pops of target practice.

Courtney tugged her gaze off the stairwell—and her eyes collided with Deadeye's. She did her best not to shrink under the fire in that golden orb.

Red chuckled. Drawing her arm up, she planted a firm kiss on the side of the owl's head.

"Lighten up." She clicked her tongue. "You're lucky he only took off three feathers. You should've seen Torch's ear."

A hard poke at the back of her arm made Courtney jump. She turned to see Books returning his own arms to a folded position, stepping back. This close, she realized they were the same height:

short, unimpressive. His cool gaze made up for the intimidation factor.

"You gonna stand around all day?" He reached out a palm, and Red handed him the gun she'd taken from Courtney. "I won't rip my trainees' arms off, but I don't let them waste space either. Put that thing down and let's go again."

Straightening her shoulders, Courtney set the tranq gun down on the range wall, took the Glock from Books, and let out a steadying breath. "I'll aim higher."

She did.

Jasper had gotten used to Oliver dragging him out of the station on lunch breaks over the busy year they'd known each other. Most days, they'd head to Jessie's Joe, find a spot near the window—since his precinct office had none—and his best friend would force his headspace out of whatever case he'd sunken into. Today, they sat stuffed into a corner booth at Cream & Sugar, down the street from Courtney's old café, listening to the hum of unfamiliar customers and baristas around them. Jasper couldn't stomach the thought of going back to Jessie's. Not when he'd see a stranger's face behind the counter.

"*Ayoo*! That's our boy!"

The sudden whoop erupted into claps and more cheers, applause multiplying across the tables around them. Jasper glanced up to see the TV mounted in the corner of the café—not featuring a game, but a news report. A huge, telltale black-clad man hopped from rooftop to tiled rooftop, racing over the buildings of lower Eastside. The shaky footage cut to a reporter and the headline rolling across the bottom of the screen. *Orion Giant wreaks havoc on Eastside Triad drug-house, destroys 1,000 lbs of narcotics.*

His teeth ground together.

Across from him, Oliver turned in his booth. Catching sight of the TV, he paused a moment, the still-visible side of his face twitching in an expression Jasper couldn't see. He turned back around with a politely neutral expression.

"Clap if you want to," Jasper sighed. As much as Oliver tried to hide it, Jasper knew he was a fan of the colossal vigilante.

"Aren't you happy?"

"McCoy and Patton were monitoring that ring. Now they'll just relocate before we can move in."

"The OCPD should've moved in a long time ago," Oliver countered. "The Giant just took a thousand pounds of drugs off the streets. I'd call that a win, no matter who did it."

"It's not a *win* when a vigilante's flaunting to the whole city that he can break the law to get stuff done, just like those criminals."

"The vigilantes do more for the streets than the law's done in a decade. You can't deny that."

"The law's the only thing this city has that's stable, Oliver." Setting down his sandwich, Jasper leaned back to look his friend in the eye. "What happens when one of those vigilantes decides to use their freak power to keep the next drugs they bust? Or take advantage of an innocent person? What's to stop another maniac like the Torch, blowing up half of Eastside for kicks?"

Oliver's jaw flexed, muscles jumping in his cheek. "Then I guess we'll just have to trust the ones who *are* fighting to do what's right, and back them up."

The two glared at each other a moment. It was odd—Oliver had been treading into the unspoken No Man's Land between them more and more lately, forsaking his usual easy-going demeanor to poke at Jasper's convictions in not-so-subtle ways. They'd always held a silent respect for the other's views, however opposite, as long as they'd been friends. Jasper wondered what had changed.

Their strange, stiff silence didn't have long to fester. The snap of high-heels pounded toward them, followed by a familiar voice: "*What* the hell is this?"

Jasper looked up just in time to see a flash of black-and-white before Dina slapped the paper against his chest. He caught it as she let go, and stared down at the colorless print of a painfully familiar smile.

"You have a warrant out for Courtney's arrest?"

Tearing his eyes away from the shy glimmer of teeth and reluctant sparkle in Courtney's dark eyes, laughing at whoever had taken the photograph, Jasper set the poster face-down on the table. "It's out of my hands."

"Bullshit! You *turned her in*. With *no* proof."

"St. Barnabas submitted their CCTV footage to the police station. It clearly shows Courtney Spencer holding a man at gunpoint in the med supply room." Finally looking at Dina's flushed, angry face, Jasper continued, "Someone even gave her the codes to the room. Wonder who that could be?"

Scarlet stole over Dina's already darkened cheeks, making the spark in her eyes flare hotter. "There's got to be some mistake. Courtney's not a violent person."

Jasper's fist curled over the paper. "How well do you actually know her?" Wincing at the pain behind his sternum, he took a breath, and let his voice soften. "You say you're best friends, but has she contacted you since she left?"

Dina's voice wavered. "She's... still the same person." Eyes fixed on the paper under Jasper's hand, her throat bobbed. "I trust her *because* I know her. Whatever's going on, she's still Courtney."

He sighed. "I want to believe that."

"You *have* to believe that." Lowering her chin, Dina balled her own fists at her sides. They trembled. "I have to believe that," she whispered.

◆

Books' straightforward, no-nonsense way of teaching went a lot farther with Courtney than Deadeye's chilly instruction. By the time they'd finished at the gun range, the blisters on her hands burned more fiercely than ever, and her ears hummed when she pulled out the foam earplugs. But her muscles ached in a satisfying way.

She climbed the stairs with Books and Red, listening to their tête-à-tête bounce back and forth ahead of her. Deadeye had gone off on his own after shifting back to human form. Refusing to look at her, which she at least preferred to his freezing stare, he slunk off to the third floor alone, leaving Red to head up to dinner without him.

"Aw, let him nurse his pride," Red said, stomping up the last step to the ground floor. "Probably energy better spent regrowing his feathers, but that damned ego of his will need some coddling before he heads up Friday's raid."

"I didn't mean to hurt his ego," Courtney said.

"You didn't," Books replied. "W did."

"He needs a few knocks to his pride once in a while," Red said. "Boss' whole sharpshooting bit put him back in his place. He shouldn't have come after you like that."

Courtney waited for the qualifier, the harsh side-eye sent her way, but it never came. Knives clinking against her hip in their belted leather cases, red-streaked braids flipped over one shoulder,

Red clacked her gum against her teeth—she'd retrieved it from between the stones on the wall, much to Books' disgust.

"My guy's always been a little jealous of Boss," she said. "He was never second-best anywhere before the Dugout, but W's the real deadeye when it comes to marksmanship. Then, getting replaced by Four-Eyes didn't help. Boss might've rubbed it in a little hard today swapping him with the kid, who's nowhere near Deadeye's level—no offense, Books—"

"None taken."

"—but he was getting a little aggressive." Red sighed. "Sorry about that. He just… doesn't like your style. Rubs him the wrong way, I guess."

Courtney frowned. "My style?"

"You know. The soft, *I-can-keep-my-hands-clean* act. It won't last long here in the Dugout, and he gets pissed whenever somebody tries to keep it up. Takes it personal, I dunno. None of us could keep ours clean, so it sorta rubs wrong when a new-blood waltzes in thinking they can do better than us."

"I'm… sorry." She wasn't trying to hint she was better than anyone. She had no idea her goal to avoid killing might cause someone who did to take it… personally.

"Don't apologize for it." Red's voice firmed. "In my book, that's what'd make you soft. Stick to your guns—heh, your *tranq* guns—and show him you belong here. Show him you can bring something to the team, and he'll warm up." She paused. "And if he doesn't, well, tough luck. For him. 'Cause I think you belong here."

Warmth touched her throat in an unexpected squeeze, and Courtney took a few steps to chase down her voice. The toasty scent of pizza swelled as they neared the second floor.

"You said Deadeye could regrow the feather's W's bullet clipped?" Her memory flickered with an image of W crumpled on her blood-soaked sofa, teeth gritted, half conscious as she fought to stop him bleeding out. She remembered her panicky call to Dina, whose medical expertise gave way to stunned disbelief after they examined the fading wound. "Can Changers heal themselves? I mean, more than a normal human body can?"

"That's a complicated question," Books said.

"Some can," Red answered. "I can't. Deadeye can, sort of. At least, he's recovered from some pretty bad scrapes and slices." She fired a sideways grin at Courtney. "I claim responsibility for a few."

"How?" Before Red could elaborate on what kind of weird stuff she and her boyfriend got into, Courtney clarified: "How does healing work for a Changer?"

"You need to be able to focus the Change in isolated parts of the body," Books said. "Most of us don't have that kind of control. It's intensifying the Change—and keeping it controlled enough to hijack the process of tissue transfiguration, concentrating the Change into all the cells in the affected area, from skin to muscle to bone. Usually, Changing triggers like an instinct and the whole body follows that first wave. But if you get good enough, you can dial it back until you have control over just one area of the body. Basically, you speed up the body's natural process of healing by forcing tissue groups to shift back to their original state. It takes a lot of practice and only a few people here can do it. Nobody's as good as W."

"Yeah, well, he ripped his body apart ten times over before starting the Dugout," Red noted. "Put yourself through the kinds of hell he did, and you either learn how to heal or become a bloody mess stuck to the pavement in some back alley."

"Now *that's* a cute image." Strings' voice echoed down the stairwell. Courtney looked up to see her bounding down the steps toward them, balancing a pizza box on her head.

"I swiped this from Reggie; I'll trade pieces for backup in case he's hangry."

"Picking a fight with the Torch is not on my to-do list today," said Books.

"Shut up, I wasn't asking *you*, I was asking the real fighter here."

Red threw up a hand. "Last time I crossed Reggie, he burnt off half my weave. I'm still saving up for another one."

Courtney couldn't help but glance at the shaved side of Red's head; she'd thought it was a style choice, but now that she really looked, she saw the red-painted stripe on the side of Red's scalp covered up an uneven patch. She wondered why Red didn't arrange her braids to hide the bald spot.

"Oh, you think you look more badass this way and you know it." Strings spun the pizza box atop her head and caught it before it tipped. "I promise I'll share."

"He might have a soft spot for you, but I wouldn't push it," Books said. "He'll happily light up the rest of us to get his pizza back."

"He doesn't have a soft spot for me."

"Haven't you noticed? You look like his little dead Joanna."

Strings gasped, and almost dropped the pizza. "Are you crazy?" she hissed, tucking the box under her arm. "Don't say her name."

"She's right, Books, lower your voice." Red reached out and swiped the box from Strings. "Whatever. The new girl's with us, and he knows not to mess with her unless he wants another impromptu ear-piercing from W."

"Learn some sensitivity," Strings muttered to Books, falling in with them as they headed up the stairs.

"Sensitivity?" Books sounded genuinely confused. "It's obvious."

"He just likes that I mess with him; no one else has the balls to treat him like a real person."

"Yes, because he lights them on fire."

Red shushed them as they reached the top of the stairs.

The second floor sprawled out in front of them. Courtney paused in the doorway as her three companions strode on, taking in the space. The open middle level served as the center of activity for the Dugout, converted daily into a mess hall, game room, and anything else the crew wanted it to be—from sparring floor to napping space. The couches strewn about were almost all filled, save one in the corner. Her friends headed for it.

Catching up, Courtney sidestepped a game of cards taking place in the middle of the floor, muttering a quick apology as she shuffled between the wide circle of players. She spotted W on the edge of the circle, and their gazes brushed as she passed. A quick, crooked smile, and he returned his eyes to the players. She found herself grateful—she didn't want to stand out any more than she already had at the gun range today, and she wasn't sure how the rest of the Dugout would react if they suspected a deeper relationship between the latest new-blood and their leader.

Joining her little band on the couch, she found a spot big enough for her on a section of threadbare cushion between Strings and Red. A slice of pizza soared her way, and she caught it just before it splatted on her lap.

"Eat up!" Strings bellowed around a mouthful. "He can't take it back if it's already in us."

"I wouldn't issue that as a challenge," Books said from his perch on the back of the couch behind them.

Across the room, Courtney spotted the fiery-headed man in

question. She debated tossing the incriminating slice of pizza out of her hands, but she was already sandwiched between the culprits.

Yellow-tinged eyes skimmed over her, narrowed, and landed on Strings. The Torch shook his head. No real malice showed in his stare, and when her roommate gave him a cheeky wave he only scowled, turned to snatch an entire two boxes of pizza away from the trio of poker-players, and shuffled away with his prize.

"See?" Strings garbled through her mouthful. "It's all good."

"Displacement," Books returned. "You'd better not pester him while everybody's gone on Friday; I don't want to be stuck in a quiet Dugout with just him and you."

"W will be here, too."

"Yeah, well, Reggie's not going to displace his aggression on W, is he?"

Courtney turned to look between him and her two other couch-mates. "The Torch isn't going on the job either?" She knew Strings wasn't on this raid, and she might've guessed Books would stay behind. He didn't often go out with the "fighters" on operations, she'd learned; he worked a more digital angle, supporting the team on the ground with remote surveillance and intel from hijacked camera systems.

"Reggie's a loose cannon," Red said. "W's saving him for the big job. Where a leash won't really matter."

"Big job?"

"*Augh,*" Red coughed, looking down at the pizza in her hands in horror. "Dammit, Strings, you got us jalapeños! You *know* I can't do spicy."

Strings snickered. "You ate half a slice before realizing that?"

"They were buried under the cheese—*Ugh*! That's so hot!"

Tossing her offensive slice into String's lap, she launched her-self off the couch. Strings and Books both chuckled as she marched across the room, stole the entire jug of soda off the table and chugged straight from the bottle. Gripping the bottleneck with crackling force, she marched back to the sofa where Books and Strings sat, not bothering to hide their smirks, and glared at them through watery eyes.

"I'm armed, you know." She waved a knife in Strings' unrepentant direction.

"You're not as scary as the Torch," Books said. "She knows she can get away with anything around here."

"Oh yeah?"

Red lunged, and Strings' cackle of surprise squeaked into a low rasp when she Changed, a black cat dancing away from the blade's feinted swing. The cat darted across the room, snatched a slice of pizza off someone's plate near the card circle on the floor, and trotted off with it swinging from its teeth.

Courtney laughed.

Red and Books' bantering reignited behind her, and she let herself settle back into the couch to nibble on her own pizza slice. A warmth settled in her chest that had nothing to do with the jalapeños. Her gaze roamed the Dugout, settling over each member in turn. She recognized most of them now. The inseparable trio playing poker by the pizza table either boxed or practiced martial arts every morning—Diamond, Fitz, and Blue. They'd not yet spoken to her, but she was proud she'd at least learned a few more names. Beyond them, those new recruits by the duct-taped window spent every day together. A few other cliques she'd started to recognize, too, and as she listened to her two couchmates argue over who Strings annoyed most, she realized she could call one of those cliques her own.

Her lips twitched into a smile. She'd never been part of a clique before. In school, Dina had always been the star in social circles;

scholastics or extracurricular, she'd shine bright enough to draw a crowd. Courtney couldn't remember finding people she *wanted* to fit in with. People to challenge her, to push her toward a common goal. Her only goal then had been to survive. But here, something had shifted. Honing her skills at the range with Books, proving to Deadeye she deserved to be here, tripping up the steep learning curve in training with Strings and Red, she felt... sharper. A competitive edge she'd never before experienced hemmed her focus. Each day, she wanted to beat her own skill level from the day before, challenge herself to go farther, harder. Here, she wasn't breakable. No longer tiny and inconsequential. She *would* be big enough to make a difference. Not because she was big... but because she was part of something bigger.

Somehow, in this strange haven of loons and deviants, she'd found a place she belonged.

A laugh rang out, high and clear and familiar. Courtney's gaze settled on the circle of card players in the center of the floor. A mismatched dozen of new recruits and old members sat cross-legged around a pot of crumpled cash, grumbling as W dealt them a fresh hand of cards. Sliced into funny shapes or folded at different angles, the cards still slid through his hands with surprising fluidity. Someone shoved the cash toward him with their foot. Still laughing, he shook his head with a wave, motioning for people to put more in the pot. *All or nothing.*

Of course, he'd win again. Courtney recognized this game. *Life*, he'd called it, when she'd first seen him shuffling a deck of chopped-up cards. Won by changing the rules, every minute of ridiculous play. She shook her head with a grin.

It warmed her to hear his real laugh again. Since her arrival in the Dugout, he'd seemed tense and preoccupied, and before that... she hadn't seen this lighter, playful side of him since before he'd tried to push her out of his world. Looking at him now, she felt a surge of gratitude that he'd let her back into it.

She noticed Margo sitting cross-legged beside him, tucked so close to his side she hadn't spotted her little frame until now. The child watched him shuffle the broken cards in wordless fascination. The white reflections flickered off her dark eyes. W laughed again and tilted the cards back, angled so only Margo could see, and tapped a long finger over one with a conspiratory grin. The corner of Margo's mouth ticked up. She nodded. No words, just the fingers of her tiny hand bunched in the sleeve over W's elbow.

Something in Courtney's chest tugged. A sweet sting that snatched her breath for a moment.

Pale eyes flickered up to catch hers. Holding his gaze, she watched that unguarded grin soften. Warmth fluttered again behind her ribs. She dipped her chin, hoping to convey a silent thanks for earlier. Lips pressing in acknowledgment, his eyes dropped to her friends sitting around her—and shifted. She could no longer read the mixed expression behind them: pride, contentment, clouded with a strange tinge of apprehension.

His gaze skipped away from her before she could send a silent question his way.

8. THE JOB

THE GRIP OF the gun burned under Courtney's palm. If she squeezed any tighter, either it would snap, or her fingers would. She honestly couldn't decide which would be worse. She held the only non-lethal weapon in the group, and if it broke—or she did—nobody else would be lining up to fire tranqs in her place.

The hallway yawned empty and dark in both directions. The six members of the raid team filed out, one by one, from the grated stairwell door. Stand-by lights glowed along the edges of the ceiling, dimmed to an eerie half-fluorescence that made too many shadows. Not that there was anything to hide behind. Or any*one* left to hide. Red had taken care of that already.

Four and a half minutes ago, Courtney had watched Fitz and

Blue—the twins who made up two-thirds of the Dugout's insepa-rable trio—snap the neck of a guard on the ground floor and drop him unceremoniously into the dumpster behind the building. It had taken less than a second. Diamond had walked up, asked the time, and before the man could glance at his watch, Fitz had swept up from behind, grabbed his head and twisted. He'd dropped without a sound.

They'd only reached the third floor, and already Courtney had seen enough of her team's methods to know she was a fish out of water—so miserably, hilarious so, she wondered if she'd even make it to the roof. How had she ever thought she could do this?

Even Des had stayed behind. The hulking, soft-spoken wall of muscle waited two blocks away, parked in the getaway van. His only job was to watch for their signal. He had no desire to be inside this building. Courtney remembered his quiet words down on the Dugout's paint-splattered training floor. *I am a protector. A de-fender, not destroyer.*

Meanwhile, Books watched them, safe behind his laptop in the Dugout, surrounded by a hundred gadgets and gizmos. Depending on the complexity of the security system, he could hijack cameras and open locked doors from a distance, acting as an extra, pixelated pair of eyes to supplement Deadeye's super-hearing and sight on the ground. The cameras had blind spots, though, so Deadeye had to stay vigilant.

Maybe she should have stayed back with them. At the very least, down in the van with Des. Watching, waiting. The five hu-man-death-machines around her wouldn't blink before putting a bullet in someone's face. Or a knife. The tranq gun in her hand felt like a toy. Deadeye's narrowed eyes had certainly looked at it like one as they'd peeled out of the Dugout an hour ago, the moon slash-ing down through the clouds in quiet bursts of silver that glinted off the rifles slung across the trio's backs, and Red's knife belt, making her feel like a cartoon dropped into a black-and-white Hitchcock film she didn't belong in.

She was supposed to shadow Red. While Deadeye was technically lead strategist, he'd be shifted as a scout for most of the op, which meant Red was acting lead. Which meant: Courtney would be trying her best to stay out of the way, sticking to Red's heels without Changing, for sixteen stories of heist. The top of the Pierce & Bailey law office—the tallest high-rise in Orion City—housed AITO's latest shipment. Weapons, medical equipment, records; they needed all of it. Or, more importantly, they needed AITO *not* to have it. Whatever they couldn't get down to the van, Red planned to detonate. The charges clinked against her knife belt, making Courtney wince with every step she shadowed.

The rest of the team was no less nonchalant. Fitz looked almost bored as he climbed the stairs. The trio was recruited for every job, and it didn't take a genius to figure out why. Fitz and Blue were seasoned raiders who knew each other's movements so well, the rumor around the Dugout was they were telepathic. Identical save for the way they wore their sandy brown hair—Fitz in a ponytail, Blue closely buzzed—both had the same unique mutation. *Freak genes*, W had called it, like his own or the Orion Giant's. The brothers' Change looked normal in every way but size: a golden eagle that doubled its weight and wingspan to something big enough to carry off a small human. They couldn't use their shift indoors, however, so until they had open access to the sky, the twins stuck to their second-best asset: martial arts. No one could stand against them in close combat.

Diamond was equally formidable. Almost as inseparable from the brothers as the twins were from each other, the female member of the trio had *two* shifts. Small, but stocky, muscles standing out in her sleeveless dark arms, Diamond wore a nylon suit that hung so loosely on her body she had to tie it with a thin belt, which looked designed to snap when she Changed. Her exposed arms were pockmarked with scars. Courtney wondered if it had something to do with her Change; she'd never seen Diamond's shift. Though her original Change was an adder, the fastest striking venomous snake in the world, Diamond preferred to use her second form over her smaller, serpentine one. All Courtney knew from Red about Diamond's second shift was that she'd gained it through the blood process, which meant she'd somehow acquired the DNA of the creature she desired. The process was painful and risky. But a few members of the Dugout—like the Torch—had undergone the transfusion to earn a new Change. Whatever Diamond's Change was, it was big enough to need a nylon suit large enough for her human form to swim in.

"Shadows don't drift." Red's low growl snatched Courtney out of her speculations. "Stay on my six."

Hurrying to catch up, Courtney rejoined the edge of the group in time for Deadeye's feathered head to swivel around and pin her under a molten stare. Fighting the urge to shrink back behind Diamond and Blue, Courtney tugged her gaze away from the owl on Red's shoulder and focused on the hallway instead. She squared her shoulders.

She deserved to be here. She'd proven herself on the gun range, hit enough targets under the ticking clock Red had set and earned her spot on this raid. Even Deadeye hadn't scraped up a solid reason to veto her attendance. The tranqs sat heavy in her pistol, and she gripped it with two hands, willing them not to shake. She had ten rounds. Ten chances to fire first.

Better hit 'em before we do, Red had told her.

She had to be faster.

"This your first shadow run?" Courtney looked up at the soft voice to see Fitz walking beside her, his own gaze sweeping the dark hall ahead. "You're a newbie, right? Usually recruits don't come on these for a few more months."

Courtney swallowed. It was the first time any of the trio had spoken to her. "Yeah. It's my first."

"You got prior experience or something?" Brown eyes flicked over her. "Or a secret super-Change we oughtta know about?"

"No. I just spent every day on the range or the training floor to make sure I could come."

"Itching for blood that badly, huh?"

Her fingers jerked around the gun's grip. "The opposite," she whispered.

"Eh?"

"Fitz," Diamond snapped. "Cut the chatter. Deadeye heard something."

Courtney stopped before she thumped into Red's back. The rest of the team had paused, every eye fixed on the shadowed bend of the hallway ahead. Red's shoulders tensed, and the great horned owl leaned forward, legs bunched, wings lifted out to either side, prepared to spring into the air.

Red reached around to grip the watch on her wrist. Books had created the little device for raids like this one. Ripping out a cell phone's tiny vibration motor and microphone, he'd replaced the time-keeping compartment with a concoction of his own making. When he had access to a camera system, he could send alerts and simple messages to the watch's wearer through silent vibrations, and receive a constant stream of audio. He'd originally designed it for covert operations like the "Needle in the Haystack" job Courtney had heard about, where W had infiltrated AITO for months wearing a different face. But now Red and Deadeye wore it on raids with multiple levels and blindspots Books could warn them about.

"How many?" Fitz whispered, sidling up to Red.

"Sh." Whatever secret code she and Books had worked out, Red's face tightened in calculation for a few seconds, counting the buzzes before she dropped her arm. "Two." She flicked two fingers out toward the twins. "You've got the first one. Deadeye and I've got second."

Fitz nodded, stepping back. In silent unison both he and his brother unslung the rifles from their backs: big, streamlined automatics with long suppressors on the barrels. Courtney froze.

Red slid a knife from its sheath with soundless speed.

The shadows ahead appeared first, on the floor beyond the edge of the hall. Slow, meandering steps, the scuff of boots trickling into Courtney's ears a second before the voices. A low conversation. Someone chuckled at an unheard joke.

Deadeye launched himself off Red's shoulder.

The two security guards rounded the corner. The first man's face barely had time to register surprise before a dull snap echoed in the hallway; Blue's silenced shot hit him square in the chest. He jerked backward, glasses flying off his face, hit the far wall and slid down. His partner scrambled for the gun at his hip. Deadeye got there first. Wings flapping, he yanked the man's pistol to one side, just as a metallic hiss sang through the air.

Red's knife sank into the guard's neck. Buried to the hilt, it struck home with a sound Courtney knew would replay in her ears for the rest of her life—a gurgling, choking rasp sputtered off into a half-gagged wheeze. Deadeye kept his talons on the firearm as he dropped, flapping, keeping it from clattering to the floor. The man went down slowly, dropping to one knee, then the other. He hit the floor face first. A thick pool of crimson spread out around him. Releasing the gun, Deadeye vaulted back into the air.

The floor tipped under Courtney's feet. She grabbed the wall before she fell, fighting the heave that clawed up her throat. If she vomited, this was the end of her first job. All her jobs. They'd never let her on another raid.

"You good, newbie?"

A hard finger poked her shoulder. Courtney fought to clear the spots in her vision, and looked up to see Fitz's face above her own. One thick eyebrow raised.

"Yeah," she choked.

"No, she's not," Diamond hissed. "Give her a push and she'll fall over. Where'd you pick this one up, Red? It's like she's never seen blood."

Thick, coppery and salty, the hot scent a dozen yards away seeped into her nostrils; the wolf's senses edged in against her human ones. Her stomach rolled again. Courtney smashed her eyelids shut, and pulled in a deep breath. The gargling noise echoed in her head. Deep in her gut, the Change trembled.

"Hey." Red's voice swam in, closer than expected. Fingers snapped in front of her face. "New-blood, I stuck my neck out to get you on this op. Don't make me regret bringing you."

Forcing her eyes back open, Courtney met Red's dark, gleaming gaze. Behind her, Deadeye fluttered to a landing on her shoulder, ruffling the few stray braids in Red's up-do. Wide orange-gold eyes stared unblinking: challenging.

Courtney pushed herself off the wall. "I'm good." Her voice came out in a rasp. She cleared her throat. "Promise."

Diamond rolled her eyes. Adjusting her own automatic over her shoulder, she tromped down the hall, pausing a few yards up to wait for Red. Fitz followed, then Blue. Tilting forward, Deadeye gave one of Red's braids a tug with his razor beak, then took to the air again. He glided up to land on Blue's shoulder, feathers ruffled.

Courtney clutched her gun and started forward. Red fell into step beside her, letting the others walk ahead.

"It gets easier," she said. "You're doing better than I did my first time."

"First time? Your first raid?"

"Nah, my first raid I did great." Red smirked. "Shadowed Boss himself, made Deadeye jealous with how much I impressed him on my first day."

"Oh." Courtney tried not to stare at the crumpled heaps as they approached the end of the hallway. "Then, first time…?"

"Seeing a man get shot. You're holding up better than I did." Red snorted. "Granted, I was five, and no snot-nosed kid handles that well. But you didn't barf. Props to you."

Courtney glanced at the girl beside her. She remembered Red was only two years younger than herself, nineteen; she wasn't much taller, either, but she carried her shoulders straight back, stride long and sure, not a waver in her step. "Did you…?"

"Barf? Oh, yeah. All over my light-up shoes. Last time I ever wore those."

A tight, raw question slid to Courtney's lips, but before she could ask it, the bodies to her right magnetized her gaze.

The man Red had downed with a knife to the jugular lay sprawled halfway across their path. His face tilted to one side, cheek squished onto the bloody tile and his nose bent like it had broken in the fall. His eyes were half open. Crow's feet fanned out around them, laugh lines etched beside his mouth. Round apple-red cheeks, hair graying at his temples, under the hat that read *Bailey's Security*—the same firm her father had worked for. She stared at the little crossed batons stitched over the embossed shield.

Her shoes stuck to the ground, inches from the spread of blood.

"C'mon." Red's voice softened the slightest bit. "Longer you stare, longer it'll take to fade."

The footsteps continued beside her. Then away from her. Ripping her feet back into motion, Courtney shuffled after Red. Her insides shook.

She'd frozen. She'd held the tranq gun in useless hands, and watched two lives snuff out in front of her. They'd been in range; she'd had plenty of time to raise the gun, to fire a tranq across the space and hit one of them. At least one could've been lying there now, still breathing.

The roar between her ears drowned out Red's next question.

"Yo." Fingers snapped again under her nose. "Do we need to dump you back off at the van? If this isn't your speed, you can wait for us down with Des."

No. Her throat clamped on the word. *No, I can do this.*

"I'll be faster next time." Courtney lifted the gun, squeezing the barrel with her free hand. "I'll hit one."

"If we make an opening, go for it," Red said. "But you don't shoot unless I say so, got it?"

"Why?"

"What do you mean, *why*? Because I'm your lead, and because you'll get somebody killed if you fire that off too soon." Red sighed, sharp and short. "Damn, you're lucky it's not Deadeye leading today, or you'd be back at the van already." Her shoulder twitched. "Just... don't look at their faces. Stick to me, let the others handle the messy stuff, and you'll do fine."

Doing fine wasn't the objective. *I won't freeze.*

She could make it to the sixteenth floor, finish the job behind the others as a shadow, leave no trace, no consequence of her presence...and waste every drop of sweat she'd poured into getting here. No. She'd let others handle the messy stuff for too many years.

I won't.

Their footsteps were the only sound in the stairwell as the group climbed to the fourth floor. According to Books, only one security guard had access to the sixteenth level, and they'd need to locate him somewhere between the second and fifth. Once they swiped his key card, they could head straight up to the top and lock the doors behind them, sealing themselves off from the rest of the building. Deadeye had a separate plan of escape, and apparently it didn't involve going back down the way they came. Courtney didn't want to think about what that implied.

"Heads up," Diamond whispered. "Around the corner. I smell smoke."

Red paused at the top of the landing, gripping her watch again. Her jaw twitched. She shook her head. "Books can't get a read. There's at least one guy hanging out in the camera's blind spot. Maybe more."

Fitz stepped forward. "Then we go in quick and quiet."

"Hang on. Let Deadeye scope it out first."

Inching out into the hallway, Red held an arm out toward Diamond, and the owl leaped off her shoulder to settle on Red's leather-braced forearm.

"Shadow, you next," Red muttered.

Startled, Courtney ducked forward, squeezed around the twins on the narrow stairs, and joined Red on the landing.

"Stay behind me."

The others slipped out of the stairwell one by one, falling in line behind them. Courtney couldn't figure out how each one kept their footsteps so silent. Even barefoot like the rest of them, she still couldn't manage to make her feet hit the concrete without sound. No Changer wore shoes on raids, apparently; it jeopardized the ability to Change fast and run. She winced at the faint scuff of her steps, wondering how far it carried down the hall.

This hallway looked identical to the one before. The only difference was at the end of this one stood an elevator, surrounded by three uniformed men lounging against the wall. Two stood, one sat cross-legged, passing a joint back and forth. A haze hung over them, muting their figures in the dim lighting from the stand-by bulbs above. The sharp, chemical waft of smoke reached Courtney's nose. Her Change-heightened senses recoiled, and she fought the urge to cough. At least they'd have trouble spotting her team's silent figures down the dark hallway through the haze.

The slow slither of Red's knife from its sheath froze Courtney's feet. Her team-lead was a shadow against the wall, melting forward on a catlike tread. Deadeye tipped forward off her shoulder and swooped up on silent wings, floating along just under the ceiling.

Someone laughed. A young, squeaky laugh, cracking on the edge of adolescence. A boy's low tenor echoed out of the smoke at the end of the hall, followed by the older voices of his coworkers.

Courtney's lungs unlocked.

She lifted the tranq gun before she knew what she was doing, lining the face of the youngest guard above her sights. They were twenty yards away. The distance of her training dummies in target practice. If she hit them first—

She squeezed the trigger. Once, twice, three times.

The first tranq hit the young man in the shoulder; he stumbled sideways with a yelp. The second two bounced off the walls with noisy *plinks*. Startled shouts ricocheted. An owl's screech rocketed down the hall, and Courtney saw Deadeye take a dive for one of the two men still standing. But they'd already reached for their weapons.

"Dammit!" Diamond yelled. Someone shoved Courtney from

behind. She hit the wall and ducked, just as a bullet whizzed over her head.

"Fitz! Blue!" Red dove sideways. "Take 'em out!"

She pressed low to the ground, hands shielding her head. More bullets screeched off the concrete wall behind her. Diamond coughed.

Dammit. Courtney flinched back into the wall. The Change thumped in her bones, hot under the cold adrenaline. Above her head, a thunderous splatter of *pops* exploded, automatic rounds muffled by the twins' silencers. The two men at the end of the hall dropped. The unconscious youth on the ground twitched. Courtney's stomach lurched; they'd hit him anyway.

"You idiot."

Courtney twisted around. Diamond crouched, gripping her shoulder, crimson wet ribbons snaking down her arm. Her face was eerily calm, narrowed eyes locked on Courtney's with a chill that stopped her breath.

"Aw, shit," Fitz said. He dropped to a knee and clapped his larger hands over Diamond's, applying pressure. The hissing flutter of wings approached.

"What the *hell* were you thinking?" Diamond growled.

"I—" The metal scent of blood invaded again, snatching the words off her lips.

"New-blood!"

Courtney looked up at the hoarse voice, still half-crouched, just in time for a shadow to blot out the hallway. The air moved in front of her face.

Crack. The blow snapped her head backwards, sent her tumbling onto her tailbone. The concrete floor rattled up through her skeleton. Her teeth buzzed. Ears ringing, she fought to blink the person above her into focus. A fist tightened in the collar of her suit and yanked her upright.

Deadeye's human face materialized inches from hers.

"What did I say about dragging us down with you?"

9. SOFT

A SECOND, DARKER hand appeared between them, grabbing Deadeye by the chin and forcing him back a step. The tight grip on Courtney's collar released.

"Back off." The back of Red's head eclipsed Courtney's vision. "She's *my* shadow. I'll handle her."

"Then *handle* her," Deadeye snarled. "Before she gets the rest of us killed." Shaking her off, he stalked away and Changed mid-step, shifting in a whorl of feathers and shadow. The owl soared off down the hallway.

Growling a curse, Red turned and stabbed a finger toward Blue. "Follow him. Take care of anything up there that heard us."

With a terse nod, Blue gripped his rifle and took off at a jog after Deadeye's receding form. Courtney flinched when Red's gaze dropped back down to her.

"I was tr—"

"Save it," Red barked. She looked at Diamond. "Can you shift?"

"It'll be hell." Peeling her hand off her shoulder, Diamond tucked her chin down to try and see the dark wet gleam above her collarbone. Her breath wheezed through gritted teeth. "But yeah, I should be able to. It grazed me."

"Blood loss will get worse when she shifts back," Fitz said.

"Then don't shift till we get to the roof," Red said. "We still need our bulldozer. Books said there's too many up there."

"Look." Fitz jerked his chin toward the end of the hall. "Looks like one of those was our guy."

Red turned. Deadeye was circling back, dangling something from his talons. She held up a hand. A blood-splattered lanyard with a key card dropped onto her waiting palm.

"At least this was worth something," she muttered.

Courtney got to her feet. Deadeye didn't even look at her. Banking a few yards down the hallway, he returned to the elevator where Blue stood, rifle ready, and perched on the end of the long barrel. Even from this distance, the look he sent Red simmered the air.

"Fitz, give Diamond a hand." Red looped the keycard around her neck. "We're taking the elevator. Damn the stairs."

"But—" he said.

"We'll come out shooting if we have to. Diamond's gonna lose stamina fast, and we're not climbing twelve more floors like this. Faster we get to the roof, faster this job's over. Now move your ass." Pivoting, Red snagged Courtney's sleeve. "And *you* stay on *my* ass."

Cheeks stinging from more than Deadeye's backhand, Courtney lurched forward, half-jogging to keep up with Red's long strides as the other girl released her arm. She forced down a deep breath. She'd screwed up. But she could still recover this.

The image of the young man she'd tranquilized, jerking on the ground as a real bullet found him, blazed across her thoughts. Her gut clamped.

She *had* to recover this.

Diamond moved surprisingly fast for someone losing so much blood. She barely leaned on Fitz as they reached the elevator. Courtney pressed herself to the side as the rest piled in, wishing she could disappear into the cold metal wall. Fitz shot her a glare, but no one else looked her way. Even Red kept her eyes forward as the numbers ticked up on the green dial above the door, a tendon in her cheek flexing and unflexing. Only the sound of Diamond's labored breathing filled the tight space.

Ding.

The air squeezed in as everyone inhaled. Courtney's fingers bit into the pistol grip. With agonizing slowness, the elevator doors rolled back—to reveal an empty hallway.

Blue darted out, Deadeye on his shoulder. Fitz followed with Diamond. Red turned to Courtney.

"You get these." Hands lifting on instinct, Courtney jumped when Red placed three small cylinders in her open palm. "Don't drop 'em. That's nitroglycerin in there."

"*What?*" Courtney squeaked, fingers jerking closed around the tiny metal cases before they slipped.

"Don't worry, Boss stabilized them—sort of. Enough to carry them around *gently*."

"What am I supposed to do with these?"

"Tail me, and when I say so, stick them on top of the supply crates as soon as we get that freight open." Red slid two more knives from her belt. "Once we get to the roof, stick by the wall.

Use your tranq if anybody gets close, but stay out of the fighting. Kay?"

Courtney stared down at the little explosives, mouth dry.

Red sighed. Balancing a knife between two fingers, she dropped a hand over Courtney's shoulder. "Look, that was a dumbass move back there. But we're not done yet. Remember what I said—*prove* you belong here."

She let go, turned to the hallway, and broke into a jog, bare feet silent on the concrete. Courtney clutched the cylinders with cold fingers and followed as fast as she dared. Her pulse jumped with every tiny *clink* against her palm.

They caught up to the other four stopped at the end of the hallway, pressed to the wall on either side of a wide set of double doors. Fitz held Diamond by her uninjured shoulder. The smaller Changer leaned against him, her face an ashen gray undertone. Switching both knives to one hand, Red gripped her watch.

"Six," she whispered. "This is a job for the big one."

"I know." Diamond's faint whisper eked through clenched teeth. She hunched forward, breaths shortening.

Fitz's hand hovered over her back. "Di, you don't have to—"

"Yes, she does," Red snapped. "Let her work."

Fitz stepped back, forehead creased. Diamond grunted. Her back arched, and she hit the floor on all fours, a low wheeze ripping into a growl deep enough to rumble the concrete. The folds in her nylon suit flattened. Stretched. Courtney stepped back with the others, unable to look anywhere else as her shape tripled in size.

Striding away from Diamond's contorting form, Red tugged the lanyard from her neck and slipped the keycard into the door lock. A high-pitched beep answered the movement.

"Ten seconds, chief." She gripped the door handle and looked back, her lips pressed into a firm, grim line. "You ready?"

What used to be Diamond's tiny frame now blocked the whole of the hallway. Five feet at the shoulder, wide as a car, thick gray skin and massive horns. A... rhinoceros. Courtney should've been used to it by now, but she couldn't keep from staring. Stretched to its limit, the nylon suit gleamed under the dim lights, the tear across Diamond's shoulder stretched further. Dark blood trailed from the enlarged bullet wound. The three-thousand-pound beast groaned, sides shuddering. The massive snout bobbed.

"Fitz, help me with this door," Red said.

Jumping forward to grab the opposite handle, Fitz yanked forward as Red did. Cold air and moonlight spilled into the hallway. Head down, Diamond lumbered forward. They both dove to either side, tugging the doors with them. Metal squealed.

A shout echoed from outside.

Diamond bolted through before the doors were fully open, slamming the metal doors against their hinges.

The yells came first. Then the heavy, sickening thumps. Horrified cries bled into shrieks of pain. Gunshots followed, peppered between the voices. Courtney jerked forward—and a hand clamped around her elbow.

"Ten seconds aren't up," Red said.

"She's alone out there."

"Diamond can thicken her skin for short bursts during her Change. She's got Freak Genes, *you* don't. You go out there now, you'll be swiss cheese in two seconds."

"But she can't be bulletproof," Courtney said.

"No, but she's got a hell of a lot better chance of making it through there than any of us. Trust her—she's come back alive every raid before this."

The final gunshot cracked out, behind one last brutal thud, and the rooftop went quiet. The night filled with the distant thrum of the city below. A new sound scraped the eerie stillness. Pops, clicks, and inhuman groans petered off into a dull whimper.

Courtney tugged away from Red. Ducking around the metal doorway, she stepped out onto the rooftop.

The cold bit through her nylon suit. Sixteen stories up, the wind slammed in, whipping her hair around her face, into her eyes. The concrete stung her bare feet. Moonlight stabbed in through the breaks in the clouds: bright enough to paint a scene Courtney wished she couldn't see.

Bodies—broken, crushed, twisted in ways they shouldn't be— lay strewn about the rooftop. Steam rose off fresh pools of blood to swirl on the frigid air. In the center of the mess, a small figure huddled, shivering, torn nylon suit hanging off one bloodied shoulder.

Fitz pushed past Courtney. "Di!"

A siren screamed, echoing down the street below.

"Shit," Red said. "Someone triggered the alarm."

Blue jogged out onto the roof, and Deadeye leaped from his shoulder. He Changed with fluid speed in midair, dropping to human feet and striding past the woman on the ground without missing a beat. "Get her down from here." His low, hoarse voice carried above the building siren. "Drop her at the van, then get back, fast, so we can get this load down before AITO's lap dogs get here."

Metal banged behind Courtney, and she turned to see Red slamming both doors closed. "This should hold them for a minute."

"If they catch Des first, it doesn't matter if they can't get to us up here," Deadeye said. "We'll take what we can, and torch the rest before that siren reaches the block."

"Fine by me." Red tossed him the keycard. "Less to carry. Books'll be pissed."

"If you can't pull a trigger, you don't get a say in the calls we make on the job." A pair of mismatched eyes swiveled to Courtney, and she mustered up a glare before they rolled away. "Better in smoke than in their hands."

Across the rooftop, a huge, steel freight container stood, green metal sidings glowing under the moon. Deadeye headed for it.

Red put a hand to her watch. "Books heard; Des is pulling the van around now. Blue, take Diamond. Fitz, you get started on those charges."

Blue set his rifle on the concrete beside Diamond. Doubling forward, he hit one knee, tucked his head to his chest, and Changed. Enormous copper wings erupted out to either side and beat downward, launching him up off the ground. An eagle four times its regular size swooped over Diamond. Wide, careful talons closed on the back of her too-large nylon bodysuit. With a powerful series of flaps, the Changer lifted his teammate off the ground. Dipping and bobbing under her weight, he slammed his wings against the air, cleared the edge of the building, and dropped away into the night.

The siren's steady wail grew louder.

Courtney gripped the charges in her hand and headed for the opposite end of the roof, where Deadeye had slipped the keycard into the freight's lock and started unlatching the doors. He looked up at her approach. His cloudy eye twitched.

"Red told me to help set the charges," Courtney said, holding up the little cylinders like a peace offering.

Deadeye let go of the door, snatched them from her, and turned back to the freight container. "Go stand by the edge of the roof with the rest of the deadweight Fitz and Blue have to carry down."

Anger simmered under the fear. "I can help."

"*You* can stay out of the way, before I make you."

The chilly growl nearly doused the tiny flame of bravado she'd mustered. The corner of her jaw still stung from the back of his hand. Refusing to cave to the probably smarter instinct to back off,

Courtney held her ground.

"You said we've only got a few minutes."

Deadeye hauled the freight doors back with a grunt, then turned. "What?"

"Give me some of the cargo, and I'll help carry it to Fitz and Blue. You need the extra hands."

Stepping up into the dark interior stacked with crates, Deadeye hung onto the edge of the freight container, smashed a bare heel down on the slatted wooden box, and reached down into the splintered crate. He yanked out a rifle.

"Fine." He tossed it to her so fast she barely caught it, almost dropping the tranq pistol as she fought to keep her grip on both. "Get that to Blue. And this one."

To her surprise, he extended the next one to her, tapping his foot on the crate in impatience while she scrambled forward. Blood painted the back of his heel. When she stepped close, hand closing around the barrel, he yanked the rifle back, tugging her into the shadow of the freight container.

"You're done." Sharp breath skated over her face. "After this, you're out. I don't care if you've got the Boss in your soft little pocket; I'm his field lead, and *I* keep this team alive on the ground. You turn them soft, I'll turn you inside out. This is your last raid. Ever. Got that?"

Courtney's fingers whitened on the gun barrel. "You think I'll turn your team soft? Have you *seen* your team?"

"Hey!" Red hollered from across the roof. "What's the holdup? That shit's not gonna load itself!"

Deadeye released the gun, and Courtney stumbled back with both rifles in her arms. They clacked together against her chest. When he turned back to the freight container, her tongue moved on its own.

"I'm not soft." Her own voice startled her: sharp and stern. She gripped the guns as she stepped back out of Deadeye's reach. "Not in the way you think. I didn't come here to sit tight and watch. So— no, I'm not done." Adrenaline rushed over the words; she barely got them out. "Not until I say I am."

She darted back to the center of the roof, blood thumping half in horror, half in thrill at her own brass. Gone was the girl who froze down in the hallway.

Prove you belong here.

Red marched past her, snagged an armload of rifles from Deadeye, and returned to dump them beside Courtney. A cross-shaped shadow glided over the growing pile. Red waved down Blue, who'd just reappeared over the edge of the roof.

"Get this stuff down," she called. "I'd say we got time for three loads before we really need to hoof it."

Enormous talons landed on three rifles. Bundling them up together by the barrels, Blue swept back into the air, hauling them like they weighed nothing. Fitz swooped down next. Changed to an identical form as his brother, he grabbed the remaining four. They both disappeared over the edge of the roof, to the van no doubt waiting below.

Red jogged back to the freight container to get another load.

A sound behind Courtney yanked her focus back around to see a figure by the door. Her gaze locked with his—and they both froze. She hadn't heard him over the sirens, rising in pitch every second.

There were seven, not six.

The young security guard pressed flat against the door, tendons standing out in the back of his hand as he fought with the handle. Red had jammed a knife into the keycard holder; the little light above the lock pad flashed red, prevented from opening. The guard blanched when he met Courtney's eyes. Fingers shaking, he didn't even reach for the gun at his hip, just threw all his weight onto the door handle. The error light above the door's lock system blinked again.

Courtney lifted the tranq gun. If the others hadn't seen him yet, she just might be able to save—

The gunshot cracked off the surrounding buildings, jumped back to pierce her ears twice over. The security guard's terrified face slackened. Darkness spread out over the beige front of his uniform, a fast pulse of scarlet over his heart. He crumpled like a marionette. The sound of his head smacking the concrete sliced even over the sirens.

Courtney's balance tipped. She took a hasty step back, tripping over her ankles, and caught herself. Her head whipped around.

Moonlight glinted off the end of Deadeye's gun, extended from his place inside the freight container. His golden eyes seared in the shadows. Not fixed on his target, but on her.

I'm not soft.

Her muscles shook, even as she fought to steel them. She couldn't yank her gaze free.

"Books must've missed one," Red shouted. The sirens blared full-force now. "Those things are moving fast. Two loads'll have to do. We're out of time." As if on cue, an eagle glided back up over the edge of the roof, talons empty. "Blue! Grab the newblood."

Courtney didn't have time to stiffen, or even inhale. The wind changed above her head, the moon disappeared, and in the space of a blink, expert talons wove themselves into the nylon across her shoulders. The concrete dropped out from under her feet. Stomach in her throat, Courtney left her scream behind with gravity as they hurtled over the roof's edge.

Above, Red's figure appeared. Stepping off the roof all on her own, she pitched downward, arms out to either side. Fitz's huge wingspan appeared behind her silhouette. With a jerk, he arrested her descent, angled downward, and sped the two of them past Courtney and Blue. Courtney craned her neck to try and see the van below—and felt her insides roll at the dizzying height—before a blast of heat from above prickled the air around her. They were halfway to the van when the concussion thudded through her bones, gusted the hair across her face. She twisted back to look up.

White-hot tongues of orange raged against the night sky. Squinting up through the stinging heat toward the roof, Courtney fought the urge to shield her face. She strained her eyes. Was Dead-eye...?

An owl screamed out of the fiery cloud, followed by a trail of glittering smoke.

Seconds later, her feet hit the roof of the van. Cries echoed in the dark. Drowned under the approaching howls. Blue lights flashed around the corner.

"Punch it, Des," Red screamed.

She'd barely made it through the open door before the tires shrieked against the pavement, hurtling them away from the curb.

They left the sirens behind, wailing after them.

10. LOONS

"**D**AMN, YOU MUST'VE stepped in it big time to get yourself blacklisted after your first shadow run. I've never seen Deadeye this pissed over a newbie. What'd you do, shoot Red in the back?"

Courtney slouched over the edge of her bed, focused on lacing up her boots to avoid her roommate's curious gaze.

"Not quite," she muttered. "But close enough."

"Seriously? I was joking." Strings swung forward off her perch on the ceiling beam, caught herself by the backs of her knees, and hung there, ponytail swinging. "What happened?"

Courtney tied off the last knot in her shoelace and braced her elbows on her thighs. "I failed."

"Failed?"

"I didn't save anyone." Her throat tightened. "I had three

chances, and I froze up, then moved too fast, then didn't move fast enough."

Strings' brows knitted. "Weren't there six of you? Six came back. I mean, I know Diamond's getting stitched up, but six out and six in again, still breathing, is a pretty good raid."

"That's not..." The words tangled. Jaw clenching, Courtney fought with them a moment, before realizing Strings' rapt, confused gaze made the words she could find irrelevant. She pushed herself to her feet. "Do you have any idea where I could find W?"

It was two a.m., but he wouldn't be asleep. The whole of the Dugout had been burning with activity when they'd returned an hour ago. She hadn't seen him then, when the twins had rushed Diamond up to the fourth floor for medical attention, nor when Red had swiped some eager new recruits to help unload the stolen weapons. Even now the buzz had died down, he'd be up, somewhere, brainstorming his next move. Courtney knew W well enough now to know sleep wasn't his best acquaintance.

"Try the roof," Strings said.

Courtney blinked. "It's freezing."

"If you haven't pieced together that Boss is crazy by now, you might need your loon-radar checked." Strings looped her arms up over the beam she hung from and tugged herself up, settling into a cross-legged perch. "Rain or snow, that's his favorite spot in the city. He goes up there sometimes to get away from the rest of us. Y'know, like when mommy needs to hide from the kids."

The idea of W as a harried mother hiding away from rambunctious children hit funny. Courtney forgot the anxious knots in her stomach for a second, amused by the image.

"There's a trapdoor above the ladder on the fourth floor, at the back of the broom closet," Strings said. "Fair warning, we've all learned not to even try bugging him when he's up there. But it's your neck."

"Thank you." Courtney turned for the door.

"Hey." Above, Strings' voice shifted to something lower. Softly urgent. "Whatever happened out there, don't let it get to your head. This place needs you."

The tight feeling under her ribs crept back. Her lungs needed room to expand, and it wasn't here.

"I'll be quiet, in case you're asleep when I get back," Courtney said. She slipped out into the hall, shutting the door behind her.

The fourth floor was empty when she hit the landing. She knew she wasn't the only one up and about, though, from the murmured voices leaking under closed doors. Torch's soot-smeared wooden door with the ripped-off room numbers loomed on her left, and she scurried past it faster than the others. Footsteps light, she made it to the end of the hall and turned toward the little closet that stood an inch ajar. Cold air whistled from behind the door. She edged it open and slipped inside. Dim light trickled down from a half-lit square on the ceiling, and when she reached out, her hands hit wooden ladder rungs. She gripped the sides and climbed up, wobbling when a few splintering clicks sounded under her boots.

The trap door took two hands to lift. Heavy, groaning metal eked upward, and the thin line of indigo and gold spread into a wash of chilly colors.

The cold air hit her first, followed by the noise. A hollow, echoing rush of sound swept up from the city below, honks and distant cries and sirens driven on the wind. A grumbling engine rattled by, followed by the squeal of brakes. No one heeded curfew in this part of town. A peal of sharp, hair-raising laughter screeched out a few blocks away, dancing on the night. A dog barked. Somewhere not far off, down where the laughter had come from, a duet of bellowing, wildly off-key voices burst into drunken song. Someone yelled at them to shut up. A faraway crash, metal and glass. The whine of a car alarm.

Yet, above it all, in *spite* of it all, a stillness filled the rooftop, at odds with the chaos below. Courtney pushed herself off the edge of the trapdoor and onto her knees, letting it fall quietly shut. Her jeans sucked up the cold damp of the concrete. She scraped to her feet, and her vision clouded with the golden swirls of her own breath bouncing back at her. A single light glowed on the top of this building; it didn't reach far, but it was close enough to cast the rest of the rooftop in hazy shadow. She ventured away from the trapdoor, toward the edge of the roof. The stars burned through the gloom as her eyes adjusted.

She finally spotted the silhouette perched atop a raised concrete fixture at the other end of the roof. W sat with his arms sprawled behind him, long legs hanging off the ledge, looking out over the city. He didn't seem to hear her until she'd crossed the empty field of roof to stand below him.

"You should be in bed." His low voice sounded too loud in the weird pseudo-silence.

"So should you," she called up.

In the distance, an inhuman wail rang out: a wild, lonely sound that sliced a pang of unknown longing through her. A loon. The creature's call almost drowned under the clamor of the city. Courtney shivered, and curled her arms inward. In her haste to escape the Dugout, she hadn't thought to bring a jacket.

"Deadeye told you, didn't he?" she said.

"Mm." W's gaze remained on the skyline. "A lot of things."

"Then you know I'm banned from future raids."

At last, his head turned down toward her. She couldn't make out his expression in the dark, but his voice sounded strange. Stretched tight, deceptively flat. "Do you want to be banned?"

"No." Her answer came out hard and fast. She bit down against the rush of words. "But does it matter what I want?"

He didn't respond. The city's dull thrum trickled between them.

"Why did you let me go in the first place?" Courtney gripped the backs of her elbows, fighting the urge to shake. "You were dead-set against it, then all of sudden, I got the green light. What changed?"

He straightened as he turned away again, sharp profile unreadable against the stars. "You needed to see for yourself. You're not one to hang back and watch from a safe distance. That's where your little cop got it wrong." Leaning forward over his knees, he peered down at the dizzying drop off the ledge where he sat. "Can't cage a bird to protect it from falling. Pretty soon you'll realize the bars only were there to stop it flying away... then you'll know it was never yours to begin with."

Courtney frowned up at the silhouette. "Flying away?"

"Can you look me in the eyes and tell me you don't want to? After everything you saw tonight."

Her throat tightened. "You still think I'm going to run." The realization punched through her, ripping against the tender memory of that night's conversation on the shooting range. "That's why you're hiding up here. You don't want to see *me*."

His shoulders stiffened.

"James, look at me."

The dry calm of his voice was too careful to be real. "It'll make it a lot harder to give you space if I do."

"I don't need space! I need *you*." Her explosion surprised them both, echoing across the rooftop. W's head turned. "You think what I want right now is to be *alone*? After tonight? I need to—to *talk* about this with someone, to figure out what the hell I'm feeling, what I'm supposed to do next." Her voice wavered. She ground her teeth. "Give me a hand up."

"What?"

"Your hand. I can't climb up there on my own."

Staring at her for a wary moment, W finally pulled his legs off the ledge. He shifted to her side of the concrete rise and extended an arm. She gripped his wrist, and he closed his long fingers around hers. With surprising speed, he tugged her off her feet and up to his level. Boots braced on the side of the concrete fixture, Courtney scrambled over the edge, landing on her knees beside him. He kept a loose grip on her wrist until she'd regained her balance.

"For all the reasons you should be mad at me," he said. "You pick the strangest one."

She settled to the cold concrete, tugged her knees to her chest and wrapped her arms around them, shoulder bumping his. "Why should I be mad at you?"

"That shake in your voice, to start."

"I'm just cold."

"I thought we had a no-lying policy."

She swallowed. As before, with Strings, words got stuck somewhere in her chest, jumbled together in a hard knot. She didn't know where to start unraveling them.

W shifted beside her, moving away. In the darkness, she thought he'd started to stand, leaving her there on the cold cement by herself. Then she felt two arms encircle her from behind. Warmth enveloped her as he gently drew her back, between his bent knees, tucking her against his hard chest. The open cocoon of his coat swallowed her. Windchill vanished, along with her breath.

"Better?" His voice tickled her hair.

He had to feel her heart thumping in all the spaces they now shared. It took her several beats to snatch back her voice. "Yes."

His own heartbeat, strong and steady, rippled against her spine, soothing her own uneven rhythm. She found herself relaxing into it, nestling deeper into the warmth. She'd forgotten just how much *bigger* than her he was; this close, she almost disappeared inside his arms, hidden away from the night and the wind and the sirens below. Nothing could touch her. For the briefest moment, she almost let herself believe that.

The icy, raw edge of leftover adrenaline from the raid ebbed, if only a little.

"I'm sorry." The whisper skimmed her ear, so low she wouldn't have heard it any further away.

"What for?"

"I'm the last person you should be talking to about what happened." His arms tightened. "As much as I want to ease the burden from you, I'm the one who put it there in the first place. I…" The air fluttering past her hair caught on itself. Slid out without a sound. Courtney waited for it to move again. "I told you, once—this city should've broken someone like you. But it never did. Not after all these years. Now I… I'm in for some new kind of damnation if I've become the one who finally does."

The faint, rustling moan of wind scoured over the building. It tapped on the thick gray edges of W's coat, brushed them against Courtney's face. Her hair blew across her eyes. But the cold remained banished.

"You think I'm breaking?"

"No," he said. "Not yet. But I can already see, in your eyes, the change. Deeper than the first one." Muscles tensed against her. "I don't want you to lose who you are. Not like I did."

Inside the wind, voices carried. Cries from the street below. Courtney couldn't tell if they were happy or afraid. Sleep was far from many others in this part of the city, it seemed.

"And it'd be your fault," she whispered. "If I did. Is that what you believe?"

"I brought you here."

"I chose to come. And I chose to *stay*."

The heartbeat thudded a little harder against her back. "Do you regret it, now?"

"No."

"You remember the rules."

"I'm not lying." Reaching up to curl her arms around his, where they rested over her knees, she threaded her fingers between his longer ones. His skin was so much colder. "But... Deadeye told you what happened. I'm banned from future jobs because I haven't changed *enough*. I need to become someone different, someone stronger, if I'm going to make any kind of difference here."

His fingers clamped around hers. "No."

"I couldn't save anyone." Tight, cold, the shame squeezed in, that fierce grip of powerlessness she'd felt earlier in that blood-soaked hallway. "You know why I wanted to go, what I thought I could try to do. But I was useless. It felt like swimming against a tidal wave. I couldn't do *anything*. They killed, and I watched, and when I tried to move, I failed each time. I..." Her lungs hitched. "One of those security guards worked for the same firm as my father. They could've been colleagues. Then there was the other, barely more than a kid... and the last." When she squeezed her eyes shut, she still saw his face. The young man on the rooftop, trapped and terrified, desperately trying to escape back through the door Red had jammed shut. His wide eyes, wet and pleading. The scream that never got off his lips before Deadeye's bullet found his heart. "I made no difference. I may as well have been a real shadow."

W remained silent. His thumb, the only digit free from their interlocked grip, ran slow circles over the back of her hand.

"You said, before, that you still remember the names of Margo's parents," she said. "Do you remember their faces?"

"Yes," he said softly.

"Of everyone you've killed?"

"No." The reply was hollow, brittle. "Not the ones before. They're... a little harder to forget now."

"Since Margo?"

"Yes."

She shuddered. "I don't think I'll ever be able to get those faces out of my head."

The circles across her hand stopped. "I hope you never forget." As she frowned in the darkness, she heard him reaching for words, struggling to find them for the first time since she'd known him. "As much as I wish you would... the day you do, I'm afraid I won't know you. You'd have become the same kind of monster I am."

"Monsters don't raise their enemy's orphaned child," Courtney said.

"They also don't hesitate to make the orphan in the first place."

She turned, wishing she could make out his expression in the shadows. "You liked my idea of using tranqs. Even if I failed at implementing it." The arms around her remained tense, hard. "If you were dead-set on killing every person in the way, you'd have turned it down at the start. You want to make a change. I saw it in your eyes." She hesitated. "Why not enforce non-lethal raids?"

"It's a long road to anyplace where change isn't bloody." He sighed, and she felt the weariness ripple through his frame as if it were her own. "Protecting my people comes first. Non-lethal methods are risky, and sometimes more dangerous than erasing the enemy."

Disappointment seeped through her, and he must have felt it, because his arms tightened.

"I'm not saying it's impossible," he added. "I... truly would like to move in that direction. Someday."

"It could be today."

A low chuckle rumbled at her back.

"Why are you laughing?"

"Because you're still you. It's a relief." Slowly, the tension bled out of the frame behind her. She felt his breath move to her cheek, and the warm seam of his lips skimmed her temple. Her pulse skipped again. "You're a start, you know," he murmured against her hair.

"What?"

"Of that change."

She looked away with a sharp swallow. "I failed miserably tonight. I got Diamond shot."

"It was your first raid. You used to keel over at the sight of blood, but you held your own with a team of trained fighters, all the way to the top of Pierce & Bailey's. You let an eagle carry you off a *roof*. And you climb up here, mere hours later, and try to talk with me about improving future raids."

His hand untangled from hers, and reappeared along the edge of her jaw. The cool pads of his fingers traced her cheek. She shivered.

"I'm still nowhere close to the person I need to be," she said.

Gentle fingers slid back beneath her chin, tipping her face up toward his. Warmth skittered through her veins.

"You don't need to become someone else to make a change," he whispered. "Trust me."

The words brushed her lips, a soft tickle of air. Her breath stuttered.

"I thought we had a rule," she whispered back.

She felt his smile in the dark. "You'll never see me break it."

His lips were warm, in contrast to the hand that cradled her face. Courtney closed her eyes, feeling the heartbeat against her jump in tandem with her own. But the kiss was slow. Less urgent than their first one, a quiet confidence in their embrace that had been lacking before. Long fingers threaded through the hair behind her ear. He held her like something that wasn't about to disappear, this time. Something he could be sure of.

When they finally drew apart, she let her forehead tip against his, breaths shared, eyes still closed. "I'm not planning to change who I am." Voice shaky, she filled her lungs with his scent. Metal and peppermint, and a faint, wild outdoor kind of smell, like distant smoke on the wind. "But I'm going to get stronger." Forcing a small laugh, she added, "And I'm not going anywhere. Who would be there to piss off Deadeye, if I did?"

He chuckled against her lips. "Who, indeed. Those feathers don't ruffle easily, either. More proof you're a force to be reckoned with."

Opening her eyes, Courtney caught the faint glimmer of his gaze above hers, reflecting the city lights. "You still haven't answered my question."

"Oh?"

"Does it matter what I want?" She tightened her fingers around the hand she still held. "Because I told Deadeye I'm not done. I want to stay in the fight against AITO, and I'll be prepared next time. Faster, with better aim."

"Hm. Red told me you disobeyed orders on the job today."

"Yes."

His laugh tingled through her again. "Not a shred of repentance. You'd do it again, wouldn't you?"

"If I was trying to save someone's life, yes."

Lifting his face from hers, he pressed his lips against her forehead. "We'll see."

"When?"

"When you've recovered from this one, we can reevaluate your plan on improvement. Maybe a few more lessons down at the shooting range, first."

His arm fell back around her, and she turned back to the city below, deciding that was the best she'd get for now. She laid her head back against his shoulder. His heartbeat had lilted back to its original rhythm, gentle and strong. She listened to it for a moment, letting her gaze wander up over the indigo horizon. The stars glowed brighter than she was used to. Perhaps it was the frozen winter sky, or the fact that the light pollution from the streets below, her usual vantage point, felt thinner this high up. A familiar triple belt constellation blinked down at her from the ink. The city's namesake.

"I get why you come up here," she murmured.

He hummed behind her. "Do you know the story of Orion?"

"Not really. Some old Greek myth about a hunter, right?"

"There are a million different versions of it," W said. "The way most go, he dies fighting a beast. The gods set him up against a monster he can't defeat. He's the best shot with a bow, unrivaled anywhere, but in every myth, he always dies. A bull, a scorpion, however the story gets told, it ends the same way. He loses the fight. The beast destroys him, and he gets thrown up into the stars to commemorate a valiant death."

Courtney traced the faint string of stars with her eye. "Why did the gods send a beast to fight him?"

"Vengeance. A challenge. Boredom. Who knows." He paused, and an odd weight settled in the silence. "There are some versions that say Orion took the beast down with him. I was always partial to those."

Something under W's voice unsettled her. The dark, somber note felt too heavy for a conversation about constellations.

They watched the distant glitter of Orion's belt for a long moment, letting the sounds of the city fill the rooftop around them. A siren wailed through the night. Mournful, echoing. She listened to it, a strange sense of dread stealing over her. The cold sharpened. She pressed a little closer to W.

"I guess it's ironic that he got a city full of beasts named after him," she said.

A hint of the lightness returned to W's voice, though the shadowed note remained. "It is, isn't it?"

As the sirens faded, the hollow cackle of a loon rang out again. Courtney waited until the eerie, inhuman laughter petered out, before shaking her head with a wry twist to her lips.

"I think it's funny how you let Strings' little nickname catch on," she said. "I would've thought you'd shut it down, since you're not exactly a fan of the word."

"I think it's fitting."

"Really? Because the Dugout *is* full of crazies?"

He chuckled. "No. Though that doesn't help our case."

"Why, then?"

"Loons are loners. They might band together at night, to stay safe, but as soon as the sun comes up they abandon whatever flock they're with to go it alone. All that crying in the dark is really just a call for temporary allies. They're the loneliest critters I know of."

Courtney frowned at the skyline. "You think that fits Orion?"

"I *know* it fits Orion. Down on those streets, it's everyone for themselves. Even on my team, it's the stamp of this city. We might have a common fight, and we can band together when it's dark— and it's been dark, believe me. But survival's a game you play alone. As soon as they see a light at the end of the tunnel, a way out that doesn't involve me…" His words trailed. "There's no cage holding them here. The Dugout's a temporary flock. We might look like a family, to you, but each one of these Changers knows at the end of the day, freedom's the end goal. Peel back all the poker nights and off-time shenanigans, and you get a bunch of scarred fighters who'd put that goal over trust any day. Makes for a bunch of lonely creatures." Pausing while another loon's call answered the first, W let the cries echo and die before he continued. "But when you've got a beast to fight that can't be taken down alone, you team up with whoever you've got. Right now, I'm their best chance against AITO. So, hopefully this flock'll stick around a while longer."

Courtney traced the backs of his knuckles with her fingers. "That… does sound lonely."

"It's a side effect of living in this city." He shrugged, the slight movement rustling her head where it lay against his shoulder. "Anything else you want to know? Apparently, at this time of night, I turn into an encyclopedia of random facts. Loons, legends, all the odd things in between."

She let herself smile. "You always did get the most talkative those late nights at the cafe."

"You were bored. I had to entertain you."

"Is that what you're doing now?"

"Best way to clear a bad night out of your system is to keep boredom far away."

"I guess it is working a little." The sinking feeling in her gut had lessened. "I'm surprised you know so much about kooky birds and old legends."

"Takes one to know one."

"Are you calling yourself a legend or a loon?"

"If both shoes fit, I've got two feet."

She laughed. Her eyes drifted down over the faint silver edge of horizon, to the few glimmering stars at the edge of the dark.

"What's that constellation?" she asked.

"Where?"

"Down at the bottom of the sky, that straight line of stars."

It was his turn to laugh. The sound came out warmer than before, tingling through her. "It's not. That's Chicago."

The breath in her throat caught. "We can see over the Wall from here?"

"Just that side, there. This part of the city's on a higher incline than the rest. You could probably see over from parts of Eastside, too." He paused. "You've never seen over the Wall?"

Speechless, she shook her head. The tiny string of not-stars on the horizon shimmered. Beckoning. Now that she really looked, they gleamed more golden than the silver constellations above. Her chest tightened.

A whisper surfaced at the back of her mind. The gentle, hazy image she hadn't seen in a while—in reality had *never* seen, though its familiar, soft colors felt like an old friend. The dream had come less often in recent years. On rare nights she felt safe, hidden in the warmth of her apartment after a day that wasn't horrible, a shift that didn't suck her dry, it would sometimes visit. She'd forget for just a few hours the shadow of the Wall looming behind. Her brain would dip into that unknown place. She could see it now, as she closed her eyes. The familiar images cocooned her: an endless road, the smell of sea salt on the air, stars above and the headlights ahead, hills and wind and horizon for a hundred miles. Throat tight, she opened her eyes again.

Always the same dream. She knew the curves of that road, the flicker of lights, the smells, like the back of her hand. Though she'd never *known* them at all. She wondered if, somewhere out there, this scene was real.

"You will someday," W whispered into the back of her hair. "In person. Close enough you won't be mistaking the city lights for stars."

She kept her eyes fastened on the horizon, staring so hard the night began to swallow the tiny gleams of gold. She blinked, afraid to lose them to the dark. They reappeared.

"Are you following the rule?" she whispered.

His arms pressed her closer. "Hope to die," he murmured. "We're going to get out."

The quiet promise settled on the still air. The wind had stopped, and the sounds of the city felt strangely soft. Courtney listened to the firm, sure cadence of his heartbeat, and willed herself to believe it as much as he did.

PART II:
THE IMPACT

11. PRICE

"YOU'RE LOSING your touch."

Cassandra let the body hit the floor with a crimson smirk in W's direction, wiping the blood from the cuff of her sleeve. She slipped the knife back into her belt, the heels of her boots clicking down the now-empty hallway.

"Am I?" W replied, stepping over the fallen man.

"That's *two* I've had to save you from," she sang over her shoulder.

"That's a reach. You were closer. He'd have hit you first."

"The fact that I kept his bullet from finding your neck still stands."

W chuckled, longer strides catching up with ease. "My body count's higher than yours."

"You *knocked* that last one over the head." Cassandra's melodic laugh echoed down the hall. "He's probably still breathing, down there, ready to get up in a minute or so."

"We'll be long gone by then."

The two of them kept pace in silence for a moment, eyes alert, guns ready. The small facility tucked behind AITO's string of nondescript warehouses on Westside Orion wasn't heavily guarded—likely, the Director thought weapons and medical equipment invited more risk than a tiny research repository. But it still had a solid layer of security to get through. In the two months since their attack on the main AITO compound, W had kept his raids strategically unpredictable. Jeanine's resources were spreading thinner and thinner across the city to try and keep up.

Adjusting his grip on the gun, W let his gaze slip over the woman at his side. His oldest field partner had no Change-enhanced senses or abilities—no Change at all, in fact—but W knew Cassandra would sense a threat as fast as he did. Reflexes rivaling his own, her skill on the field was matched by none. For this two-person job, there was no operative in the Dugout better equipped to be at his side. Yet, W would have almost rather gone alone. Beneath the airy banter, he felt the strain between them like a chill wind. His old partner, once able to read his every move with telepathic accuracy, now watched him through the distant, curious eyes of a stranger.

Perhaps *he* was the stranger.

"The file room should be just up ahead," he said, more to fill the silence than anything. They needed only one file—one that would augment his own research in fine-tuning the drug he'd painstakingly created to trigger a dormant Change—but the rest of the research stored here might prove vital down the road. "Take what you can, and then set the charges. We'll have two minutes."

"I'll have us out in one. To keep to your *long* gone aspirations."

The corner of his mouth lifted. "You always were the ambitious one."

"I seem to remember that description fitting you better." Dark eyes flickered up to him beneath long lashes. "The dethroned don't soon forget upstarts who swept half a city out from under them."

"You sound almost as if you're still salty about it."

"*Tsk*. All's fair in love and war, darling, but to see those same ambitions sinking..." Her heels clicked into harder, quicker strides. "It's quite a disappointment."

The silence fell between them again, cold and heavy. W slowed, his grip tightening on the gun in his hand. A *tranq* gun he couldn't quite believe he was carrying. The impulse to grab it that morning on the way out the door had startled him, but he hadn't fought it.

She'd noticed the green band around the barrel, no doubt, but hadn't commented.

Cassandra reached the door first. An old-fashioned steel one with a lock requiring only a key, no biometrics. Few of AITO's lesser facilities shared the fancy new tech of the main compound; funding from the Outside was limited, so many of their outposts and repositories had been converted from pre-Quarantine infrastructure. Convenient, as old warehouses and disused storefronts made for easier break-ins.

Tugging two slender steel picks from her bloodstained sleeve, Cassandra slid the points into the lock and set to work coaxing it open. W watched her, studying her pensive expression.

"I never told you how I ousted *my* predecessor," she said. The faint scratch of the lock beneath her careful maneuvering filled the space between them for a moment. "It happened a good five years before I met you."

Curious at the glint in her dark eyes, focused resolutely on the lock, W was returned to the memory of the night he'd first met her. A young woman, standing a head taller than himself at the time, cold fire in her eyes and a band of devoted killers at her back. She'd found him fascinating that day, nearly as fascinating as he'd found her. A scrawny street rat who'd single handedly killed two of her best thugs, then masqueraded with their faces to steal food and weapons throughout her territory—he'd either become a lucrative asset, or a serious threat. To the young James Wilder's eyes, Cassandra Silver had looked like the ultimate antithesis to powerlessness. So, of course, he'd accepted the more alluring offer between joining her ranks or dying on the spot.

Little had she known he'd rise to replace her leadership within three short years. Not only would he loosen her iron grip on her hard-earned kingdom, he'd become someone she didn't want to fight to win it back from.

"I've heard rumors," W replied. He'd been around early enough to catch the whispers of how Cassandra had usurped the infamous mob boss before her. "Always did wonder if I'd ever hear the story from you, though."

The smooth line of Cassandra's jaw hardened under her olive skin. "He got soft."

W waited, watching her hands tilt and shift the lockpicks.

"He wanted to build a family on the outside," she continued, voice flatter than her usual silky cadence. "Above the underworld, beyond the reach of the shadows he lived in. Had a daughter, and a granddaughter, who knew nothing about his empire below their feet—and he thought he could keep it that way."

A cold slither started in W's veins. The Hasegawas, Margo's parents, had also tried to live in two worlds. Killing for AITO, then assuming they could keep their family on the outside away from the bloodstains. The chilled note under Cassandra's voice told him exactly where she was going with this. He kept his face neutral.

"It didn't take much manpower to put the threats in the right places. His granddaughter was the hole in his armor he couldn't fortify. Replacing him was as bloodless and quick as asphyxiation. Of course, I couldn't leave him alive, even after he stepped down. So once the pawns were in my hands, I took him off the board."

Click. The lock gave, and Cassandra twisted the handle, swung the door inward and glanced back at him with a solemn expression.

"He didn't start out soft," she said. "But once something soft got under his skin, the fiercest ambitions he had didn't matter." Eyes flickering down to the gun in his hand, the one that felt too light, she pressed her lips together. "I would hate... to see your armor fail you."

"It's not going to."

The words sliced out of him, hard and cool, and they stared at each other for a moment.

"Good," she said.

She turned and walked into the darkness of the filing room, pulling the charges from her pocket. They glinted in the dim light.

"There's a price to be paid for freedom." Her low voice echoed back to him. "Forgetting it puts all of us back in the cage, no matter how close we were to destroying the bars."

The chill deepened. Opting for silence in light of the job they had to do, W stepped into the shadows after her.

She dreamt of Annika.

Jeanine's glasses dug a hard line into the bridge of her nose where she leaned across her arms, head down on the papers strewn about her desk. At the light touch to her shoulder, she jerked upright with a sharp gasp, startling the assistant who'd woken her. The young man backed off with a sheepish apology.

"S-sorry, Director. I wasn't sure if you could hear me."

She couldn't remember his name. Nor the names of the other two young scientists behind him—she didn't want to, after the last. If she learned a name, trust might creep in. And trust was fatal.

"Did you... spend the night here?" the first assistant asked.

The young man and woman behind him shuffled on their feet. Clearing her throat, Jeanine adjusted her glasses and bun, which had slipped out of its sharp up-do to fall in scraggly blonde strands across her eyes. A pen rolled off the desk to hit the floor as she straightened the mess of papers.

"There was a lot to be done." Her voice emerged clipped and alert, no hint of the sleep still crowding her brain. "Why are you here? You shouldn't be in until noon, at the earliest. Have you completed your salvaging tasks already?"

The assistant who'd woken her hesitated. "We wrapped up the salvaging last week, actually. There wasn't much to recover from the Bailey building. They knew what they were doing; the blast took out both the new shipment and the storage unit beneath. All the research located there is gone, save a few files."

The cold, heavy feeling from her dream came back, a slow crawl of ice in her bones.

"And the storage facility the Torch attacked last month? Their first strike after he escaped."

The assistant looked down at his feet. "Still nothing."

"And... last night? The file room in the Westside district?"

He pressed his lips together. "They burned everything that was left."

No. This confirmed it. Everything. All her fears, that the Whistler was still alive... only *he* had known about that research facility, the storeroom of every last file she'd kept on the Changers they'd collected since the program started. The dropsite atop the Bailey building—again, only he had known their secure supply location. She'd deluded herself long enough into hoping that officer had gotten off a lucky shot. Of course the Whistler had survived. He was phenomenal. His genes were incomparable. He was everything she needed, and everything that could destroy what she'd built.

Behind the assistant who'd braved approaching her, one of the scientists leaned in to whisper to the other.

Jeanine stood. "Go down and see if Todd needs anything in the Z-Ward. You're dismissed."

Scurrying back with short nods, the three scientists left her standing beside her desk, her fist shaking atop the pile of papers. She hadn't realized she'd clenched her fingers until now.

Jerking away from the desk, she strode to the tiny bathroom unit attached to her office, and locked herself in. She braced her hands on either side of the sink and breathed.

The instant her gaze met her reflection in the mirror, she winced. Her gray-blue eyes were bloodshot, the hair escaping her bun in a snarled halo around her face. The pink imprint of a pen shadowed the underside of one cheek; she'd fallen asleep with it pressed into her skin. The thin layer of makeup she wore had smeared across her eyes and lips, a bloody smudge at the corner of her mouth. Leaning over the sink, she turned on the tap and pressed two palms of frigid water to her face.

The dream lingered on the achy edges of her thoughts.

Jeanine hadn't touched the memory in years. The foggy scene had stolen across her unguarded mind, sinking her back into the body of a fourteen-year-old girl sitting in a hard metal folding chair next to a hospital bed. Her sister's tiny, frail hand felt like something made of paper inside her own. An origami doll, fingers fragile enough to crumple at the slightest wrong movement. The plastic tube under Annika's nose took up half her face. The twelve-year-old's chest rose and fell, so faintly Jeanine worried if she blinked, she'd miss it.

"*I promise.*" The thin, soft words had felt foreign. Jeanine's voice hadn't sounded like that in decades. "*I'll find a way to save you. I promise.*"

The tinny beep of the bedside monitor had been the only response.

She'd never managed to keep her promise. But she was so, so close to making up for it.

Erasing sickness. Death. The logical next step after finding human cells capable of healing themselves, of rejuvenating after dismemberment and even cellular disintegration. The outside world thought AITO was here to find a cure. And they were right. She was.

A cure for death.

It was possible. Her research was at the edge of finding it— this ultimate solution tugged from the cells of a creature mutated beyond human, beyond mortal. A creature that could stitch itself back together and regenerate cells from scratch in a matter of days. The Torch's DNA was something so close, yet not quite there. If only she'd had access to a theriomutant of his caliber with more human in his cells.

If only she'd had access to *him*.

She needed more time. But he was making sure she had none. Evan—the Whistler—stole more time from her every day. Already, he'd erased thousands of hours of research, hundreds upon hundreds of files of collected data and priceless breakthroughs dissolved into ash. Last night's raid hadn't been the first, and would be far from the last. The Whistler had gathered too much deadly knowledge during his stint inside AITO's walls. In the last week alone since he'd "liberated" half their subject population of theriomutants, he'd targeted with systematic, ruthless precision every hidden AITO facility this side of the city. Burning, destroying, stealing. And every day, more theriomutants appeared on the streets, joining his cause. She had no idea where they were coming from, but the reports kept flooding in, and with so many of their checkpoints going up in flames, neither AITO nor their partners in the OCPD could keep up.

He nearly had an army.

And the stealing. It was one thing to destroy the files. But there was no telling how many he'd absconded with, or how damning the information inside. Should the wrong records be thrown into the light of day...

He could bury them. All of AITO.

Everything she'd worked for.

Her fists tightened on the porcelain rim of the sink.

She knew what she had to do. But for the first time, a pit of frozen, nauseating shame coiled in her stomach. She'd signed orders like this before. But for so many... No. There was no other way.

She'd come too far to let him take this from her now.

Releasing the sink, she slammed open the door to the bathroom and strode across her office, snatching up her ID badge along the way.

Director. She was Director now.

The gruesome weight of this decision fell on her shoulders alone.

It was forgivable. That was what she told herself as the hard clip of her heels clacked off the concrete walls, echoing down the corridor toward the stairwell. It was a price to be paid for the greater good of the rest of her species. For the hollow promise she'd made so many years ago.

It was forgivable.

12. THE FALLOUT

ASPER WADE HAD never before wrestled with the law. Once, back in second-grade PE, his dodgeball team had won by mistake, and he'd been the kid to raise his hand and announce that the other team had scored the final point. The ball had barely grazed his pant-leg. No one had seen it. But he'd felt it. His teammates had groaned and pummeled him after, but he'd never felt sorry. It was right. It was honest.

In the police academy, he'd run silent laps around the training field when someone else had made a mistake, stood for hours under spittle-flying shouts when he'd made his own, and learned the rulebook by heart until he made no more. He knew the law inside and out. Concealing evidence, no matter how small—or how personal—was an obstruction of justice.

And Jasper lived for justice.

Yet here he stood, outside Commissioner Van de Graaf's door once again, debating walking away without a single knock.

The arrest warrant was already out for the woman who'd held a nurse at gunpoint at St. Barnabas. Motives and whereabouts unknown. They'd questioned him briefly after his ex-girlfriend's disappearance, but Jasper had been kept off the case, for good reason.

He had yet to report the connection between Courtney Spencer and the Whistler.

His conscience lacerated his insides. For all his talk to Dina and Oliver about keeping the law above personal feelings, he'd managed to evade the inevitable until now. Sitting on the information was wrong. He should've reported everything he knew about Courtney's affiliation with the Whistler two months ago, as soon as he'd put two and two together. Despite everything in him screaming otherwise, he'd kept his mouth shut and watched his colleagues struggle without leads in a woman-hunt he'd hoped would fizzle out. It hadn't. They'd even dragged Michael Spencer into it, questioning a disoriented preteen still grieving his missing father. Enough was enough.

It was time to put weakness aside.

As Jasper lifted a hand to knock on the dark wooden door, the roar in his head dwindled to a resigned, painful quiet. But his raised knuckles stilled when he heard the voices.

"Dr. Campbell, I assure you we're doing everything we can to find him."

"That's not good enough." A woman's voice, tight and sharp. "He's been inside my facility. There are *moles* inside AITO. He's systematically dismantling our security points around the city. With the number of theriomutants we lost in the break-in, there's a risk of—"

"I'm sorry, thar-ee-o…?"

"*Changers*," came the irritated reply. "Your units failed to recover half of our subject population. That's over one hundred theriomutants loose on the streets. Not just loose, but in *his* hands. We can't risk losing any more. There's no other option. The longer we wait, the bolder he becomes."

"I don't understand your request, doctor."

"This isn't a request. It's a notice. AITO is suspending its conservative methods. From now on, our response teams will be using lethal force."

A silence followed.

"You're saying, then, that all the people in your subject population at AITO—"

"Theriomutants, commissioner. Not people."

"They'll be... disposed of?"

"They're too great a risk to keep alive with moles inside our walls."

Another pause. "And if a Changer is identified on the streets, your response unit will..."

"Terminate them."

"In front of the public?"

"The *public* is in more danger than they realize. If we don't curb this now, there won't be a public to protect."

"Surely one man doesn't threaten AITO to this extreme." Van de Graaf's low chuckle made the woman on the other end of the door bristle—Jasper heard her voice drop to an icy register.

"He isn't just one man. He's managed to accelerate the production of Changers. Since he first appeared on our radar, they've multiplied seven to one. And they're not just multiplying. They're getting smarter. They're learning about us faster than we can learn about them—targeting our facilities, destroying research warehouses and supplies, killing scientists. You want a cure, Commissioner? If this city is overrun by infected lab rats, the only cure we'll have left in our arsenal is extermination. Every citizen will be infected. You may think my methods extreme, but I assure you, they will prevent a disaster even more so. It's more than a virus now, he's created a biological weapon."

Jasper stood so close to the door now, he could hear his breath bouncing off the surface. He shut his mouth. Silence. For one horrible second, he worried the two people in the office had heard him. Then he heard the commissioner's heavy exhale.

"I don't like it," came the faint rumble. "But if you're right, if these freaks truly are threatening the safety of Orion citizens, there may be no other recourse. We can't afford a second raid on the AITO compound. You have my department's support." Another, longer pause. "God help us all, at least they're only halfway human anymore."

Jasper took a step back from the door. Then another, turning to walk away.

He didn't know where he was going until he hit the lobby. Rain mixed with sleet drummed against the station windows, a dull roar intensifying as he neared. Air. He needed air.

A small person blocked him halfway to the door. "Jasper."

"Dina?"

She looked up at him, so close her short hair slipped back from her face at the motion.

"What are you doing here? Is everything okay?" The question spilled out automatically, disconnected from the building thunder in his brain.

"No." Worry pinched her expression. "I swore I wouldn't do this, but—she's in too deep. I need your help. I didn't know who else to…"

Her words faded out, even as she continued speaking—because Jasper's eyes locked onto the station doors swinging open. An icy blast of water swept in behind three figures.

Two of his fellow officers dragged a young man between them. His head lolled on his shoulders. He was barefoot, his skinny body covered in a tight black suit of some kind. A loose loop of fabric hung around his neck, swinging as they walked, revealing eye holes punched through the black. A mask. Torn at the corners, like someone had ripped it down his face and let it hang from the broken knot at the back.

The man stumbled, and the officers yanked him upright. The cuffed man lifted his head. His battered face caught the light. It tilted at an odd angle, his face blackened with bruises. One eye was swollen shut. A nasty cut leaked blood over his left eyebrow. But Jasper would recognize him anywhere.

Oliver.

His friend offered him a feeble smile, and Jasper felt the floor tilt under his feet.

He was moving forward before he could think, the shout tearing out of him. "What's going on here?"

The trio stopped. "Didn't you hear?" Weary triumph colored the officer's voice. "We finally caught the vigilante. The Orion Giant's not getting any more headlines."

For a brief second, the precinct around them faded away. He and Oliver stood alone, face to face across a rainy street, a cop car rumbling under Jasper's clammy hands and the dark figure in the alley opposite staring him down in defiant challenge—the Triad symbols on his jacket glowing under the flash of blue lights. The memories crashed into him. Hours stuck on stakeouts together. The day Oliver saved his life on a nightwatch gone wrong. The reluctant respect that grew between them, as Jasper learned why Oliver had betrayed the Triads, and in turn told Oliver why he'd moved to Orion City. That unexpected first invitation from old Grandma Lee to celebrate the Chinese New Year with them, being forced to eat until he might explode. That first sense of belonging, of having a real connection here in this city that had once tried to drown him— a rock under his feet, a place he could stand even after other places wavered.

The memories snapped back into Oliver's dimmed, swollen dark eyes.

"What…" Jasper's thoughts short-circuited at the look on his friend's face. "You've got the wrong man."

"That's how he got away with it so long," the officer grunted. "You'd have to see it to believe it. This little runt turns into the twelve-foot freak show we've been chasing for months. Took fifteen tranquilizers to bring him down to this size—and somehow he's still walking."

Jasper couldn't rip his gaze from Oliver's. His best friend stared back, his injured eye a little unfocused, but fixed valiantly on Jasper's face.

A sluggish laugh bubbled up from his friend's chest. "Don' looksss….ssso b'trayed," he struggled out. "If I'da told you, you'da locked me up withhhhout…" He wheezed. "W'thout a blink. Law first, with you. Even if that law's more broken than the onessss who have to *break* it… to save the sssstup'd idiots who *made* it…" He dissolved into drugged laughter. A tear slipped from his good eye.

"Step aside, Wade." The officers adjusted their grip on Oliver as he slumped. "This one's got an order for immediate transfer to AITO. We can't hold him in this facility."

The air was gone. He couldn't breathe, couldn't lunge forward and grab, couldn't protect, couldn't serve. He was useless. He was so horribly, utterly useless.

"*Now*, rookie."

A small hand closed around his arm, pulling him back. Jasper stared after them, fighting to think as the officers hauled Oliver away. Every thought in his head had winked out. There was only the sound of the sleet on the windows. The hum of the department getting back to work. The number of yards growing between him and the three figures retreating down the hallway.

Dina's hand tightened around his elbow. "Was that…?"

Oliver grew smaller and smaller. He'd never looked so small. *The Orion Giant.*

"Are you okay?"

Courtney's voice stabbed in again. *If you have to break the law to do what's right…*

"I need to—" he sputtered out. He stumbled out of Dina's grip, tipping for the door. "I'm sorry, I just need—"

He flung the doors open and staggered out. Stopping a few paces from the entrance, he sank back against the station wall. Ice pelted him. A frozen dribble of sleet caught the back of his neck and dripped down into his collar. Jasper dug his fingers into his hair. He tried to force himself to feel something. *Think* something.

Only once he'd started to shiver did he notice he wasn't alone.

"I'm sorry, Dina," he rasped. "Now may not be a good time for me to help you."

She stood in silence. Arms wrapped around herself, her little figure bobbed as she shifted from foot to foot. She leaned back against the wall beside him.

"That was your best friend, wasn't it? His name was…"

Jasper's voice cracked through his dry throat. "Oliver."

"I'm guessing he never told you about his nightly escapades?"

"He never—he's not…"

The rain thrummed, an icy murmur silencing his denial.

"The Orion Giant is a hero," Dina said. "Your friend saved a lot of lives. When his trial comes, they'll have to mention that."

"He won't get a trial." His throat closed off. Who could he tell? The words he'd overheard behind the commissioner's door drummed against his skull. He had to tell someone. Courtney was out of the picture. His colleagues? Not a chance. And now Oliver…

"She was right."

Jasper looked down at Dina. "What?"

"You really do wear everything right there on your face." She studied him. "Something was wrong the minute I saw you. Before Oliver ever walked into the station. What happened?"

Her brown eyes were darker than Courtney's, more direct, relentless and unwavering as she waited for an answer. Jasper tried to look away, but found he couldn't.

A whole year in the city, and he'd only managed to find confidantes in Oliver and Courtney. They'd been lights in this city's relentless dark. But now… he couldn't tell them apart from the rest of Orion's shadows. His muscles clenched in the cold. His jaw hurt from locking his teeth against the chatter. He could see Dina's breath turning to fog on the air, little swirls that squeaked past her trembling lips, though she didn't make a move to leave his side.

If he couldn't trust Dina Ramirez, he really had no one else.

"What if all the structures you thought were solid…" The words bled from him almost against his will. "Everything you trusted your whole life, right and wrong, the good guys, the bad guys… What if all of that was a lie?"

Dina blinked at him. She crossed her arms and stared out into the rain. "That would suck."

"I don't know what else to…" His jaw clenched. "I have to believe in the law. It's the only thing that brings good and keeps it there."

"No, people bring good and keep it there." Dina paused. "They also bring the shit that hits the fan."

"My best friend is going to lose his life because he tried to go outside the law to bring good."

"Lose his life?"

"AITO. The White Coats, as you call them—I just learned the OCPD is working with them to turn in every Changer and have them executed."

Dina's hand flew to her mouth. "Courtney."

"What?"

Her eyes flashed to his, wide and shining, then dropped. The CCTV footage flickered in his mind.

"You knew." Suspicion crystallized, sharpened his voice. "You knew about her."

Dina stiffened. "*You* knew?"

"St. Barnabas caught her Change on the security camera."

She winced. Jasper saw the guilt flash across her face before she could hide it.

"What do you know, Dina?"

"Nothing! I came to *you* for answers."

"You know I've got none. I think you came to tell me something."

Dina's lips parted. Something flickered in her eyes. She turned away and stared out into the rain. At last, Jasper spoke in a flat voice.

"She's with him, isn't she?"

Dina's throat bobbed. "I think so."

The two of them stood, listening to the distant rumble of sirens. The rain hissed between them.

"Do you know anything else you're not telling me?"

Dina looked up. Through narrowed eyes, she measured him. "I

know pieces of things. Whether I tell you or not depends on what you're going to do."

"About what?"

"Your friend."

Her head barely came up to his shoulder, but Jasper felt like the small one under her stare. It pierced straight down into that place he wanted to close up, lock, and bury deep down where it couldn't burn anymore. But he couldn't. Because this wasn't justice. This wasn't some shifty acquaintance he could resign himself to lose, consoling his conscience that they stood on opposite sides of the law. This was Oliver.

"They're going to kill him." His voice snagged, almost swallowed up by the pattering sleet. "They're going to kill my best friend. I don't care if he lied to me, or if he isn't... if he's not who I thought he was. I can't let that happen."

Dina pursed her lips. "You know *why* he lied to you, right?"

Jasper's mind drifted with the image of the mask hanging down Oliver's front. Two tattered eyeholes.

"There was a doctor I used to work under," Dina said. "Brilliant guy. Unconventional. One day, he did a crazy stupid thing on the job. A patient came in critical condition. He was going to die. Cardiac arrest, no chance of making it another ten minutes despite all our equipment and training. So this doctor tried something that broke every rule in the book. I won't confuse you with the medical details—they were kinda gory—but long story short, his unorthodox method both saved the guy's life and cost him his medical license." She paused again. "Why am I telling you this? Because, Jasper, if you were a doctor, you would've been one of the ones so attached to the rulebook you might've stopped him saving that man's life. You would've watched him die on the table and told yourself—and everyone—you couldn't do anything else."

The rain pitched higher. A fierce whine, digging into his eardrums.

"There's a right and wrong," Dina went on. "No one's debating that. But maybe it's time you step out of your two-dimensional world and realize your friend was fighting for the same thing you are. Just a hell of a lot more efficiently."

Jasper locked his jaw. Half a dozen prepared answers boiled up, echoing what he'd told Courtney all those days ago: *You're talking like a criminal.*

But the words of Commissioner Van de Graaf edged in ahead of them. *Halfway human.* Rationalizing the massacre they were about to commit. Justifying it. In the name of the law.

God help us all…

The breath slipped out of him in a cold, unbroken stream.

"Dina," he whispered. "I never thought I would have to choose between the lesser of two evils." He fought with his words. "Would you be willing to help me with something… insane?"

She raised an eyebrow. "Insane seems to be a running theme these days."

He swallowed. The rain seemed to increase with his heartbeat, a building roar that thumped in his head, filled his bones. A burn began to drive away the cold. "I need a nurse. And about half a dozen tranquilizers."

13. VILLAIN

T WAS RAINING.

W watched the rivulets split and track down the window, leaving muddy forks on the dusty glass. Ice swam inside the miniature rivers. He could feel the chill despite the rickety space heater in the corner of the room. Winter whispered through the cracked brick wall.

Four stories below, the pavement shimmered in the dim afternoon light. Pale gray slush rimmed the fence, the edge of the building opposite. Layers of sleet stacked up until it looked like snow. Ice was good. On any day like today, it should have made him happy. Wheels danced on ice. Streets slick and deadly, his people could move while the police froze. Even Des, with all his skill, struggled to drive in these conditions. But that wouldn't stop his team. Padded paws and treaded boots worked just fine. As for the rest of the plan—to an amateur arsonist it might've posed a problem. But Torch was no amateur.

It was as if the Fates were smiling down on him, dropping down a freezing sign that this night, this final push, would topple the castle. The corner of his lips twitched. God, the Fates, whoever was up there, didn't sympathize with him. If anything, the ice flaunted a sick reminder of what waited on the other side if he did fail.

If he lost them, he could live. Years upon years of freezing the pain into numbness had taught him how to let go of people. He didn't *like* to lose them. Cheap hires, hit men, disposables like the goon he'd shot in Courtney's café could be replaced. But this was a team he'd built over half a decade. He knew Red's fiery temper, Deadeye's dry humor, Strings' pitchy violin tunings. If he didn't act, he would lose them.

But if he did act… he would lose her.

The ice seemed to thicken on the air at the sound of footsteps behind him. An arm slipped through his, warm fingers curling over the backs of his knuckles.

"You're more brooding than usual." Cassandra's husky voice hummed near his ear. "I hope you're not worried about the change of plans."

W studied the silver webs forming on the window.

"My source is good," she said. "They're scared, they're weak. Killing all of their subjects is a desperate move. If we catch them now, before they regroup, we could put them down for good. We have enough momentum. If we wait any longer, we'll lose our edge."

"When do they do it?"

"Every Changer in AITO is scheduled for termination by the end of tomorrow."

He listened to the tap of ice on the glass. The slush had crystallized into hail.

"The Triads agreed to the acceleration of plans. The team's ready to move out by sundown."

W turned from the window. Cassandra's arm fell from his as he walked back toward the desk, where blueprints of the original storage facility they'd planned to raid had been replaced with floor plans for AITO's main compound. He looked at them for a moment, studied the hastily scrawled game plan.

He'd received the information an hour ago. An hour to strategize, an hour to tear apart and reconfigure the plan he'd had in the works for ten years. Less than twenty-four hours to change his entire operation before AITO terminated every last one of their captive Changers. He still had people in that compound. People he couldn't save, hadn't been able to spring when the last raid had ended so abruptly. He brushed a hand over the fading scar at his ribs.

Not all Changers could heal themselves. Not all had such direct control over their faculties, forcing every cell and sinew of their body to align and reshape, to warp at their command. Not like him. He'd seen the Orion Giant recover from bullets one or two times. A few other vigilantes were working to perfect the technique— Deadeye, the Torch. But none had spent twenty years mastering the Change, bending it to their will instead of the other way around. More often than not, the Change warped the mind. W had spent the last two decades fighting that insanity. The break that always threatened. It had been a standstill battle up until the day he found his real enemy. When, all those years ago, that battered boy had moved beyond fighting to *survive* the Change and realized he could *use* it.

Twenty years of training. Ten years of plotting, building and careful preparation. The Wall would come down. He would be the one to raze it.

Now, all that planning was about to fly out the window. Because AITO had made a suicide move. A move that would win them the game if W didn't do something equally suicidal.

"It'll be close," he said. "We don't have the numbers. The new recruits aren't trained to control their Change. After the amount we lost in the last raid, we'll be pretty evenly matched with AITO's forces. And that's only if Torch takes the police out of the equation."

"He will," Cassandra said from behind him. "Untrained or not, the recruits will at least slow down their forces."

"Yes." His voice tightened. "They'll run around like confused beasts caught in the crossfire."

"If they don't come, they'll die anyway. AITO will hunt them down if we fail."

W scratched at one of the diagrams with a knife lying on the table. "I'll ask for volunteers. They're here of their own free will."

The sigh hissed behind him, sharp and thin. "Play it however you like. Leave the girl behind if you're worried about her."

There it was. The center of her razored tone, tightly hidden under a layer of indifference. W drove the knife through the center of a blueprint, right above the layout of AITO's control room.

"She stays. Along with anyone else on this team who isn't a killer."

"Will you tell her what you're going to do?" Amusement warmed her voice. "She struck me as the flighty type. A little blood, a little gore, and she'll run screaming for the hills."

Do you see me running?

W traced the edge of his knife with a fingertip. A small bloom of red lifted from his middle finger. Pulling back, he watched the skin seal itself in a slow, smooth line. The smallest tug of energy drained from his core. Practice.

"She knows she's not invited on the facility raid," he said. "Which was scheduled for tonight. As far as what she doesn't need to know..."

He let the words hang on the air, until he heard Cassandra's soft chuckle.

"Are you leaving a babysitter behind? Strings, maybe? She was always a little squeamish when it came to pulling the trigger."

"Like I said, this one's on a volunteer basis. Everyone on this team knows what they're heading into. Strings, Des, Books, anyone who doesn't want to take a life won't have to."

Silence followed his statement. Turning, he saw Cassandra staring at him with her red lips slightly parted. She approached him with slow steps. Her heeled boots were silent on the wooden floorboards, a cat's tread. She stopped a few inches away from his face. Russet eyes swept between his, back and forth, wide and disbelieving.

"You don't actually..." Her whisper slid over his skin. Once, a long time ago, he'd enjoyed the scent of her this close, the sweetness of her breath, the wild smoky tint of her hair. Now, he resisted the urge to step back.

"It was amusing at first. Your pet project, that young moldable little mind—always so fun to corrupt." Her brow furrowed. "It was obvious when I met her your hooks had sunk in deep. But now... she's become more than a side project. She has hooks in you, too. You're trying to change things. For *her*." Confusion, more than envy, more than anger, clouded the dark wells of her eyes. "She can't change what you are, James. Giving the soft ones on this team the choice to shy away from the job, the chance to try and keep their hands clean… it doesn't erase the lives you've taken." Gaze burning, she leaned in even closer. "We're alike, you and I. We lead because we're willing to do whatever it takes. You don't get this far in the business without stains."

He studied the sympathetic downturn of her mouth, noting how calculated the angle was. "Nothing has been erased," he said. "She knows what I am. What I was."

"Does she? Then by all means, tell her about tomorrow. Perhaps she'll volunteer."

He measured her. She measured him right back.

"I would say she's deluded you," she said. "But she doesn't have the guile. You've deluded yourself. You actually think you're…" She stopped. The amusement in her eyes drained, pressed out by a stunned—almost pained—stare. With an unusual tremble in her hand, she touched his arm. "James," she whispered. "People like us aren't capable of love."

W looked down at the hand on his coat. Gently, he slid his fingers around hers and removed it, keeping her smaller hand inside his for a moment.

"Speak for yourself," he whispered. Leaning forward, he pressed a chaste kiss to her forehead. He released her fingers.

She made no move to follow him as he headed for the door.

Rain knifed out of the sky, hardening into hail. Courtney frowned up at it, feeling her nose turning red, the sting against every inch of exposed skin. She jammed her fingers into the pockets of her jeans. *Not* her jeans. A dead girl's clothes she hated to remember she was borrowing. People had died going up against AITO. A lot of young, reckless Changers like herself. Maybe Strings' old roommate had bitten off more than she could chew. Maybe she hadn't been ready for the raid that had killed her.

Or maybe she'd prepared for weeks, nailed every shot to the center of her targets. Maybe she'd been the best fighter in the Loons, and that still hadn't been good enough.

Courtney sighed, watching the steam of it slide and shift on the air until it disappeared.

Save the raid on Pierce & Bailey's, she hadn't gone outside in the entire two months she'd been at the Dugout. Granted, this didn't really count—she stood on the metal platform of the fire escape on the second floor, hugging the brick wall to avoid the rain. W's team didn't trust her to just leave and come back, knowing the location of the Dugout. Despite W's promise earlier that she was free, she figured that didn't mean she could tromp around the city at will, leaving trails for all of AITO to follow. She was a fugitive after all. After that stunt at the hospital, she wondered if Jasper would have a warrant for her arrest if she saw him again. Her throat panged.

Oh, well. At least it was fresh air.

An engine snarled to life across the courtyard. Courtney looked down to see a van grumbling around the corner of the condemned building opposite, moving painfully slow across the ice. It stopped in the middle of the yard. Steam curled around the wheels. The driver door opened, and a man slid out. Courtney expected to see Des, but this man was much smaller, and he wore the fitted nylon suit Strings had designed for Changers on raids.

Courtney frowned. She'd heard Red mention something about another raid tonight—which she was exclusively not invited on— but that was still several hours away. And where was Des? She'd never seen anyone else drive the van.

Moving to the back of the truck, the man opened the rear doors and let the taillights glow in the steam, engine idling. He unloaded a huge black assault rifle. Then a second... then a third. He glanced up. Courtney shrank back on instinct, feeling his gaze scrape along the side of the building where she stood.

Was he one of theirs? She didn't recognize him from the Loons. Retreating back into the Dugout, she barely had time to analyze the thought—*theirs*; how she'd attached herself to "them" without a beat of hesitation—before she crossed the room she shared with Strings and exited to the hallway.

It was crowded. Though she knew plenty of people lived on this hall, she'd never seen so many out all at once. The new recruits down at the end came and went from slamming doors. Men and women she'd only glimpsed a few times. Courtney frowned as she watched them mill by, noting the way they'd dressed themselves—loose clothing, a few workout stretch pants, and several wore Strings' nylon suits.

The raid. It was the only explanation. But... there were so many. And W didn't let new recruits tag along. She'd been an exception, as Red's shadow, before she'd been banned from all upcoming raids until further notice. Most of these people hadn't been here any longer than she had. She'd resigned herself to staying behind this time, already concocting a plan of how she could train and convince Deadeye to let her on the next raid. It made her itch to know that in a few hours the team would be out fighting AITO without her. And, just as sharp as the idea of Red or Strings catching a bullet in the chest, was the idea of her new friends gunning down another human being. The idea that there might be another Margo by the end of the night. Some kid without a father or mother in the name of vigilante justice.

And she would be sitting here, in the Dugout, unable to do anything about it.

The people in the hallway split and shuffled around her, heading for the stairs. A few shot her cursory glances while she stood like a fish trying to stay upstream. She watched them pass, stomach sinking when she saw some toting guns. This didn't make sense. The raid wasn't until tonight. And why were the new recruits going? Hadn't W said he didn't like to waste people? They couldn't be any more trained than she was.

A gleam of red hair stood out among the rest.

"Courtney!" Her father zigzagged toward her. She took his arm as he reached her and pulled him inside the doorway.

"Dad," she shouted over the flow of people. "What's going on?"

"It's a riot." His eyes looked as wild as they had the morning she'd first seen him. "This Boss of theirs is starting a revolution or something. It's bad, Court, they're going to kill everyone—all those poor people in Chinatown, all of Eastside, it's going to be a—"

"What?" She tugged him closer. "Who's going to kill who? Chinatown?"

"They explained it all to us. Said he was asking for volunteers. Said anyone who didn't want to go was free to leave, but that nowhere was safe anymore, not the Dugout, not our homes, not the streets. AITO…" He gripped her shoulder. "Courtney. It's going to be a bloodbath. They're going to storm the compound. They're in league with the Triads down in Chinatown, they've got a riot staged to distract the police, and that crazy demon the Torch is setting fires all across Eastside, spreading the authorities thin so no unit will be able to come to AITO's defense."

"Why?" Courtney's hollow yelp disappeared under the din of the hallway. "What does he hope to accomplish? The last raid he launched on AITO killed half his team—"

"That's just it. The people AITO captured before—every Changer, whether or not they were part of his group—AITO's going to kill them all. After tomorrow, there won't be any of his team left to rescue. They've started combing the streets. Killing people without question, no quarantines, no more trying to find a cure."

"*What?*"

"They shot a man dead in the street yesterday. They went after a kid in Eastside, the youngest Changer I ever saw on the news—a group of people hid him so he got away in the crowd, but they would've killed him, Court. A child."

Her eyes darted over the people in the hallway. No sign of Strings. "Is everyone going on this… this mission?"

"I don't know. Every recruit I met is on board—they've got families to worry about, kids they're terrified might Change."

"It doesn't work like that. They'd have to be…" An icy thought slammed into her. *At least ten years old.* The reservoir had been contaminated ten years ago. W's voice rocketed back: *Anyone old enough to have the serum in their system ten years ago has potential.*

"Michael," she gasped.

"I'm going back to him right now."

"What? Dad, you can't! You were on the news, if they're hunting for you—"

"They'll find me protecting my son! If this Change can happen to anybody at any time, who's to say Michael's not in danger right now?"

Words crumbled as her brain surged ahead, spinning through horrific possibilities and pictures. She gripped her father's arm so hard he winced. "Where is he?"

"Michael?"

"No. *Him.*"

He blinked. "Upstairs, I think. They're about to leave—"

She took off, tripping and slamming through the crowd. Her father's voice bellowed after her. "Wait, you're not going to *talk* to that madman—*Courtney!*"

A woman cursed at her as she stumbled, knocking into the recruit's shoulder so hard she almost dropped the gun slung across it. Courtney righted herself without an apology. She speared her way through the final cluster of people, bursting into the stairwell. She made it to the relative clear of the second landing... and almost crashed into Red coming down.

"Ho, where's the fire?" Adjusting a belt of knives on her waist, the girl tossed her a curious smirk. "You suiting up with the rest of us?"

"The fires," Courtney panted. "Is Torch already setting the fires?"

"Uh—I think he's still mixing the C4. Are you okay?"

Courtney dove past her. The old wood splintered under her crashing steps. She hit the third floor, then the fourth. Her lungs burned as she sprinted down the hallway. The last room, that final door on the left where a crack of light spilled out across the floorboards.

She banged it open without a knock.

For a dizzy moment, she was terrified she would find Cassandra. But W stood alone at the window. His back was to her, silhouetted against the angry sky. Hail drummed on the roof, so much louder here on the topmost story.

"I wondered if the ruckus would tip you off."

His soft tone was totally at odds with the pounding in her skull. Courtney slipped into the room. The door drifted shut behind her.

"Is it true?" She crept closer, half wishing the hail would drown out his answer.

"You'll have to be a little more specific."

"The riot. The fires." She held her breath. "AITO."

Drumbeats of ice. The gurgle of the space heater across the room. Then: "Yes."

No emotion. Not a hint of remorse. The air slid out of her, a knife from a wound.

"You've been planning this the whole time, then?" Damn her voice for sounding so small. "That note Deadeye gave you when I first got here, about the Triads being ready. The raid tonight was all a ruse."

"Sharp memory." He didn't turn. "It wasn't a ruse. Circumstances changed, and plans shifted with them."

"So all that talk about change?" she bit out. "Last night. I thought we had a rule. No lies between you and me."

"I told you the truth," he replied. "Change is bloody."

Her stomach tightened. "All those people, W."

There. Finally. The faintest, almost imperceptible rise of one shoulder. She wouldn't have seen it if she hadn't been staring at him so hard, her eyes drilling into his back as she willed him to turn around.

"We're in a war, C." Despite the tension in his stance, his voice continued unchanged. "I don't have the luxury of keeping my hands clean."

"Like me?" She marched further into the room. "Is that why you planned on leaving me behind? In the dark? While you go out and murder half the city to get your revenge on—"

"This is *not* about revenge." He turned, and she flinched back. His pale eyes burned. A hard, dark energy crackled behind them, electricity that threatened to arc out and destroy whatever it touched. She'd never seen a crack in his mask this wide. "In fourteen hours, every subject in that compound is going to die. Not only every last one of my people, but every disgruntled shopkeeper and bank manager and janitor and *barista* who had the misfortune of drinking tap water ten years ago. Who had the misfortune of being average nobodies caught up in a biological war, unwitting test subjects for a genetic weapon brewing in their own blood. A weapon deemed so inhumane by the government it was buried, then resurrected again right under their noses in an enormous cage of cement where AITO gets free reign to observe and manipulate their guinea pigs. In case you missed it, that picture is a whole lot bigger than me. Than my father, than *any* of us." His jaw twitched. "It's bigger than you."

"I know." Her breath hitched, seeing the ice behind his eyes. They pinned her where she stood, a weight that crushed the words she'd gathered, pressing them out of her brain. How could she argue with him? He'd been planning this for years—decades, even. Long before she'd had the nerve to do anything but keep her head down, pretending she couldn't see the news, the horrors going on around her every day. Before she'd met him, back when it was easy to let her desire for normalcy blur and fade the realities in the background that didn't match, didn't fit the world she wanted: a world that was safe and sane and fair. A world most of the other citizens in this city preferred to see, as well.

All except W.

"I know," she repeated, stronger. "What AITO is doing is evil, and we have to stop them. But—"

"No, not *we*. Never a *we*, Courtney. You were *never* supposed to be a part of this!"

The words stung for only a second. She saw the pain in his eyes a second after: the rage, the fear, the vulnerability he masked with a hand over his face, dragging his fingers down across his hair and eyes. He laughed, and the sound was a gunshot, cracking off the walls with a violence that chilled her bones. "I'm supposed to be down there right now. I can't believe it's finally set to go, the bomb is ticking and all the chips are down, and what's holding me back is an ex-medical-student-barista who cowers at the sight of blood."

Anger sprang forward, a hot lash fighting for control of her tongue. She clamped her teeth down on the flare-up of words, and stepped toward him. "Those people out there in Eastside are just as innocent as the Changers AITO is killing." Her voice shook. So did her hand, as she crossed the steps left between them and lifted it to his arm. "James, you set out to stop AITO in order to save people. You told me. And when you look at Margo, you said you—"

"Don't," he hissed.

"You said killing her wouldn't be like killing someone from AITO—someone who'd already lost their conscience, lost their humanity." She swallowed. "And... Margo's parents, you said you still remember their names. They were human. They were trying to have a family, maybe thought they were using science to make the world a better place, in their own twisted—"

Fingers closed over hers, crushing them. Peeling them off his arm. "At what price?"

"At what price are *you* going to stop them?" Her throat tightened. "How many more Margo's will you make?"

For several long seconds, the hail muted above them, all sound sucked out of the room as she tried not to wither under his stare. She watched the light change behind his eyes. Flicker and darken. The dull roar faded back into her awareness. Ice thundered louder than ever.

"I'm not the hero." The low snarl slid into the space between them, seething with an energy that frightened her more than she ever remembered feeling around him. "I'm not your *cop* with all his righteous ideals, or the Orion Giant in the tabloids, the hero who saves the town at the end of the day *and* stops the villain. I *am* the villain, Courtney. Wake up." He stepped back from her, strode around her with a speed that left her spinning, struggling to track with his words as he clipped: "I tried to push you out of this. Now you're not just a liability, you're..." His jaw flexed. "I can't let you compromise my operation."

Before she could register his meaning, could absorb the weight behind the look he gave her, he was standing in the doorway. One hand slipped into his coat pocket. A key glinted in the light.

"And I can't let you hurt yourself trying."

Understanding blasted through her. She sprinted for the door, a yell building in her throat just as it swung shut. Her fists thudded against the wood.

"W!" Her fingers found the handle, scrabbling at the knob. It squeaked, immovable under her hand. "*James!*"

Footsteps clicked away down the hall. She screamed, slamming her palms against the door until the old frame made a cracking sound, but it didn't budge. Wheeling, she ran to the window and pressed her nose to the glass. Little spirals of hail swam past her vision. Below, a smear of taillights stood out in the fading light. Figures pressed in around the van, too dark and blurry to identify.

Doors slammed. The red glow flickered, brakes squealed, and then the vehicle was rolling forward, the swarm of people parting around it. The van bumped carefully over the ice as it exited the courtyard. The figures converged again. After a minute of indistinguishable shuffling, the group started forward after the van.

Her nose began to ache. Refusing to pull away from the cold, Courtney cupped her palms around her eyes and held her breath to stop the fog on the glass, straining her eyes to see if W was among them. He could've been anyone. He'd probably Changed his face going down the stairs, preparing for the departure.

Anger and dread battled for dominance. Curling her fist against the glass, she cursed.

A dark, frozen feeling yawned behind her ribs. The breath left her lungs in a hard jerk when she recognized it: the frigid shadow she'd thought she'd left behind in Westside, beaten for good under her newfound spark.

Hopelessness.

14. NOBODIES

THE ANCIENT SCREWS keeping the handle in place wouldn't budge. Even if she'd had a screwdriver, such a heavy layer of rust sealed the knob, she'd never jimmy it off the door. Courtney found a knife on the paper-strewn table, stabbed into what looked like a map. She poked and wiggled the tip around the tiny keyhole. Too wide. Scouring the rest of the room, she abandoned the idea of lock-picking when she found nothing thinner than a pencil. Even that was too fat for the hole. If only Strings' dead roommate had left behind some bobby pins—Books had shown her a thing or two about locks, even if she had broken nine out of the ten picks he'd given her to practice with.

She crossed back to the window. The light was fading fast, the imprint of her nose and hands dark on the glass. She squinted down at the courtyard again. The single light above her head made it hard to see, brighter inside now than out. The slush-covered lot looked abandoned below. No sign of the van. No sign of anybody leaving the Dugout. W's half of the Loons had left, and she was alone.

Bastard.

She forced her chest to rise. Shut her eyes. Her phone was lying on her bed downstairs. She hadn't needed it the entire week, so she hadn't thought to shove it in her pocket. Her father might still be here. Maybe. If she could make a loud enough racket—stomping on the floor, throwing a chair through the window—but it was hailing, and anybody who'd stayed would be two stories down...

The window. Her eyes flew open. Pressing a palm to the glass, she watched the fog spread around her splayed fingers. She leaned forward. It hadn't looked so high until now. As she strained her eyes through the scummy shield of glass, she caught the frosted edge of the fire escape below.

Her fingers skimmed the window ledge. Mold and dust met the edges of the glass, like no one had opened it in years. She searched for a latch and frowned. Her window downstairs opened. Strings went out there to swing off the fire escape all the time. Granted, their room was much closer to the ground. Maybe W didn't want anyone sneaking into his room from outside. It struck her as paranoid. But then again, in the circles he ran, there was probably plenty to be paranoid about.

She turned around and trailed her eyes across the room, landing on the space heater in the corner. Its groan was faint, an old rattling hum she hadn't noticed until now. She walked toward it. The clunky piece of metal looked heavy. But maybe. Just maybe...

Yanking the plug from the wall, she tested the exterior with a fast tap of her hands, checking the temperature. The outermost edges on either side were hot to the touch, but not unbearably so. She could hold it for ten seconds. Gripping with firm hands, she hefted it from the floor. Her back arched under the weight. Damn, these old-fashioned ones were heavy.

Okay. Ten steps to the window. Courtney walked as fast as she could with the load, palms sweating. She bent her knees and heaved.

The space heater bounced off the window ledge, knocking her backwards with the momentum. She let it hit the floor with a thud, and shook out her stinging fingers. She had to commit. A low-confidence swing wouldn't cut it.

Grasping the heater again by the edges, she stepped back, swinging her arms until gravity gave them a pendulum lift. She swung it again. On the third swing, she stomped forward and thrust every muscle into the upward motion.

The heater crashed through the window with a brittle crunch. Glass spewed. Courtney stumbled as it left her grip. The heater clanged off the fire escape, skidded, and hit the ground two seconds later with a wet thud. Metal clattered. Courtney brushed the shards from her pants. One palm stung, and she picked out a glass triangle from the lifeline of her hand. Bracing herself on the wall, she lifted a shoe to scrape off as many of the shards from the base of the window as she could. The top had punched clean out, but the bottom stuck up in clear jagged teeth. A few stubborn bits resisted her shoe. She shrugged off her jacket and folded it over the ledge. It would have to do. Gripping the edges of the window, she looked down.

Icicles hung from the fire escape. The hail had thinned again to rain, but that made this somehow worse. Slicker, more deadly. Two more platforms stood below this one, one story apart. Slush clung to the grated floor.

The topmost was *missing* a *ladder*.

Either it had rusted to oblivion and fallen right off the side of this condemned building, or it had been deliberately removed.

Icy wind whipped the hair back from her ears. No ladder between her and a ten-foot drop.

It was still her best plan.

Squeezing her lips together, Courtney climbed out onto the ledge. The hard points of the glass dug into her thighs, but didn't slice through the jacket or her jeans. She let go of the window and wobbled on the slick platform.

The square hole in the grating yawned at her. Every instinct screaming not to, she sat down on the edge. Then slid over onto her stomach and let her feet dangle.

Crap. This was a stupid plan.

Wind sucked at her legs, flapped the edges of her shirt around her stomach, where slush had started its freezing crawl against her skin. She felt a vague sting near her arm. Glass? She closed her eyes, inching out a little further. Her chin dug into her hands. Her triceps screamed from supporting her weight. She dangled awkwardly for a second, unable to let go. If she fell and slipped, if she rolled right off the platform...

Two seconds suddenly felt like a long time to fall.

She wiggled her elbows off the edge, trying to extend her grip to only her hands so she'd have one foot less to fall—and slipped.

A soundless cry cut off in her throat. She hit the platform below with a rattle that crunched her knees. Her body pitched forward. Both hands flew out to catch herself against the side of the building, the same moment her feet skidded off the other edge of the platform. Courtney slammed onto her stomach, fingers stabbing between the holes in the grating.

She lay there until the metal stopped shuddering beneath her. A tiny prickle of light danced beside her face. A slush-coated shard of glass, caught in the metal slats. Her lungs tugged at her insides in harsh scrapes.

Too many seconds passed before she staggered to her feet. She hugged the side of the building with both hands, though the edge of the fire escape was now several feet away. Her whole body trembled.

The distant wail of a siren echoed through the rain.

Gritting her teeth, Courtney pushed herself off the wall. She held the freezing rail tight beneath her hands. The stairs below had no railing. Slush and chunks of hail covered the steps. She went down on her hands and feet, gripping every stair as she descended.

A hinge squealed. "Courtney? What are you doing out there?"

She almost fell off the ladder. Looking down, she saw Strings sticking her head out the window near her feet, squinting up at her with a mix of shock and amusement. Another face appeared beside hers. Rain plinked off his glasses. Books.

"Strings!" Courtney scrambled down the last few steps. "Open that window wider!"

"Why are you even..." Strings stepped back as Courtney crawled through. She collapsed onto the floor, then pulled herself back up on soaking, shaky feet.

Books watched her with a neutral expression.

"You didn't go on the raid." Strings looked her over. "When you weren't in the room and I couldn't find you, I assumed you left with everybody else."

"You're both still here?" Courtney panted.

"Several people stayed behind," Books said. "Des, Daisy, a few of the new recruits."

"What were you doing out there?" Strings demanded. "You got a death wish?"

Courtney's gaze darted past them, taking in the empty common room. Usually every couch was crammed full this time of evening.

A scattered deck of playing cards lay abandoned on the floor. The stained, stringy couch cushions stared back at her.

"You're soaked." Strings swatted at her shoulders. "Don't tell me the shift's already getting to your head. You're gonna be as crazy as Torch by the time—"

"She was locked in an upstairs room."

Courtney and Strings both looked at Books. He pushed his glasses higher up on his nose.

"She has glass on her pants. She busted out a window. I assume the thud we heard before we looked outside was the space heater? Upstairs only has two of those. Torch's room, which is on the other side of the building, and W's. Since no one else is allowed up there, and I'm assuming it wasn't Cassandra—she left an hour ago to prep the Triads—that means the Boss locked you up there before he left." His clinical gaze flicked over her with a new hint of suspicion. "Which means he probably had a good reason."

"He thinks I'm a threat to his operation."

"Are you?"

"Yes."

The word jerked out of her before she had the chance to think. Before she recognized her own resolve. Because... it *was* resolve. Something heavy and warm, building in her chest, spreading outward through her body like adrenaline, but different. Hotter. Fiercer. She didn't have time to analyze it. Her thoughts had pulled a hundred miles ahead, sifting through a dozen half-baked ideas. She wasn't W. She didn't have ten years to plan a better alternative to his masterminded, horrible operation. But... she *wasn't* W. There had to be another way to look at this. And she wasn't the old Courtney, either. She wouldn't sit by and watch while a terrorist from a different direction tore up her city. No. This time, she was going to move. And maybe... for the first time, she wouldn't have to do it alone.

Books studied her with unblinking eyes.

Strings swung her gaze between the both of them. "Okay. I'm lost."

"I need to know who's left." Courtney's heart beat faster with every word, the plan taking shape in her mind. "Des, Daisy—who else, Books?"

He arched an eyebrow.

"You're not a killer," she shouted. "You stayed behind because he gave you a choice, and you're not a murderer. I know Strings isn't. Des isn't. Daisy... how many people are still in the Dugout who won't kill for W?"

He regarded her. "You want to start your own miniature revolution? Right now? After they've already left?"

"You're a hacker, right? Strings, you're the scout. Des is the best getaway driver in practically all of Orion City—and Daisy..." Courtney hesitated. The girl who'd fried her brains from Changing too much. The plan was already unraveling in her mind.

"Wait a minute," Strings snapped. "You're not seriously thinking of stopping the riot? That's the only thing keeping the cops from ripping our team apart. Do you *want* AITO to kill everyone?"

"No. I want to burn AITO to the ground. But I want to do it in a way that won't make any more Margo's."

Strings glanced sideways at Books, and stage-whispered: "She's going the way of Daisy and Torch."

But Books was watching Courtney with a faint glimmer inside his narrowed eyes. "You know, I never could piece together where she came from. But hearing you say it out loud... it makes sense. She's more than an orphan. She's his collateral damage."

"I am *so* lost," Strings complained.

"You won't be able to stop them," Books mused. "The riot or

the invasion. Even if, hypothetically, I thought it a worthwhile idea to help you, I'd have to be onsite to hack AITO's security mainframe. Too many layers. You'd never get inside before W did. Logistically you'd have to have enough people to stop the riot downtown, then combat the now unoccupied cops as they poured in to defend AITO, *and* take down AITO's existing security to... what, exactly? What's your master plan? Provided you actually got inside. Force them to open the Wall? To surrender? With what army?"

Courtney swallowed.

Strings let out a funny sound between her teeth. "Wait, Courtney, you weren't thinking of..."

"A Change is only a weapon if you've got the brains to control it," Books said. "Otherwise you're just an animal up against a network of trained killer humans. You can barely control your Change. Even if you managed to recruit some of the other newbies..." He sighed. "You don't have enough teeth in your bite."

The plan was a ball of strings now. Maybe they were right. Maybe her mind had started to unravel too. Just like Daisy and Torch.

From across the empty common room, a voice rumbled. "I'll be your teeth."

All three of them turned. A figure stood in the shadows, dark skin almost hiding him, paused in the entrance to the hallway that led to the Dugout's only exit: that old shattered window above the fire escape where Courtney had first arrived. The huge man hesitated. He inched forward, the tentative step at odds with his massive form.

"Des," Books said. "I thought you went home to be with your family."

"I was on my way out. But then a window crashed upstairs,

and I heard you guys talking, and…" Des took another step forward. "I want in."

"There's no *in* to get in on," Strings groaned. "This entire conversation has been pure nonsense."

"The new girl had an idea. I want to hear it."

Courtney swallowed again as Des crossed the room, coming to a stop at the edge of their little group. He towered over them, huge shoulders hunched as if to make himself smaller. Dark eyes pinned her with their attention.

"Well…" She fumbled for words as all three gazes landed back on her. "It's not a plan, per se. Yet. We're outnumbered on both sides. W's group stands a way better chance at fighting through AITO's defenses, and we'd have no chance against the police if we tried to mess with the riots in Chinatown."

"Wow, I'm loving the sound of this so far," Strings intoned.

Courtney barreled on. "W's relying on that diversion to steer AITO's backup away. But he's going to kill a *lot* of people." She squeezed out a breath. "Everyone left in the Dugout—you, me, whoever didn't follow W—we stayed behind because we're not killers. I know you three believe in something. I don't know what, or how, but there's got to be another way to destroy AITO without becoming them. Justifying all this blood as a means to an end— we're taking lives to reach our goal just like they're taking lives to reach theirs."

Strings wrinkled her nose. "You're firing an awful lot of shots for someone sitting on the sidelines. I didn't go with W, but that's because I'm weak. I own that. I'm not judging the only man who can get the job done!"

"You're not weak," Courtney shot back. "AITO's sudden move forced W into an endgame nobody was prepared for. He's trying to do the right thing. But so are you. And me. We didn't go into battle for him. But that's not enough. We can't sit by and let him kill anyone caught in the crossfire."

Books released a measured sigh. "You talk like someone behind a pulpit. But you don't know your audience." He paused. "You assume I didn't go because I'm not a killer. You're wrong." The fading light from the window glinted off his glasses. Courtney shivered at the blank expression behind them. "I didn't go because, in spite of all his careful planning, W is blinded by the conviction that this has an end. That somehow, some way, he can force down the Wall and pave a bloody road to freedom. But it doesn't. AITO's compound is located on the only exit through the Wall. Clearance to go through that gate doesn't even apply to their top scientists. The new director Jeanine Campbell has the sole link to the outside. The operating system is coded to her voice; she alone can open that gate. And she'd never in a million years do that—even at gunpoint. But W is desperate. He's enlisted not only the Loons, but the Changers on the fringe—the rabid ones, minds that have already frayed. They won't have control. They'll kill anything and everyone, possibly even each other." Books pushed his glasses higher up on his nose. "It's a suicide mission. For everyone involved."

Courtney swung her gaze to the others. Des looked uncomfortable. Strings' face still held a pinched expression, but her eyes looked more uncertain than before. Books returned his gaze to the window, shoulders relaxing like he'd won the argument, but wasn't happy about it.

That old spark resurfaced. Stubborn and bristling, a pinpoint in the dark.

"What about that link?"

His eyes slid back to her. "What?"

"You said you can't hack AITO's security. What about communication? You said AITO has the only direct link to the outside."

He gave her a slow blink.

"Jas—a person I know from the outside," Courtney stumbled. "Said that people in the rest of the country have no clue what's really going on inside Orion. We're famous across the country as a hazard zone. The media likes to blow it up with crazy theories: they think we've all been infected by an ultra-contagious virus. Something so dangerous we're a threat to the entire country without AITO's intervention."

"Really?" Strings snorted. "For ten years? And we're all still alive? Obviously we haven't turned into zombies and eaten each other if there's still a big Wall up, keeping us in."

Courtney speared Books with her gaze. "Has W thought of hacking that direct link to the outside?"

Books gave her a pitying look. "W has thought of everything. If he thought that were a remotely useful idea, he'd have done it years ago. The people on the outside don't care about Orion City. Even if they knew what was going on, what do you think they would do? Tear down the Wall in righteous outrage? They wouldn't believe us if we told them."

"W is the most cynical person I know," Courtney fired back. "He once told me there were two people in the whole world he trusted, and I'm pretty sure one of them is himself. He wouldn't consider asking for outside help. Even if all his other options ran out." She sucked in a breath. "There's got to be someone in control of AITO. They answer to an authority on the outside, right? What if we went to them?"

Strings scoffed. "You want us to send out an SOS to the people who've been ignoring us for a decade?"

"I think they've been ignorant of the truth for a decade. W said everyone thinks AITO is controlled by the CDC. But AITO has gone completely rogue. If Jeanine Campbell controls the messages going out from Quarantine, she could divulge—or conceal—anything she wants. What if everybody truly thinks this is all a virus? What if they really have no idea AITO isn't helping us, but using us as human guinea pigs?"

"Don't you think that's a little naïve?" Books' voice took on the first hint of an edge. "W—and *myself*, which is nothing to sneeze at—have examined every inch of AITO's weaknesses, their strengths, and how to dismantle them. He's planned since the Wall went up. I came later, but I've studied every strategy, every probability and outcome. It took years to get him inside AITO that first time. You think you're going to solve it in one night?"

"The new girl makes a fair point," Des rumbled. Courtney jumped at his voice. She'd almost forgotten he was standing there: a big, silent shadow to their conversation. "She's suggesting a different approach. Not attacking them from the inside, but sending a message to the outside. She's right. W would never have considered it. He's too jaded. As are you, my young friend." He nodded down at Books, who stiffened. "But…" He turned to Courtney. "You do not have a team. W took a small army with him, but you have only two."

"Two?" Courtney held her breath.

Des nodded. "You and me. A wolf and a bear. Perhaps, if we had a mouse and a cat… we might have a little extra staying power."

Strings' nose twitched. "Our shifts aren't going to do us any good up against trained soldiers."

"Maybe. But I am a driver. That's what I am good at. You are a scout. Books is a walking computer."

Hope swelled within Courtney with such warmth she could've hugged the enormous man. She looked at Books and Strings.

"You're both idiots," Strings grumbled. She chewed on her

lower lip. "We're all going to be dead soon anyway. Dead or on the run for the rest of our lives, which'll be impossible in a concrete fish bowl." She lifted her chin. "You told me once you were a nobody. Remember that, C?"

The use of her nickname—W's single initial for her, the mark of infinite potential—put a sting in Courtney's chest. She'd forgotten how he'd introduced her to the Loons.

"I told you to stay because the Loons didn't have enough good people. And a good person isn't a nobody." Strings blew out a gusty breath. "I guess that makes this whole thing my fault. You were bound to rock the boat if you stayed." She glanced at Books. Then she laughed, the sound somehow light and brittle at the same time. "I can't believe I'm saying this, but... I've got nothing else to lose. Count me in."

Courtney slid her eyes to Books. Hands in his pockets, gaze firmly on the window, lips pressed in a thin line. Des spoke first.

"You with us, or against us, brother?"

His lips got thinner.

"Thomas," Strings said. He started at the name. She sidled closer to him. "If you do this, I'll finally go on that date with you."

His ears turned bright red. One hand darted up to push the glasses up his nose. "Wh-what are you talking about?"

"Come on. You might be more obnoxious about it, but you're not the only one who can read people. I know you've had a crush on me for ages. You do this—you rack up your guts and do the right thing, screw the odds—and I'll go out with you. I trust Courtney. She's one of the good ones. So, help my crazy roommate and you've got yourself a date."

Crimson spread from the young man's ears to his entire face. He took off his glasses, cleaned them on his shirt, and mumbled, "I've, uh... got to go check and see if I have the right equipment."

He walked away as fast as his jerkily dignified steps would allow.

Courtney stared after him. Warmth welled up stronger as she glanced sideways at Strings. Her roommate had her lip tucked between her teeth, hiding a smirk.

"Always thought he was cute, in a dorky way. Knew he'd never get up the courage to ask." Strings shrugged. "Some people only do the right things with a really dumb motivation."

W's face rose up in Courtney's mind. A cracked mask, fire burning behind. The frightening energy beneath that cool exterior, when she'd glimpsed the driving force behind his plan to demolish AITO. To free all the people like himself. Preventing any more lives being warped, stolen, used, snuffed out. Terrorizing the terror until it terrified no more.

No matter the cost.

"And some people with the best motivations," she whispered. "Do terrible things."

15. TERRIBLE THINGS

THE ODD TRIO stood at the edge of the darkening street. Ice still swirled on the wind. A hulking form crouched in the alcove of a doorway. Above him, a small figure in a black bodysuit perched on the rim of the fire escape. Tucked into the opposite shadows of the alcove, a third figure leaned against the wall, glasses winking in the dim light of the streetlamps.

"This is not going to work," Books muttered.

His attempt at aloof disapproval was ruined by his skinny frame shaking in the cold, arms firmly tucked against his ribcage. Strings glared down at him.

"You hashed out the plan with her yourself." Her teeth chattered. "If it goes south, you're as much to blame as she is."

"There'll be no blaming. We'll all be dead."

Des' low growl cut over the faint drum of hail. "Doubting her won't increase our chances. Get to your positions. It's nearly time."

As if on cue, an inhuman howl echoed down the street. The mournful sound hovered on the wind for a moment. Books and Des looked at each other.

"How long do you think it'll take?" Strings whispered down. Books shushed her.

The sound came again. Rough, sheer, hair-raising.

"She's got about five minutes." Des' whisper echoed in the alcove. "Which means we have less."

"How close is it?" Strings called down. "I don't hear anything."

"Shut up, shut up," Books muttered. "The vans have audio surveillance. It's how they find the Changers so fast. But they pick up little sounds too, so unless you want to tip them off—"

"Shut up," Strings snapped. "We get it."

The wall rumbled. Though the disturbance came from several buildings down, the pavement vibrated all up the street. All three figures tensed.

A panel opened in the side of a warehouse. Corrugated metal slid up like a garage door, and a white van revved out onto the street. It moved fast for the elements, wheels crackling on the ice. The empty street spit dirt and sleet as it gathered speed. It skidded toward the source of the Changer's cry.

Strings tightened her stance at the rim of the fire escape. As the van fishtailed past, she leapt.

The Change happened midair. Body fluid, her black-clad limbs contorted into feline form, and she hit the roof of the van with soundless grace. She slipped sideways for half a second as the van's momentum caught her. Then she was flat to the roof, moving low in a hunter's creep toward the windshield.

She dropped to the front of the van. Paws on the windshield, slipping on the wet glass, blocking the driver's view.

The van jerked. Taillights flashed. Then Strings was off—springing back to the roof of the van, flattening herself to the surface as her body morphed a second time. The nylon suit clung to her human limbs again, black and glistening in the rain.

The van slowed.

Strings reached forward. Tapping the windshield with a fist, she leaned down and tipped her head into view. An upside-down grin.

"Hey! You take hitchhikers?"

The van lurched. Strings flew forward. The wheels screamed as she recovered her grip, half spread-eagled on the windshield. She scrambled back to the top.

The passenger door opened. Just a crack—indecision freezing the movement halfway. Voices echoed in the van. Rough, angry. The door opened wider.

That was all it took. Strings tipped sideways. One arm clung to the roof while the rest of her slid off the van, pouring into the passenger side door.

Curses rocketed across the street. The van shuddered up and down on its wheels.

Des launched to his feet. "We should move in."

"Not yet." Books grabbed his arm. "She has the tranqs. Let her do her part."

The van rocked back and forth. The dark-tinted windows revealed nothing inside, the passenger door bouncing on its hinges until it swung shut. Ten stiff seconds passed. The van settled back onto its wheels, shaking subsided.

Des pulled his arm out of Books' grip.

The opposite door sprang open. Strings poked her head out, one arm gripping the roof, and shot them both a distinctively catlike grin over the top of the van.

"Two snoring AITO bums ready to go."

Des bolted from his hiding place. Books followed, eyes scanning the street even as triumph broke out across his companions' faces.

"We need to get out of range of this outpost. Des, tie them both up and dump them in the alley. Strings, you've got five minutes to get our fearless leader back to a coherent state. I'd give us thirty minutes, tops, to get this van's tech into range of the main compound before they figure out something's wrong."

Sirens blared in the distance.

"I'd say we have enough of a diversion." Des reached into the van and hauled out an unconscious white-jacketed driver. "They won't have time to notice we hijacked the van with Torch's Armageddon starting up down the street."

"Never rely on anything but Murphy's law," Books muttered. He turned. "Strings?"

Strings tugged on the collar of her bodysuit, popped the joints in her neck, and nodded. "Ready."

Down the street, another bone-chilling howl echoed off the bricks.

"Go get her."

Turning with the same fluid grace with which she leapt from the fire escape, Strings broke into a run. She Changed before her second footstep hit the ground.

The black cat raced away down the street.

She huddled alone in the middle of the road. Ice crept beneath the black bodysuit where it hugged and stuck to her foreign body in awkward places.

The howl had poured out of her without any premeditation. The plan—the steps involved, the positions to stick to—all had vanished the moment her paws hit the ice. She was only instinct now.

Five minutes ago, she'd been Courtney. Five minutes ago, she'd been confident—if not in the plan itself, then at least in her own determination to carry out her part. They needed something loud and fierce to snag the attention of the closest AITO post; Des was essential for the van hijacking, and Books' and Strings' shifts wouldn't cut it here. Despite having the least control over her Change, Courtney's idea to pose herself as the bait made the most sense, even to her reluctant teammates.

But now, the haunting wails slid from her throat like a hysterical question, ricocheting off the buildings and falling back to pierce her. Primal fear slid in with the ice. Where was she? Nothing smelled familiar. Smoke stung the air, distant but caustic, burning acrid in her nostrils. A faint cry. Almost undetectable, floating to her new senses from far off in the night. Another cry joined it. Her ears went flat. Human. The sounds were unmistakable in any language, man or animal. Fear personified.

A low whine built in her throat.

Something tugged at the edges of her consciousness. A memory? A thought? Instinct tried to push it out, but it pushed back, fervent and alive.

Theoretically, I could do it from anywhere inside their system, since AITO's emergency frequency can be accessed from any one of their outposts throughout the city. Security measures, in case there's a breach of the main compound. Like today.

The memory sharpened. Sounds and syllables drifted in, divorced from meaning, familiar but just out of reach. Who was that man in glasses? And why had he smelled like fear?

We'd have a short window. Until one of their techs figures it out and shuts down our access. But with everybody distracted during W's invasion... He reached for his glasses, tapped the bridge of his nose, and held them there. Squinting. *W's brash move may have created the opportune window for a more subtle assault.*

But how short a window? The memory of her own voice, strange and garbled, pulled at her. *Could we still pull this off?*

The words hazed, some syllables slipping in and out of focus, but a shadowy piece of her brain pressed the details forward with burning urgency. She locked onto the voices, the shapes of the sounds.

It'll be tight. The man's voice was flat. *I would need to get you in using the frequency AITO alone has access to. That'd be a cinch if I could do it from within the main compound. But unless you want to fight through the bloody mess W is going to make in, oh... I'd give him a half hour at most to break down their first security parameter with Red and Deadeye...* He shook his head. *No. That system will be on total lockdown to all my hacking frequencies. I'd need to already be inside AITO to hack AITO at that point.*

Then my idea with the vans might actually work.

Your idea with the vans is idiotic. But... yes, there's a small chance it might. Which is better than W's odds.

A blast of fear—the memory of excitement, adrenaline, and a foreign human emotion that burned and terrified at the same time.

She pressed her nose between her paws. The flat tenor of the man's voice put her hackles on the rise. A snarl ground past her teeth as instinct fogged over again.

Human voices pounded in her head. No humans around. Just the smell of them, the sound of them, everywhere. Smoke. Screams. *Run,* instinct shouted. *Get out of here.* An engine in the distance, rumbling closer. *Run away. Fear and fire, run away from it all, far away from here…*

Another memory fought its way in. Like a second creature lived in her brain, shoving and pointing and screaming to get her attention. The haze lifted for a moment.

I can do this.

The words were still foreign, strange barks and growls from another language. But they felt… almost familiar this time. Almost intelligible.

You'll have to keep your head. That original voice, flat and cold. *This all falls apart if your mind does, you got that? You go feral on us and it's all over.*

She struggled to focus past the press of her senses. Someone clawed her way up from deep inside, snarling at her to remember, to cling to those fragmented bits of understanding. To keep her head in the midst of the fog.

The whimper slid from her chest, suddenly just as foreign as the voice in her head. Her own voice. Which was she? Animal or human, she couldn't tell who was winning.

"C!"

The shout cut across the street. Not in her head, not in the distance. It bounced off the bricks, high-pitched and close. Courtney sank low to the ground.

"C? There you are! We've got to go, come on."

Footsteps. Light, quick, chasing the smell that hit her senses first. A girl. Human fear and excitement thick on her breath.

Courtney skidded backwards as the stranger dropped to one knee several feet away. A growl ripped from her teeth.

"C. You still in there? Come back to my voice."

Strange smells clung to the girl's strange clothes. The black suit sticking to her skin smelled like smoke and rain and metal. Slow as a hunter's prowl, the girl reached forward.

"Come on, C. How did you get out of it the last times you Changed?" A groan. "You probably just let it wear off, huh? We don't have time for that. Books and Des are waiting for us with the van. Shh... C, take a breath. This isn't you. Those fears, those instincts—they aren't *yours*. Give them back and let go. You're human. Remember?"

C.

The words blurred. Reshaped. Sharpened.

C...

An initial has infinite potential. You could be anything. Firmer than before, a new voice... an intelligible one... echoed up deep inside. *The possibilities are limitless.*

The girl leaned forward further. Fear rippled off her skin, but she stretched out a hand and set something down on the ice within striking distance.

"We're waiting on you. This whole thing falls apart without our resident madwoman."

A gun rested on the frozen pavement. Not a gun... a tranq. Her human brain pressed the information forward, battling to the surface in the current of instinct.

A new smell caught her attention. It rose off the gun, fainter than the girl's fresh scent. Someone else had touched this weapon. A while ago. Buried beneath the traces of multiple hands passing the object back and forth, his scent was still there. Familiar. Unmistakable.

Peppermint.

Her bones shifted. A jagged twist, deep inside. Courtney crumpled as the pain stabbed through her. But, as the pressure drummed up inside her limbs, she didn't fight it. She closed her eyes. She breathed in, and out, and in...

Rain slipped across her forehead. Her hair hung in her eyes, short and clumped in wet locks of copper. Courtney shivered on the pavement. The suit felt tight in all the right places now. She pushed herself upright onto wobbly elbows.

Strings exhaled. "All right in there? Thought you'd really disappeared on me for a second."

Courtney licked her dry lips. "I... thought I had, too."

Strings shoved the tranquilizer gun toward her. "Come on. Books said we had five minutes four minutes ago."

Courtney stood. Her knees wavered. "It worked? They've got the van?"

"Yeah, Part One of Operation Stupid was easy-peasy. Part Two is where I'm pretty sure we all die."

Courtney lifted a hand to the zipper at her chest. Beneath the suit, a hard lump sat pressed below her collarbone. Strings' eyes flickered to the movement.

"What's with that? You packing a weapon under there or something? I thought the whole point of this suicide mission was we *didn't* want to kill people."

Squeezing a hand into her suit, Courtney pulled out her cell phone. Strings' eyebrows skyrocketed.

"I have to make a call." Before she could object to wasting time, Courtney started in the direction Strings had come. She dialed as she walked. "We've got a minute, right? Thirty seconds is enough time to say goodbye."

Her pace sped to a jog as she lifted the phone to her ear.

Dina's fingers trembled on the plunger of the syringe. Tranquilizers were tricky. The sedatives they used at St. Barnabas were controlled, tested and safe… and took far too long to take effect. Tranquilizers like the kind the White Coats used to put down Changers on the streets, before they carted them off in their paneled vans, were risky. AITO must have perfected their drug: some kind of paralytic, she guessed, fast-acting enough to incapacitate the target's muscles without shutting down their ability to breathe. Duplicating a drug like that wasn't in her job description.

But Jasper's ridiculous plan required someone with actual medical expertise—or he was going to get himself killed. Maybe not just himself.

So, here she was. Oh why, *why* did she have to make friends with justice-crazy martyr types?

Her phone lit up on the table beside her. She spared half a glance at the face filling the screen, and then almost dropped the syringe in her double take. She scrambled to pick it up.

Across the table, Jasper's eyes connected with hers. "Who is it?"

Dina smashed the phone against her ear. "Courtney?"

Jasper launched to his feet.

"Dina," gasped a voice at the other end. "I was expecting to get voicemail. You're usually working…" A crackly breath. "This is gonna be harder than I thought."

Dina held Jasper's gaze. For once, words felt far away as she listened to the voice try to piece itself together on the other end.

"Listen, I don't have much time, but I needed to call to say I'm sorry. I'm about to do something stupid. For the right reason, but in case it doesn't go…" A breath. "You're an amazing friend, and I just wanted to tell you I love you."

Watching Dina's face, Jasper leaned forward. "Is she okay?"

"Would you keep checking on Michael for me?" A hitch in the words. "And Jasper. Tell him… tell him I'm sorry, too."

"No," Dina barked into the phone.

Silence on the other end. Just breathing, and the distant trill of a siren.

"We passed the line of something stupid a long time ago." Dina gripped the phone so hard it shook. "If you're in over your head, I'm diving down there with you. You don't get to do stupid without me. Since the hospital, remember? We're in this together. So, spill it."

Jasper's blue eyes burned into hers. Dina looked away. She held her breath while she listened to her best friend fight with hers. Finally, Courtney spoke again.

"*We're taking down AITO.*"

Dina listened without a word for the next several minutes. Jasper drummed his fingers on the table. He bounced on the balls of his feet. But she didn't look up at him, and he didn't interrupt. At long last, when Courtney had finished, Dina listened to the silence while she chose her next words.

"That," she replied. "Is the second most ridiculous plan I've heard today. Both thrown together in the last twenty-four hours, in the name of vigilante justice, with bigger holes in the center than my bagel this morning."

Jasper's hands tensed on the table. Courtney remained silent.

"You're both brave and stupid." Dina's brain raced. "And I don't think either of you is as far gone as the other thinks."

Pressing her lips together, she lowered the phone to the table and clicked *speaker.*

"So," she said. "Here's *my* idea."

Six people crammed into the back of an armored van made for a tense space. Parked lopsided in the alley behind Dina's house, hidden from view of the street, the van was already hot and stuffy, despite the chill outside. Sleet pounded out a deafening beat on the roof.

"If this plan needed to get any more stupid," Strings shouted from her position squished between Des and Books. "I would've suggested inviting a cop to our stolen spy-tech van earlier."

"You must be Strings," Dina shouted back. "Courtney said I would like you."

"You *stole* this van?" Jasper broke in.

"May I remind you all that we have thirteen minutes left to completely reevaluate our plan," Books said. "If you're going to arrest us, Mr. Wade, do it now, otherwise we'll get to business."

Courtney sat sandwiched between Des and Dina on the floor. All the seats had been removed from the back, and a grated steel wall divided them from the driver cab. The space would've been large enough to fit herself, Jasper, Dina, Books, Strings and even Des' large frame easily, had it not been for the odd mish-mash of tech jammed up against the walls. A large monitor flickered with unintelligible code. On the opposite wall, more gadgets, screens, and wires cluttered up the space. Six intimidating guns stood mounted against the grated wall. Syringes and refills of tranquilizer darts poked out of a case next to them.

"I've never actually been inside one of these," Strings said. "How are they even supposed to fit a Changer back here? One angry bear is all it would take to wreck this fancy equipment."

"They're usually unconscious," Des grunted from his awkward crouch beneath the gun rack.

"Focus," Books ordered. He looked at Dina. "You're the one who poked the holes in my plan. As it was the best I could come up with under the circumstances, I'm impressed. Tell us yours."

"Mine?"

"You said this cop had a separate plan to dismantle AITO."

"This cop's sitting right here," Jasper said. "And it wasn't a plan to dismantle AITO, it was a plan to get my best friend out of jail before he got executed."

Courtney sat up straighter. "Oliver?"

"He forgot to mention his best friend is the Orion Giant," Dina said.

Shock and skepticism rippled through the van.

"Your plan is smart," Dina told Books. "You just don't have enough people to be all the places you need them. If everything Courtney told me is happening now, the Torch is lighting fires all across Eastside, and the Triads are starting a riot in Chinatown. Those are all expert murderers. The Torch evaded the cops for two years before he finally got caught, and now he's loose again. And the Triads are famous for mass casualties when they start riots. You guys have, what, four people? How are you going to catch the arsonist, stop the riot, *and* break into AITO without getting anybody killed?"

"People are going to get killed," Books said. "It's the only way any of this will work. It's *this* one—" Here he jerked a thumb at Courtney. "—who's convinced she can do better than the Boss who's been planning this for ten years."

Dina leaned over Courtney before she could speak. "If your *Boss* is so good at what he does, why hasn't he destroyed AITO already?"

"He didn't have an army big enough," Strings cut in. "It takes years for a Changer to get enough control over their shift to use it as a weapon. W's had to sift through all the people still fighting with their sanity to find the ones who could actually help."

Jasper cleared his throat. "Argue the merits of a serial killer later. I don't see what any of this has to do with my friend."

"The Orion Giant." Dina clapped her hands together. "Now there's a Changer who's got loads of experience fighting bad guys on the streets. The city's resident superhero. He's got his Change under control, obviously. If we break him out of jail for you, he could go after the Torch while you send the rest of your guys after the Triads. You could stop the riot down in Chinatown, and he'll stop the fire-starter before he burns down every building in Eastside."

Books considered it. "Our plan was to send our new recruits—Changers with little to no control over their shifts—to Eastside to hunt down the Torch. We have eleven volunteers. Five wanted to try to stop the riot in Chinatown, and six had vendettas against the Torch. Since Des is the only Changer with real skill among them, he volunteered to lead the group into Chinatown."

"Take all of your recruits to Chinatown," Dina said. "The Orion Giant can handle the Torch."

"If Oliver even decides to join us," Jasper muttered.

"That's your job," Dina said. "Speaking of which, I'll need to borrow about six of those super-tranquilizers so Jasper can take out his buddies in blue without having to kill anybody either."

Several voices rose in response to that request. But Courtney's ears filled with the sound of the sleet pattering on the roof. Her eyes connected with Jasper's across the van.

He was watching her, too. His blue eyes had a different light than she'd seen in them before. A faint smile lifted the corner of his mouth: half regretful, half wary. She felt her own lips press into something similar.

It had been a short conversation on the phone. Dina had insisted they all meet, and with the time ticking down, Courtney had convinced Books to hear her idea to rewire their faulty plan. Jasper hadn't spoken more than two words together in the call. But even while Dina filled in his silence, Courtney could tell something had shifted. She didn't know the details. But looking at him now, he seemed... hollower. More fragile.

It was far too loud in the van to say anything to him now. But an apology pressed against the inside of her chest. She'd been so consumed with her own battle for clarity in the midst of injustice, she'd missed he was fighting his own. What had happened to make him willing to cross all his old lines? Here he sat in the back of a stolen van with his ex-girlfriend and a bunch of criminals, hashing out a plan to turn against his own police force—the whole reason he was in this city to begin with—and break someone out of jail.

Not just someone. *Oliver*... She turned the pieces over in her mind. The Orion Giant, Dina had said. His best friend. Had Oliver kept that secret this whole time? She couldn't help but be impressed. The skinny, soft-spoken young man with the unassuming grin was secretly Orion City's number one vigilante, patrolling the streets every night to put even the most hardened criminals on the run.

And now, Jasper not only knew about his best friend's double life... he was on the brink of losing him.

What was going through his head?

As she studied him, Courtney saw the same look mirrored on Jasper's face. He watched her as if seeing her for the first time. Perhaps he knew what it felt like, now, to have his worldview flipped on its head.

"Okay!"

Strings' shout sliced into her focus. Courtney snapped back to the conversation at hand.

"We've got a limited number of tranquilizers," Strings continued. "So we need to hash out who gets what, and where everyone's positions will be." She pointed to the guns on the rack. "The tranqs we brought with us are mimics of the ones AITO uses; W stole samples a long time ago and duplicated them with Books. You two can have one gun: it's only got six refills in it, so use them sparingly. Des needs the rest to control the riots downtown."

"So we know where Des and the rest of your freaky gang will be," Dina said. "What about me and Jasper? And you three?" She motioned to Strings, Books, and Courtney.

"I'll be here in this van," Books said. "But I'll need somebody to drive it close enough to AITO's main compound to get within hacking range of their frequency. I'll also need a bodyguard. I'm no good in combat on a good day, and it'll take all my concentration to hijack that frequency." He pushed his glasses up his nose. "Once we're in that close, we'll be targets—not only for AITO's security, but W's team. He's got an enormous group of Changers so untethered they won't recognize friend from foe once he turns them loose. His goal is to tear that compound apart until he finds Jeanine Campbell."

"Who's Jeanine Campbell?" Dina asked.

"The new head doctor at AITO. Now the only person with access to open the Wall."

"I'll be your bodyguard," Jasper ventured.

Books measured him. For the first time in five minutes, the sleet drumming on the roof felt almost quiet with the lack of competing voices.

"I thought your only interest in this was your friend down in police custody," Books countered.

"It's not just his life at stake." Jasper's voice took on a firmer quality. "Once I get him out, I'll rejoin you at the van. I can clear the streets with my siren to make it back to you in time."

"That won't be fast enough. W's team is already starting their invasion. If we act at all, this is the hour to do it."

"I'll do it," Dina said.

"What?" said Jasper and Books in unison.

"I'll drive the van. You hack. I'm a nurse, too, so if any of you get hurt in this ridiculous shindig, I'll be here at the van to stitch you up before you bleed out." Her sudden laugh made a few people jump. "I'm the one who stitched up your crazy Boss in the first place! I guess in a way that makes me responsible for half this mess."

The whole van stared at her.

"And if you still need a bodyguard," she added. "I'm pretty good with my pepper spray. At least until Jasper gets back."

Books took off his glasses and rubbed his eyes with harsh fingers. Strings put a hand on his shoulder.

"Park in an alley farther away from the compound to start," she suggested. "You'll only need to hack the security center to get us in, and you can do that from a distance, right? That's farther from the fighting. Unlock doors remotely for us to make it to the control room. Once we get your signal up there, you can move in closer and tackle the com system. By then the cop'll be here to watch your back." She shot a pointed look at Jasper across the van. "By that point it'll be World War III inside. W's team and AITO security will be so distracted nobody will notice one little van sitting outside the compound."

Des finally spoke up. "Strings, you'll need more than Books hacking doors for you inside AITO to make it to the control room. I can't take the whole supply of tranquilizers to the riots. You'll need some for backups in case things go south inside."

Strings shrugged. "If I get in a close enough scrape to need them, a few tranqs won't make much difference. The whole point is to sneak in under the radar."

"Whoa, you're going in alone?" Dina cried.

"What exactly is your plan once you're inside?" Jasper demanded.

Books held up a small cylinder of plastic, the size of his thumb. "Someone needs to get this frequency generator to the main control room. I can activate it from there. It'll shut down all other signals inside that room, and allow me to hijack their emergency frequency—directing it anywhere I want. That's our link to the outside. But there's a catch—activation for AITO's outside link is voice recognition. It'll only come alive to the sound of Jeanine Campbell speaking."

"But if W kills her first, that'll be tricky," Dina said.

Jasper scowled. "One small girl marching into a warzone by herself won't give the enemy anything but target practice."

"Thanks for the confidence, Five-O," Strings snapped. "But I'm pretty hard to hit in cat form. And I won't be alone. Courtney's going with me."

Jasper's expression made Courtney wish she'd never made the call.

Books frowned at Strings. "That wasn't part of the plan. You're a skilled scout with field experience; she's a new recruit with no control over her Change."

"It's not her Change we need. Actually, the fact that she *has* no field skills is exactly why we need her."

"I'm not following," Dina said in a warning voice. With one well-maneuvered scoot, she positioned herself between Courtney and the rest of the group.

"For once in my life, neither am I," grumbled Books.

"It's obvious," Strings said. "Even Changers with the most unraveled minds listen to W. He's the only one who's got them under control. And—as ridiculous as this sounds—the more I've

- 235 -

watched, the more I've realized this little nobody is the only one *he* will listen to. Don't you get it? If W gets into a standoff with Campbell, someone like me marching up there shouting and hollering won't be enough to stop him. It's gotta be Courtney. He's scared to death of her. It's why he locked her in the upstairs room, before she bashed out a freaking window to go chase after him. She's the one thing he won't risk, no matter how close he is to his end goal."

Courtney peered over Dina's shoulder at Books. He tapped a finger on the bridge of his glasses, studying Strings.

"Interesting," he said slowly. "You made that jump before I did."

"Am I wrong?" Strings challenged.

Books shook his head, looking somewhat dazed. In a voice Courtney almost couldn't hear over the rain, he murmured: "So that was the threat to his operation..."

"Courtney's the one who needs to get to the control room," Strings finished. "I'm just her escort."

One by one, every head in the van turned to Courtney. Even Dina inched back a little from her protective stance, shifting to eye her with nervous intensity. Courtney resisted the urge to shift back into the wall of the van.

"I don't know about... all of that." Somehow she managed to squeeze her voice out loud enough to carry. "But I'm going in there to stop him. Whatever it takes."

For one minute, the van seemed to still, even with the pounding of the sleet on the roof. Then Jasper's radio chirped. Everyone jumped.

"*ALL UNITS RESPOND. TEN-THIRTY-FOUR CHINATOWN SQUARE, OFFICERS DOWN, TEN-ONE. SHOTS FIRED. ALL UNITS RESPOND.*"

"Looks like the riot is starting," said Des.

Books rose to his feet. "Everyone clear on their positions?"

Six nods, all gradients of confidence.

"Good. However this turns out, it's about to be over with."

Courtney took a deep breath.

Jasper flung open the van doors.

16. THE NAME

OLIVER TAPPED A slow beat on the cold metal table. He had enough space to tap the first two fingers on either of his hands, cuffed as they were to the table, and just enough mental clarity through the thinning fog of tranquilizers to keep a steady rhythm. It was the only thing pinning him to the chair. If he wanted to, he could tear these cuffs like paper. The temptation simmered beneath his grip on control. Usually faint, it took all his willpower to fight it now.

It would be so easy. He could smash this table, break down the door of the holding cell and burst out into the hallway in all his twelve-foot glory, bellowing loud enough to send any cops in a mile-radius skittering like rats. The high ceiling out in the hall would accommodate him. If he ran into a tight squeeze on his way out, he'd simply smash the wall down.

But risk remained. A cop might show a rare streak of bravery. Despite his colossal size, someone might stand in his way. Someone like Jasper.

His fist tightened. The cuffs bit into his wrist bones. Oliver could feel his body burning through the tranquilizers. He was getting more lucid by the minute. But he couldn't Change. Not here. In a scuffle on the street, he might be able to take a bullet or two in the arm and heal himself. Yet if it came to a shootout here in the station, he would lose. Because he wouldn't fight back. As dirty as half these cops were, he couldn't kill them. That would make him as bad as the murderers he fought so hard to protect this city from.

He tipped his head back and closed his eyes. The harsh fluorescents burned an orange glow into the backs of his eyelids.

"What are you doing here?"

A muffled voice, outside the door. Oliver straightened. Through the tiny window in the holding cell door, he spotted the back of his guard's head. Nobody else.

"I got sent to relieve you for your break."

It was hard to place the feeling that ran through him at the sound of that voice. Anger? Regret? Shame?

"Are you an idiot, rookie? Nobody's doing breaks! Did you not hear the 10-34? Why the hell aren't you out there with the rest of the units? This station's supposed to be—"

The man's voice snapped off with a surprised grunt. Something thudded against the metal door. A scuffle, a muffled shout, and then a long, weird silence.

The door to the holding cell buzzed. It swung open. Jasper stopped in the doorway, reloading an odd-shaped pistol with an odd-looking cartridge. Oliver spotted a needle.

"Can you walk?"

Oliver stared at him.

"Can you *stand?*" Jasper strode into the room. He yanked out a set of keys. Oliver watched unmoving as he unlocked the cuffs bolting his hands to the table. "Come on, buddy, work with me. Are you in there? How lucid are you?"

"I'm very lucid," Oliver growled back.

"Really? Okay—good, because I was second guessing this plan the whole way here, all those tranquilizers in your syst—"

"Why the hell are you here?"

Jasper flinched. "I'm here to break you out."

"Why?"

"Can I explain on the way?"

"To where?"

"We need your help." A pause. "We... I mean, the city. The Torch is loose. There's a riot in Chinatown. AITO's plotting a massacre—"

"What?" Oliver stood.

Jasper waved at the door. "Just follow me. With everybody out at the riot or the fire there's next to nobody on the detainment floor except the ones left to guard you. And those guys'll be asleep until..." He glanced down at the gun in his hand. "I'm actually not sure. So we should go bef—"

"No."

Jasper looked up. "What do you mean *no?* I'm here to save your life. You realize once they transfer you to AITO they'll kill you."

"And I'm supposed to believe I'll be safer with you?"

The unfettered shock in his eyes made Oliver feel almost sorry. He held his ground.

"You're Jasper Wade. You stand against everything I do. I hid my identity for over a year from my *best friend* because I knew if you ever found out you'd put me in cuffs yourself. Your high horse is so far up you can't even see the ground anymore. Now here you come to 'break me out' of *your* police station. You didn't think I'd be a little suspicious?"

Jasper's jaw flexed. "I'm sorry you felt like you couldn't tell me…" His hands lifted, motioning to the tattered suit Oliver still wore.

"That I turn into a giant freak monster every night to fight the crime your department doesn't stop?"

"I didn't want to admit I was wrong."

"You aren't admitting it now."

"I was wrong."

Silence. The old heating unit in the building kicked on, followed by the distant scrape of sirens against the stillness.

Jasper ran a hand back through his hair. A muscle in his cheek jerked once. Twice. "You're not the only one I should've…seen."

"You've made it pretty clear how you see me. Vigilantes, criminals, we're all the same in your book."

"Yeah, well, maybe I'm writing a bigger book."

"Really."

"There's room for more categories. Maybe. Criminal, vigilante… superhero." The pinched lines of his face, embarrassment and resignation and anxiety all squashed together were suddenly too much.

Oliver burst out laughing. "Okay, I wasn't asking you to go that far."

"It's what every kid in this city thinks you are." Jasper fiddled with the gun. A burst of air hissed through his teeth. "Look, whatever you call yourself, there's a superhuman psychopath starting a rampage in Eastside. The police are spread too thin to stop him. We need you back. Are you with me? It's sort of now or never."

That old heat drove up inside of him, filling his chest, surging upward through his limbs, bending his bones and ripping his muscles. Oliver shut his eyes for the instant of pain. When he opened them, his hair brushed the ceiling of the detainment cell.

"Lead the way," the Giant's voice rumbled out of him.

To his credit, Jasper didn't gawk up at him. He did swallow.

"You're going to Change in here? Won't the tranquilizers mess you up?"

"I'm burning them off faster in this form."

"Can you hold that form all night?"

"As long as it takes."

The two of them looked at each other. Then Jasper nodded. It wasn't much of a nod, or even an expression, but Oliver understood. He nodded back.

Jasper turned on his heel and darted into the hallway. Oliver ducked through the door and followed, footsteps thudding in the quiet police station.

The flashing caged bulb splashed red circles over the dark parking lot, lighting up the line of stationary white vans Courtney and Strings used for cover. No siren accompanied the alarm. It was eerie. Behind that thick concrete wall, no sound escaped. The only sign of anything wrong was that single flashing light, washing the pavement in rhythmic pulses of scarlet.

Inside, everyone could be dead.

Every AITO staff member. Lab technicians, doctors, janitors. Or…the reverse. Changers, lying in pools of their own blood. People she knew. The Loons.

W himself.

"Are you listening to me?" Strings demanded in a fierce whisper.

Courtney shut her eyes. "Sorry. Run through it again."

"Ugh. Remember the cameras, okay? As long as he can see us, Books will know which doors to unlock as we move. You stick by me, got it? Once we reach the sixth level, he should have the direct link figured out."

"And if he doesn't?"

"Do you really want me to answer that?"

Courtney stared at the pulsing red light until the glow burned her retinas, straining her ears to hear anything besides the sirens drifting in from downtown. The side wall of AITO's enormous compound blotted out any other building.

"Look," Strings said. "We can't worry about whether Books does his job. We gotta focus on ours. All we have to do is show up, push the button on this thingy, and we're in the clear."

"Thingy."

"Frequency generator. Whatever." Strings held up the little cylinder. "After we get this to the control room, Books can hijack everything. That's all we have to do."

"That's all," Courtney whispered.

Six floors. A hundred rabid Changers. Who knew how many more AITO guards.

And W. All the way up on the sixth floor... W.

"Hey, Mastermind, those feet *better* not be getting cold."

Courtney gripped the tranquilizer gun. It felt too small and too big in her hand at the same time. "They're not."

Strings yanked the hood of her jacket up. "Follow my lead. I can Change fast, but you can't. I'll open the doors and keep shifting until we get to the sixth floor. You Change back when we reach the control room."

"Got it."

"Just follow the black cat. Even the dumbest doggy brain can remember that."

"I've got it, Strings."

Strings took a deep breath. "Lee-Ann. My name's Lee-Ann, by the way. In case we don't..."

The splat of the rain drummed the concrete between them. Before Courtney could think to speak, Strings cleared her throat.

"Books said to give him five minutes to get this first door unlocked. Then he'll be ready to follow us." She slipped the little cylinder into a pocket beneath her collar. "Strap that gun to your suit. You can't use it in your shift anyway."

Courtney did. Two thick Velcro straps secured the tranq behind her ribcage. It might feel weird when she Changed. She caught herself on that thought. Of all the things about today, *that* was weird.

She turned to the girl beside her. Strings had her eyes fixed on the flashing, silent alarm, lip pulled between her teeth. In the red glow, wet hair coming loose from her ponytail, she looked suddenly very young.

"I'm glad I met you, Lee-Ann."

Strings glanced sideways. Scarlet and black flickered off her eyes for several moments.

"You too, C."

Then she stood.

Strings darted across the parking lot, silhouetted in sharp red mist. Courtney watched her drop to a crouch beside the door under the flashing alarm. Before her bones could lock, Courtney sprinted to join her. She barely felt her feet hitting the pavement.

For three thick seconds, they pressed themselves against the frigid concrete of the wall. Then, from somewhere deep inside, the door clicked. Metal buzzed.

Strings grabbed the handle. "I am *so* taking him to dinner after this."

She inched open the door... and the sounds of chaos flooded out into the rain.

Gunshots. Shrieks. Animal, human... and some cries on the line between. Footsteps pounded. Metal screeched. An alarm blared, echoing down a distant hallway.

Strings turned around so fast Courtney almost smacked her nose on the shorter girl's head.

"Change," Strings hissed. "*Now.*"

Dread lurched up. Courtney slammed it down, shut her eyes, and reached...

It was so close to the surface it startled her, simmering energy, hot and ready. Deep in her bones, pain shoved and yanked. She doubled over. New sensations speared through her senses. Muscles jerked. Twisted. Settled.

She stood there, disoriented, on four feet. A foggy sharpness enveloped her. New smells and colors, the oddest contrast of brown and white and blue. One smell stood out among the rest. Blood weighed down the air, thick and heavy and copper. It flowed out on the wind currents behind the door, uncleansed by the sweet scent of rain.

She shrank back.

"Hey." Fingers snapped close to her face. "You *stay* on my six, got it? Stick to my scent. God help me, if you get lost..." The girl in the black suit crouched, head between her knees. "I'm gonna Change. Follow me and don't fall behind. These first two floors will be the hardest, W told everybody. I don't know how far they've made it up. Either way, once we hit the stairwells, I'll Change back and open the doors." She rocked on her heels. "If something happens to me… you keep going up, got it? No matter what, you *keep your brain*. You'll be more of a target as a human but just Change back and take the cylinder up. You can do this."

The words flowed in and out of her ears. Courtney stared at the girl. The girl released a short breath.

"Yeah, I'm basically just telling myself at this point."

One shaky hand reached out and patted the top of her head. A hundred instincts cried *flinch*. But Courtney didn't.

The girl took one more deep breath, and folded inward on herself. Courtney's new eyes couldn't track the process. One minute, the girl crouched human and wet in her black bodysuit. Next, a small black cat stood in a wrinkled lump of fabric.

Golden eyes drilled into hers. With a flick of its tail, the cat turned and slipped through the door.

Follow.

The order drove her feet forward before her brain could catch up. Courtney slid through after. The door bumped her sides.

The smells intensified. Metal, blood, saliva, ozone. Tinny, blaring alarms scraped through her ears. The hallway was bright. Cold. And empty. Distant pops of gunfire and growls bled through the walls. No way of telling from which direction they echoed.

The black cat darted ahead. Courtney dove after it.

Strings turned a corner. *Strings, Strings.* The name drummed through her.

Keep your brain. Keep your brain, keep your brain…

Barely discernible above the ringing in her ears, that thin thought shoved its way through the soup of instincts. Her own mind moved her onward. Half automatic, half deliberate, she forced her strange feet after the shadow she couldn't lose sight of.

She skidded around the corner.

There. The black cat trotted half a hallway ahead. Courtney gathered her muscles and closed the distance. The ground tripped and bucked under her in a dizzying way. Each bound carried her forward with startling speed.

The cat turned another corner. Courtney reached the bend in the hallway a second after. The floor slipped under her feet.

A sickly-sweet smell assaulted her senses—a half second before she would've tripped over the body. Her muscles bunched on instinct. She sailed over the heap, landing with a skid through a puddle of scarlet.

Every sinew in her body locked into place.

Death poured off of the man. White coat stained red, arm bent at an unnatural angle. The most hair-raising smell clouded the air.

A stern hiss cut the silence. Courtney jerked around. The black cat crouched five jump-lengths ahead, yellow eyes narrowed. That tail swished back and forth.

Her muscles unlocked. She sprinted to catch up.

The cat slipped in and out of the red lights ahead, a shadow elusive and just out of reach no matter how she sprinted to keep up. They turned a corner.

More heaps littered this hallway. Ugly, pungent red puddles glimmered on the floor. Alarms screeched.

Not a living soul in sight.

The cat—*Strings, it's Strings*—stopped at a door at the end of the hall. She crouched. The pulsing red shadows changed around her. In two heartbeats, a girl's form crouched on the cement, tangled black hair loose. She straightened. Eyes fixed on the ceiling, she waved an arm over her head.

The door clicked. A faint beep, and a little light blinked on near the handle. The girl yanked it open.

"Quit staring and go through, C!"

C.

That's right. Through the door, up the stairs, wait for the human to Change. Strings. The human. Her friend.

I'm human.

I am C.

Her ears began to ring again. She slid through the door under Strings' raised arm. It swung shut behind them as Strings shifted again. The black cat bounded up the stairwell. Courtney raced two steps behind.

The ringing in her ears, louder. Strings Changed again at the landing, waved her arms at the ceiling, opened the door when it clicked. Courtney dove through.

I'm me. I'm C. I'm C.

The whining subsided to a faint hum at the back of her skull. Adrenaline remained, hot and pumping, but no longer controlled her limbs. She took a breath.

Blood snuck in on the air. The ringing intensified again.

"You're doing great, C. We made it past the first floor. See? Just keep right on my tail—"

BLAM.

The window on the back of the door shattered. Glass exploded. The girl yelped, dove flat to the ground and shifted. The cat took over before she hit the concrete.

Courtney flattened herself to the wall.

A second round of gunfire split the air. Another answered it from the opposite direction. Shouts ripped across the hallway.

"Red!" boomed a voice, unfamiliar and rough. "Are you an idiot? Watch Deadeye! He can't shift and shoot at the same time!"

"Watch yourself! You're the one shooting at your own team members!"

"I can't—all these rookies with no clue how to control their shifts—hey, *watch* it!"

A splatter of gunfire.

"On your left!"

"I got him. No thanks to you."

"Less lip, more focus. Deadeye, fly up and tell them we've cleared this level."

A low, hoarse chuckle. "I love it when you're bossy."

"Hey, what about me?"

"You take the rookies on to third and take out as many more of these White Coat dopes as you can."

"Where are you going?"

Metal swished against leather. "W wants me up on sixth ASAP."

"Before the rest of the levels are clear?" A scoff. "What, a little girl like you thinks she's tougher than the rest of—"

A yelp. Then a string of curse words. Something clattered to the ground.

"Wanna switch places? Go ahead, tell W you're ready to be his first line of defense in the control room." A grumbled curse. "That's what I thought. Now, I suggest you *stick* to your assigned position and I'll stick to mine instead of sticking this knife up your ass."

Deadeye's voice returned, amused: "Don't be too rough on him, babe. We need all the able bodies we can get until sixth is clear." The faint scuffle of shoes on concrete. "But you did ask for it, new-blood. Don't mess with my girl. She's been in W's top three since this op started."

"Tch." Metal on leather again. "See you at the top."

"Beat you there."

A flutter of wind. Then footsteps pounding off in two separate directions.

Strings lifted herself from her crouch. She poked her head

around the corner. The cat's whiskers twitched.

Then she disappeared around the corner.

Follow!

Courtney's feet yanked her forward. She tumbled after Strings into the hallway, bracing herself against the smell of blood, the dark shapes scattered over the floor, white heaps of fabric smeared with red...

"What the hell is that?"

Her feet skidded on the ground, wheeling toward the sound of the voice.

"Wait, don't shoot—they're with us."

"They don't look like any of ours."

"Does it matter? Any Changer in here is either with us or escaping. Let 'em go. They'll take down some White Coats on their way out."

Strings ignored the voices. Courtney spotted the little feline shape slinking over and around the bodies, leaving her behind one leap-length at a time.

Instinct clouded. Her feet moved again.

The hallway streaked by. She had no thoughts about the warm heaps jerking past beneath her. No thoughts about the feel of something softer than the ground under her paws as she kicked off for a stronger leap. The whine in her ears had grown deafening. No room for thoughts. No room for anything else other than the driving need to *run, run, run.*

Follow the shadow.

Strings' dark silhouette stopped under the pulsing glare of a silent alarm. Or—maybe it wasn't silent. Courtney couldn't hear anything else anymore over the ringing. Perhaps she'd gone deaf. Perhaps sound had faded with her thoughts.

Strings grew to a five-foot shadow once again. Pressed her face to the window on the door. Then lifted a hand.

Click.

She yanked open the door. Braced it open with her skinny shoulders, waved for Courtney to go through. Courtney did. Her body moved so fluidly she didn't need to control it anymore. The ground slid by. She glided forward, every movement smoother than the last.

That single instinct forced all others to silence. It only got simpler the longer she listened to it.

Follow.

One level.

Two levels.

Three.

Four.

Door after door. Bodies after bodies. Hiding, listening, waiting. Shouting, so much shouting. Gunshots. Alarms.

They all blurred to a background buzz under that steady ringing. So long as she kept the shadow in her sight—black cat, black-suited human—she kept a handle on the instincts. They guided her instead of freezing her. She could think. Sort of. She could move.

That was all that counted now.

"Fifth level," Strings panted. Hands on human knees, she crouched before the big metal door at the top of another stairwell. "Can't believe we made it this far."

Shouts from the other side of the door. Alarms sprayed the smudgy glass in greens and reds, sharp and sparkling through the narrow window. Strings looked up at the ceiling.

"Here's where it gets dicey. Books can't talk to me. W took all the com systems we usually use, so there's no way for Books to tell me what's on the other side of that door. I could wing it up till now, but this last floor between us and the control room… everyone's here. There's no way to tell how many. Who's armed. Who's with us, against us. You get it. Actually, you don't, because you can't understand a word I'm saying." Strings tipped her head back against the wall. Her chest rose and fell in rapid jerks. "I don't believe this. I got us here, and I can't... I can't open that door." She slid her hands up over her face. "That's my team out there. I've never... by myself..."

Fear streamed off of her. Thick, and sweet, and acrid. Her shoulders shook.

"Get it together." The barked hiss came from behind Strings's fingers. "Books is probably screaming at the camera right now. I look like an idiot."

Anger. Hot and stabbing, flooded her system. Courtney felt her bones pinch. Twist.

Strings lifted her face. Eyes wide behind her fingers. Her hands slipped down.

"You... you Changed? On your own?"

Courtney crouched. Then tipped sideways. Both hands shot out to hit the concrete before the world spun too far. She closed her eyes.

"But how... you're a rookie!"

"You were upset." Courtney's voice rasped out of her like it belonged to someone else. "I saw you—*felt* you freeze up, and I couldn't watch. So I... Changed."

Strings stared. "You could understand me? As an animal?"

"I don't know. No, I don't think so, it was all..." The memory of mere moments before was so blurred, so watery and jumbled, it felt like trying to drag it out of the ancient past. No clear words surfaced. Just the stifling... *smell*... of fear.

"You were afraid." Courtney looked down at her hands, pink and lined and human in the flashing lights. "You Changed back and forth so much, you led us all the way here, kept your mind in spite of all those instincts trying to drag you down like a drowning person... Strings, you're amazing. You got us this far. What stopped you?"

Strings pressed her lips together. They trembled.

A gunshot cracked. They both flinched. The echo from the other side of the door reverberated through the concrete.

"If I die right now," Strings whispered. "No one will even realize it. I'm a lost girl. My name stopped being in the paper two years ago. My family will never know what happened. Even if they chose to care, they would never know. I'll just be... gone."

She pressed her face into the backs of her knees, elbows crossed over her forehead.

"I would know."

"You'll be dead too, you idiot," came the muffled response.

"Maybe. But so will every other Changer in this city if we don't do what we're about to do."

"Why are we even stopping W? His plan would've worked! He's already killed half the AITO staff! All those bodies on the ground—"

"Belong to people who might have families outside, who will never realize what happened to them either! What's to stop them retaliating once W kills the rest of them? If he takes out Jeanine, there goes our link to the Outside, and we'll look like a bunch of rabid killers—Changers gone out of control. They'll send in the military, just like Freak Week, and wipe us all out. Ending this in violence is *not* the way to stop more violence."

Strings' shoulders tensed.

"Do you really want to do it this way, Strings?"

"I never wanted to do it at all."

"No, you didn't. But you had a chance to keep your head down and do nothing, and you chose to come with me instead."

Strings' hands tightened around her knees, then turned to fists. She raised her head.

"You're the most likely one to die of us all. You have no experience leading a raid, dodging bullets or even fighting hand to hand. And *you're* talking *me* through that door?"

"I'm talking both of us through it." Courtney sucked in a breath. "If W kills Jeanine, we'll never be free. The only way he knows to get his way is with violence—it's all he knows. But it won't work this time—Books said the Director will die before she opens AITO's gate through the Wall. We *have* to get to her first."

She clenched her own fists, and stood. Her knees bumped together. The door gleamed red and green and black and silver, flashing like she couldn't trust her eyes.

"C..."

Courtney looked down. Strings looked even smaller than she had out in the parking lot huddled there on the floor. Ponytail undone, mascara smeared, she wasn't a tough violin-stealing street kid who bested every other Changer on W's team for stealth and speed. She was a teenager scared to death.

"What does C stand for?"

Courtney reached out a hand. "Crazy. Coward. Courage. Anything I make of it, somebody once told me."

Strings let her pull her to her feet. "You never picked a name?"

"I think I just did."

"Just a letter. Like..."

"Yeah."

Strings gripped the handle on the door. She filled her cheeks with air. "You ready?"

Courtney looked at the camera on the ceiling. It blinked its small red light down at her. "Should I Change?"

"No. Get your tranq out."

She'd forgotten the pistol holstered at her ribs. Reaching up, her searching fingers found it, slipped all the way behind her back in its sheath. She pulled it out.

"We're so close, it's too risky to stop and wait for you to Change at the end of the next hallway. We'll be sitting ducks for the time it'll take to pull your brain back together. I think we can make it on foot. You've got four shots so make 'em count. Stay on my six. Our goal is the final door on the left, got it? That's the stairwell that'll take us on to sixth. From there it's a straight shot to the control room." Strings inched her eyes around the edge of the window. "At least... a straight shot with a lot of enemies in the way."

"Can't we wait for them to pass?"

"No. The longer we wait, the more of W's team and AITO work their way to the top. Everybody's gunning for the control room. We're lucky no one met us on the stairs already."

"Then... now. We just rush out there, right now."

Strings' shoulders tightened. She said nothing, face close to the edge of the window, hand on the door handle.

"He hasn't opened it yet," she whispered. "There are so many of them out there. White Coats, gray suits, Changers. I don't recognize anyone."

Which means they won't recognize us.

Even if they did... there was no safeguard against friendly fire. Or not so friendly.

A threat to his operation.

What if everyone saw it that way?

"What is he waiting for?" Strings hissed. "We're not gonna get a bigger break than this..."

Would W see it that way when she finally reached the top? When it came down to it, would he deal with this threat like he dealt with all others?

Was her mission even more suicidal than his?

The door clicked.

"Now!" Strings yanked it open and dove out into the hallway.

17. THE COST

THE BRIGHT LIGHTS felt like running into a dream she'd had before. The concrete hallway spattered with blood. Dark heaps of torn fabric, white and gray, scarlet splashed in between. Mounds of unmoving fur. Feathers. Guns dropped and discarded. Greens and reds scraped over everything; harsh alarms drilled into her ears, deafening out here in the open.

Shapes moved on her peripherals. Her bare feet pounded the sticky ground.

"Hey!"

Fttt-ttt-phttt.

Something punched her in the calf, so hard she tripped and almost face-planted into the looming carcass of a bear. A hand grabbed the front of her suit. Yanked her forward, tripping and stumbling. They dove down behind the enormous body.

Phat. Phat. Phat.

More bullets tore into the backside of the bear. Courtney felt the vibrations through the thick pelt at their backs. Strings yanked her down lower.

Something hot pressed up against her leg, so close it burned. Courtney tried to jerk away, but the heat followed. She reached down. Wet nylon clung to her fingers. Hot, sticky.

"Shit," Strings said.

Courtney stared. The hole at the back of her calf looked as dark as the rest of her suit, gleaming under the lights. It didn't hurt. But it burned like she'd backed herself against a firepit, getting hotter by the second.

"Shit!" Strings cried again. "Can you walk? Run to that cover over there? We've still got a whole hallway to go!"

Courtney looked where she pointed. Another huge creature— a bull—lay against the far wall. She pulled herself forward into a crouch. The muscles in her right leg tingled.

"No, wait, stop—we gotta stop that bleeding." Strings pulled her back down. At the other end of the hallway, two men in white jumpsuits dove behind the body of another large animal. Courtney spotted a head rising above the cover—sighting along a barrel.

"Strings!" She yanked the other girl to the side. The bear behind them jerked twice. Blood sprayed the side of her face, sickeningly lukewarm. Her head spun.

"Freaking idiots," Strings screamed into Courtney's shoulder, pushing herself back up to her knees. She grabbed the tranq out of Courtney's hand. The man who'd fired ducked back down.

"We're sitting ducks," Strings yelled. "New plan. Change now!"

She shrank. The gun she'd been holding clattered to the cement. Courtney snatched it up and shoved it into the holster at her side. The black cat beside her looked up with piercing yellow eyes. Courtney Changed.

All the pain condensed into her right hind leg. The rest of her shifting bones felt like mere aches in comparison. Her muscles stitched and spasmed. She fell forward on four feet, lungs heaving. The cat darted away. Courtney vaulted after her.

Gunshots tore through the hallway ahead. They skidded off the concrete on either side of her, whistled over her ears. The cat leapt over the top of the dead beast the two men hid behind. Strings Changed mid-fall, so fluid Courtney's eyes couldn't keep up. One human leg hooked around the back of the man's neck and yanked him down with her. Then Courtney saw nothing.

She raced around the other side of the looming carcass. Strings had her legs locked around the man's neck, arms wrapped around his face as he tried to pry her off. The other man scrambled for his gun.

Courtney leaped. She cleared the distance before the man had time to look up. Her teeth closed around his arm.

"*Aaaeeeeeeuuugh!*"

Blood filled her mouth. Two instincts slammed her teeth together, then apart. The sick punch of revulsion battled with the will to tear, to rip flesh from bone.

She let go before he could shake her off. The man stumbled back as she did the same, tumbling away from each other. Her mind shook. Her body filled with the scent and taste of blood.

He dove for the gun again. She tripped backward. Stumbled into something solid, felt a rough yank on her vest. Too late to move forward or backward—the man found the gun, he was raising it—

BLAM.

He jerked sideways. Tripped over his feet, dropped the gun with a clatter, and fell. He did not rise.

Courtney turned. Strings lay half-crushed under the huge White Coat behind her. Knees still locked firmly around his neck, she'd twisted upright to a painful degree, both arms extended. The tranq gun shook in her hand.

Between her knees, the man's face glowed crimson. He scrabbled feebly at her ankles. But his lips were fat and purple, eyes beginning to close.

His hands stilled. They dropped, one at a time. Strings relaxed her knees and untangled herself from his neck. His head hit the ground none too gently.

"Come on." Strings climbed to her feet. "Still half the hallway left."

Strings shoved the tranq back into the holster on Courtney's back. Then she dove forward. The cat raced off. Courtney tore after it without a thought.

Shouts echoed. She kept her head low and ran full tilt. Her right hind leg screamed.

They reached the dead bull. Strings Changed as soon as they hit the wall, crouched low behind the narrow cover. She yanked Courtney down beside her.

"Okay, Change back. You're stuck as a human from here on, you'll bleed out all over the place if you keep shifting on that leg. Here."

Strings lifted an arm to her face, took her sleeve within her teeth and ripped off a large chunk of her own nylon suit. "This is the most unsanitary bandage ever but it'll stop the bleeding now."

She reached for Courtney's leg. Instinct ripped through her, and Courtney found herself jerking backward. Strings grabbed the front of her suit.

"Focus, C! You have to Change! Keep your mind, find my voice—listen, you have to Change or we're both dying right here.

- 260 -

Understand? You hear my words?"

Something in her voice broke through the fog. Courtney's muscles responded. Pain and scents and deafening sounds swirled around her for one moment—one breath. Then she knelt on hands and knees, concrete cold beneath her scraped palms.

Strings mumbled something in another language, voice shaky with relief. She reached out a hand. Courtney tipped against the wall for balance and extended her leg. For the second time, she got a glimpse of it.

Thick black rivulets of blood ran from calf to ankle, spidering out over her bare foot. The world spun. She turned her face to the wall and laid her cheek against the cold concrete. She felt Strings wrap the strip of fabric below her knee, then tie it off tight above the wound. She grit her teeth. The tourniquet bit into her calf.

"That should hold until we get upstairs—shit, your face. Open your eyes. Did you faint?"

"No. I'm okay."

Gunshots ricocheted through the hallway. Strings glanced up over her head. Her eyes flashed. "We've got a window now. They're clashing with each other down the hall. It's a clear shot to the stairs from here. Can you make it?"

Courtney nodded. Her temple scraped against the wall.

"You don't look good. Dammit, I didn't think you'd lost that much blood yet—"

"I'm fine." Courtney stumbled to her feet, using the wall. "This happens… every time there's…" She swallowed. "I'll be fine in a second."

"Seriously? The sight of blood?" Strings barked a nervous laugh. "You're running with the wrong crowd."

"I've been told." Courtney took a halting step away from the wall. Strings ducked forward, grabbed her arm and looped it around her own shoulders. They hobbled forward.

Gunshots clipped the air behind them. Strings flinched under her arm and picked up the pace. But the shouts seemed to echo in the other direction. They did have a window. It could close in seconds. Half a hallway ahead looked the length of a football field. Standing upright, even leaning on Strings, Courtney felt too tall.

The door with the little sign marked 'stairs' crawled closer. They hugged the wall. Behind them, the shouts grew louder.

"These freaks!" a man growled. "How many more of them are there? They just keep coming."

"At least they're easy targets. Half of them are dumb animals."

"Not on third, they weren't. They came in like a freaking army, systematic, took down half the security unit. Some of them even shook off bullets!"

"That's a load of bull. You believe those horror stories?"

"I *saw* those horror stories! They're not normal, man, they're—"

"Wait. What's that? Up ahead."

"Shit, I thought we got 'em all."

Strings yanked them along faster. The door was five paces away. Four. Three.

Phtt-tttt-phttt!

Strings stumbled into a run, Courtney right behind. Footsteps thumped after them between rounds of bullets. She heard the click before they even reached the door. Strings ripped it open. They dove inside and let it slam shut. It clicked again.

Strings let go of her. Courtney caught the wall for balance— and saw Strings stumble back into it, sliding down the concrete to the floor.

"Strings?"

"Dammit," the other girl whispered. Her eyes were wide and

black. "Dammit, dammit, dammit..."

One arm went around her middle. Face slack, Strings looked down at her hand as it came away. Crimson painted her fingers.

"Strings!"

Courtney dove to her knees beside her, the same instant the door rattled.

"Damn! My code's not working. How did they get through?"

The door beeped a harsh, hissing tone. It rattled again. Someone banged it from the other side.

"We don't have time for this, let's go around."

Cursing. Heavy footsteps thudded away.

Strings' eyes squeezed closed. Her hair fluttered around her mouth, clinging to damp cheeks.

"Move your hand." Courtney gripped her arm. "Show me."

"No time. You have to go."

"Stop that, and let me see how bad—"

"*No.*" Bony fingers clenched her wrist. "You need to get up there. Every minute you waste gives W another minute to kill Campbell."

"Well he can wait another damn minute while I make sure you don't bleed out!"

The fingers gripped tighter. A whimpered growl leaked past Strings' teeth as she shifted her weight, and then a hot, sticky cylinder appeared in Courtney's hand. The frequency generator.

"*No,* Strings."

"Stop it, C! I told you before we even left, if anything happened to me, *you're* the one who needs to make it to sixth. If you don't get that transmitter to the control room, W's going to kill the only person who could get us through the Wall, and then it's all over. Reinforcements will come storming back into AITO and we'll all be dead. Your plan will only work now."

"I'm not just going to leave you here!"

"Look!" Strings jerked her chin toward the ceiling. "Books kept those guys from getting in. He can make this hallway a bunker. I'll be fine. Now you need to go."

Courtney clenched the little cylinder. Blood warmed her palm, sending a shiver up her arm.

"Go!"

"I'll be back, I promise."

"Just get it done." Strings shut her eyes again. Her face contorted. "Go fast."

Courtney wobbled to her feet. Her right knee buckled. She caught the wall.

"The more time you waste, the more you bleed too," Strings groaned. "Get up those stairs before you can't anymore."

Fingers gripping the railing, Courtney heaved herself up the first step. Then the second.

"When Books opens the door, turn right. Don't take the straight hallway to the control room, everyone will be… clogged up in there…" Strings' voice choked off for a moment. "…keep going till you reach the second hallway on your left. The door at the end. That'll let you in the back way. Less people there… hopefully."

Half her weight on the railing, Courtney looked back. Strings' head lolled over her shoulders, arms locked around herself. She'd curled up into a ball.

"Strings?"

"Go," came the strangled whimper.

The cylinder burned in her palm. Courtney bit her lip so hard she tasted blood, and climbed the stairs.

One foot at a time. She took a step, yanked herself up by the railing, and lifted her heavy right leg to join the left. The next stair.

One foot, two foot. Ow. Heat stabbed up from her knee all the way to her hip. She kept going.

Five stairs. Six stairs. Seven stairs.

Twenty to go.

Sweat beaded on her brow. She felt the railing grow slimy under her hand. Something started to shake behind her sternum. That dull yank in her bones, burning and sizzling.

No. No Changing here. She was Courtney from here on up. Fifteen stairs.

The door blurred up ahead. She blinked the sweat—tears?—from her eyes. Strings' faint whimper echoed in her ears.

"Almost there, Strings," she called back. "I'll be faster on level floor. As soon as I get the frequency going in the control room, I'll turn around and come back for you. Books can take it from there."

No reply from behind her.

"Strings, you hear me? Hang on another minute. I'm coming straight back."

The dull, tinny ring of alarms in the distance.

"Strings? ...Lee Ann?"

Courtney's throat clenched shut. She paused on the stairs, every muscle trembling to turn around. But she didn't.

"I'll be right back," she choked out. She forced herself to take another step. *As fast as I can. For both of us. I'll run on this leg if I have to.*

Dragging herself forward until the pain put spots in her vision, she fixed her eyes on the end of the hall.

At the end of the second hallway, Courtney paused to stand on her uninjured leg. Her muscles shook. The tourniquet severed all feeling in her foot, but the building pressure at her knee sent shooting blasts of agony up to her hip. Courtney sucked in a firm breath. Bracing herself on the wall, she inched her face around the corner.

Black spray streaked the walls, gleaming crimson under the screeching pulses of light. The alarms lit up two figures at the end of the hall. An unfamiliar man in a gray jumpsuit stood against a closed door, holding the biggest gun she'd ever seen. Opposite him, Red leaned against the wall, cleaning her fingernails with a throwing knife. Neither of them looked at her. They seemed to be leaning toward the door, as if listening.

A muffled gunshot cracked.

Courtney reached for the holster at her ribcage. *Red first.* She didn't know why, but she trusted the instinct as it guided her aim. She held the tranq with steady hands and inched the barrel around the wall.

Her shot snapped the air. Red jerked backward and hit the door with a surprised yelp, one hand flying up to her shoulder. The man in the jumpsuit lifted his gun. His searching eyes found Courtney just as she squeezed off her second shot.

The dart hit him in the chest. Courtney ducked around the corner a millisecond before a spray of bullets tore into the concrete opposite her. She hunkered down with her hands over her head. Heavy footsteps thundered closer.

The next round of bullets splattered the wall again, then climbed to the ceiling. They ceased with a clatter. A heavy thud followed.

Courtney held her crouch for another three seconds, straining her ears. She peeked around the corner.

Red slumped against the wall, the knife spinning on the floor beside her bare foot. The man lay half a hall-length ahead, sprawled like a starfish. The big semi-automatic wobbled back and forth on the concrete in front of his outstretched arm.

Courtney yanked herself back to her feet. She hugged the wall and teetered as fast as she could toward the door.

Another gunshot rang out from behind it.

She broke into a wobbly run. Her calf screamed.

I have to get to Jeanine first.

The door beeped before she reached it. There was no window to the other side. Courtney stood there with the handle half-turned under her hand, forehead pressed against the metal.

No more empty hallways. She was going in blind, and everyone would see this door swing open. Should she try to sneak in? If Red and that other guy were posted outside this door, would they have more guards watching from the other side?

A muffled voice slid in from behind the metal. Faint and low and almost drowned out under the alarms, she still felt it in every ounce of her body.

W.

Her grip tightened on the handle. The cylinder in her other palm tingled. Slowly, she pushed the door open.

"I'm going to ask you again."

She slipped inside and pressed herself against the wall, grateful to emerge inside a hollow of shadows. Desks and computers and tall metal cases filled her view. Several figures stood with their backs to her on the other side of a row of steel cabinets. Courtney ducked behind a desk.

"And I'm going to tell you again," growled a second voice. Female. "No."

BOOM.

The sound exploded off the walls, bouncing back to hit her square in the gut. Courtney doubled over with her arms covering her ears. A sick feeling jerked in her stomach.

"Another brilliant mind splattered across the floor." W clucked his tongue. "From what I gather after our last visit, you've got a finite amount of those left."

"That only means you," came the brittle retort. "Have finite leverage."

"We'll see. Third time's the charm: open the gate."

"Never."

"And round we go again. You—come here. Todd, was it? I remember you from my days as an assistant. Weren't those fun, Jeanine? Todd's a nice guy. I wonder what his brains look like."

Shoes squeaked against the floor. A man grunted, under the sound of a third voice growling, "Hands on your head. Take a knee."

"You're wasting your time," snapped the woman. "Each of us signed away our lives for this research. We knew the risks. Kill him, kill me; we're willing to die to give the human race its next step into evolution."

"Evolution?" W's laugh ricocheted off the walls sharper than the gunshot. "You think we're evolved? Half of us feral, the other half empty in the head, murderers and giggling psychopaths. You remember Reginald, I'm sure. I don't remember you looking as if you'd made some kind of breakthrough when he bit off your orderly's finger and spat it out on your feet."

"You masqueraded within these walls for two months in a different skin. You learned our secrets and tore down our system from the inside, using an army of volatile theriomutants we never discovered how to control. Even with our losses, I would say our research was a success. Warfare, espionage, homeland security: all of it will be completely transformed when we use your DNA to perfect this serum."

"Ever the scientist," W spat. "Does it ever get cold, inside your head? You won't have anyone left to do the studying when I paint the walls with the rest of you."

"Whether I live or die is irrelevant. You and the rest of our subjects will be contained within these walls when our backup arrives. The research I've left behind will guide my successors in how to study you. Now that we know you're the one we're after, they'll keep you alive for further research and dispose of all other compromised subjects." Her voice colored with a smugness that could only arise from a true absence of fear. "You've handed us exactly what we've been searching for. History will thank you."

"I'll destroy your research right along with you."

"You can't. You never had access to those files as an assistant. You have nothing to threaten me with."

Courtney dared peek her head around the desk. She could make out the back of Jeanine's head, blonde bun falling out in wild strands, a spot of blood matted in her hair. Red speckled her white lab coat. Beyond her shoulder, a row of scientists knelt on the concrete with black-suited men and women at their backs. Each Changer held a gun squarely against the back of a scientist's head.

She couldn't see W. But she heard him. The dark ripple of energy under his voice caused the hair on her arms to stand up. She recognized the sound of his mask cracking.

"You were always a confident talker. Reminds me of the time when you sat across the table from the Torch and pretended he didn't scare you. But I saw your hands shaking. Like they're shaking now. Make all the speeches you want about dying for evolution, but I wonder if you'll flinch again when I put a bullet in Todd's head. Don't think I didn't notice your face after the last two."

Courtney gripped the cylinder so hard she heard a snap. She

looked down. The little plastic sheath around the wires held a hairline zigzag.

Come on, Books! How deep inside the control room did she have to get for the frequency generator to work? Books had said he could activate it as soon as she got it inside. Was it not close enough to pick up the sound of Jeanine's voice? No lights flickered overhead. No computer screens fizzled. No sign any signal had gone out at all. Courtney shoved the cylinder back inside her suit, pressing it snug against her collarbone.

Ninety seconds ago that door had clicked to let her in. Gunshots still ringing in her ears, she knew ninety seconds was an awful long window for something to happen. Maybe someone had found Books and Dina. Maybe Jasper hadn't reached the van in time to protect them. Or maybe he had. Maybe he'd been no match for AITO security—or the Loons. Maybe… there was no one waiting on the other side. No one to stop W from pulling that trigger.

"Please," a thin voice whispered from the floor. "I have a daughter."

Courtney stood up.

The instant the light slipped over her, four Changers lifted their guns. W exploded in a voice that didn't sound like his own:

"*Stop!* Hold your fire."

She stepped out into the room. Jeanine cast her a swift look from where she stood backed against a desk, but didn't move away. A thick, blue plaster cast shielded her left forearm. The force of all the eyes felt almost physical as Courtney dragged her other foot forward.

He stood flanked by six more black-clad Changers. Three bodies lay on the floor. Two white coats, one nylon black suit. The man kneeling at his feet looked up, forehead crinkling as he tried to keep his chin down. Blood ran from his temple to his jaw.

"What in the hell," W hissed. "Are you doing here?"

18. THE THREAT RESPONSE

ASLASH OF red marked his left cheekbone, just below his eye. His hair was a mess. Two bullet holes bled light through the hanging hem of his coat—too close to his chest. Was that blood on his collar?

Focus. He was still standing. Breathing. So was she. So was Jeanine, and the man on the floor who knelt with shaking elbows in the air—who had a daughter. Somewhere, in Orion City or Outside, a girl wondered when her father was coming home.

Margo's face swam through her mind.

"James." Courtney's voice fell out like something snappable; a frayed piece of string. "Don't. Please. Don't do this again."

Pale eyes drilled into her with a force enough to push her backward. She took another step.

"You were seventeen," she said. "Right? When you killed your father. The man who started everything—the one before this woman, before the Wall. The one who used his own kids as lab rats and then went on to force his sick experiment on half a million people. You've tried to fight this your way since you were eleven. At the age I learned how to use roller skates, you learned the world wasn't safe and that all you had to count on was yourself. And you got so far. Hell, you've got half this city afraid of you and the scarier half doing exactly what you say. But James—your way doesn't work." She took another step forward. Her knee nearly gave out at the movement, and she wavered on one foot. "Kill this monster," she gasped. "And she'll just be replaced. *You'll* be replaced. With something else. That monster you were becoming. The Whistler from the news. The one who killed a little girl's parents while she listened from her bedroom. The one who beat my coworker to a pulp in front of me."

W's eyes dropped to her leg. The already thin line of his lips pressed thinner, a dark heat burning behind his eyes. Courtney hobbled sideways a step. Reached for the desk beside Jeanine to steady herself, the pressure building so sharp in her calf she almost couldn't catch her voice.

"But you're *not* him," she ground out. "I know you're not. You're the man who kept an orphan under his wing because you didn't want her to be alone—the man I fell in love with. Your knee-jerk response was *compassion*. You take in broken Changers from all over the city who lost their lives and build them up again. You give them a choice. That's why they follow you. They believe in you, W." Her fingers bit into the edge of the desk. "So do I."

"Courtney." Her name snapped the air like the crack of a pistol. "Move back."

"You won't set anyone free by putting a bullet in that man's head."

"I said. Move. Back."

"What about Margo?"

Anger ripped across his features. The man on the ground cried out in a sudden burst of fear, leaning away from the shaking gun at the back of his head. W grabbed him by the hair.

"You still remember their names!" Courtney yelled. "You told me as much as you've tried to forget, their names never left you. You—what's your daughter's name?"

"What?" the man on his knees stuttered.

"Your daughter! She's got a name, right?"

"S-Samantha."

W's knuckles whitened on the gun.

"James…" Her voice wavered. "You're not the boy you were at seventeen. And you're not the man you were three years ago. You said you didn't know what Margo sees when she looks at you. I do. After everything, all she heard and saw, all those years with you… you're still someone she trusts."

The man on the floor, whose eyes had screwed shut, slowly opened them. One by one, W's long fingers released their grip on his hair. The scientist slumped forward. Forehead wrinkling further, he fixed huge eyes on Courtney.

She lifted her own to W's. He wasn't looking at her. His eyes had fixed on some point in the middle distance, gun hanging loose by his side. The mask was gone. Cracks shattered clean through, the cool smoothness splintered away to reveal a person she'd never seen before. A man with creases between his eyebrows, and a deep shadow in his pale eyes that reminded her of a well: a cold depth that whispered faint flickers of light.

Words built up in her throat. Thick and hopeful and terrified. But at the same moment they lifted to her tongue, her suit gave a sharp tug behind her ribs and a plaster-casted arm whipped around her throat.

"And here I'd prepared to sacrifice my life for this project." A woman's voice boomed two inches from her ear. Courtney flinched backwards—into a soft chest and a bony chin. "Your girlfriend here has convenient timing. And a horrible sense of her surroundings." The stillness evaporated. W's gun came up so fast, Courtney expected to feel the jerk of Jeanine's body behind her as a bullet ripped through it. Instead, cold metal kissed the base of her chin. The barrel of her own tranquilizer gun. "Tell your freaks to stand down before I fire this tranquilizer straight through her windpipe."

The thick red puddles on the ground reflected a line of statues. Beyond the walls, the faint scream of the alarms hissed through the concrete. One person finally moved. The man at W's feet scooted away from him on hands and knees, half-tumbling toward the line of desks opposite. The Changers behind the kneeling scientists glanced at him, then back at W.

"You think I won't." Jeanine's cast dug harder into Courtney's collarbone. She shifted, adjusted her feet—

—and pain exploded in Courtney's calf. Her whole leg dropped out from under her. The cry that ripped from her lungs felt foreign as she grappled for Jeanine's arm, clawing for purchase. White hot spots swam across her vision.

"Stand down." She barely heard W's voice over the roar in her ears.

As the spots cleared, Courtney made out the black-suited Changers, one by one, pulling their guns away from the hostages. The men and women on the ground lowered their arms from their heads.

"Now put the guns on the ground. All of you."

"Boss…" started a Changer from the edge of the group.

Courtney reached a hand back, blindly, stretching out for

Jeanine. Her fingers brushed the edge of a lab coat.

A second kick slammed into the back of her leg. Courtney buckled. The scream couldn't even work its way past the bile in her throat. Only the rough plaster crammed against her jugular kept her from falling.

"You heard the woman," W said. His voice sounded like paper. It wasn't his. The sound of it on his lips punched a hole straight through her, colder and deeper than any fear Jeanine could drive in.

Murmurs jerked through the Changers. A couple of them shifted their stance. But by the fourth pulse of the distant alarms, every single one had lowered their guns. Horror and awe filled her.

Not a single person had defied him. She'd sensed it before. But here it was, sharpened into knifelike relief. His was the one voice to call them back from the edge, where minds so caved to instinct no other thoughts registered. Rabid. Unhinged. Insane. None of these labels mattered with his voice at the helm. A whistle. A word. A spark of light through the darkness of the Change. If he led them straight to their deaths, they'd follow.

Jeanine sensed it too, the power magnified around the skinny man in the center of the room. Her muscles tightened against Courtney's back.

"You drop your gun, too."

W looked down at the gun in his hand as if seeing it for the first time. He blinked.

He looked suddenly so lost Courtney had the shameful urge to avert her gaze.

"This is where we divide." Jeanine growled against the back of her head. "Your father, you, me. I knew Dr. Wilder. He was a great man. Prepared to sacrifice anything and anyone for the cause. I learned all I know from him. All of us at AITO are prepared. I'll sacrifice my life, my colleagues' lives, the life of every pathetic

- 276 -

creature in this city for this cause. That's how I know we'll win, no matter how this plays out. If I die tonight, my legacy will live on. But you—you'll let yours end here, with this girl."

The cold muzzle of the gun shifted against Courtney's throat. She kept her eyes glued to W.

Dad. The thought burned its way into her mind, leaving a stinging trail in its wake. *Michael.*

Dina. Jasper. Books. Strings.

I hope you got out.

The smell of blood on the floor hit her human senses with an acrid chill. Her bones began to ache. Twisting, deep inside.

If she Changed here, could she...?

The gun bit into her jugular as she swallowed. No. Jeanine would put a needle through her throat the second she started to shift. She'd go down with a yelp like an animal, full of instinct and fear and so far away from herself, from any thought of Michael or Dad or Dina or W.

She'd be gone before she even died.

I don't know what my legacy is.

Her gaze dipped to the gleaming scarlet puddle at W's shoes. *It wasn't this.* She'd come because she could never let it be this.

"Drop the gun, Wilder."

Jeanine's voice held so much assurance, even as her body trembled. If she died, if she lived; she didn't care. She was untouchable and she knew it. The thrill of fighting death off anyway, in spite of making peace with it—whatever instinct pumped through Jeanine's veins now, Courtney felt excitement surging off the woman behind her.

"No, I don't think I will."

Not paper. W's voice lacked its usual edge, but a new sort of steel had bled into it. Jeanine pulled in a hissing breath, but he sliced off her reply:

"I have an offer."

A sour laugh jerked against her. "What could you possibly have to offer me?"

W's eyes slid the few inches left to meet Courtney's. A faint smile, sad and tight, lifted the corner of his mouth. He raised the gun. Pressed it against his own temple.

"Me."

Jeanine's whole body went stiff.

"Two decades, am I correct? Three if you count when my father first began his experiments, long before AITO formed to pick up his mantle. I'm patient zero. The first one to survive the serum altering his genes, the only one with a mutation quite like mine. Now I can think of quite a few more uses for theriomutation *intra homo-sapiens*, as I'm sure the possibilities have already crossed your mind. But—" He fluttered his long fingers around the trigger of the gun at his head, a tease that gave Courtney's stomach a little kick. "You need living cells to duplicate any sort of serum from what you find in my genes. Now I don't have your four PhDs, but I learned enough from my dear old man's research to know that any post-mortem testing you try on me won't give you a quarter as much of the breakthrough you want with me alive. So, then, what's it gonna be? I pull this trigger and put you ten steps behind where you're at now. Or you can put down the tranquilizer gun."

The only sign the woman behind her hadn't turned to stone was the steady pulse of a heartbeat in the crook of the elbow squeezed tight over Courtney's collarbone.

"You're not the only one willing to sacrifice for your cause," W murmured. "However, you wanna know what divides you and me? I don't waste people."

The ghostly feeling of his fingers against her jaw line, pale eyes scalding hers as he said those words, drifted back.

"You're bluffing," Jeanine barked. "All your years of planning, your moles inside AITO, every strategy you've built up to take down the Wall, and you're going to blow yourself away before you've even tasted freedom? You spat in the face of science because you couldn't see past your own selfish dream. Now, after getting this far, you think I'm going to believe you'll throw it all away before you even set foot outside?"

"None of it means anything without her."

The pale gray in W's eyes burned silver. He slid his eyes from Courtney's back to Jeanine's. The woman at her back remained stiff and silent.

"Here's my offer, valid only while that woman under your arm breathes. You let down the Wall. Contact your general on the outside with the news you've found a cure. AITO lifts the Quarantine and this wretched city of guinea pigs goes free, but you get to keep the one you've been searching for."

No.

"From lying, scheming murderer to selfless hero," Jeanine bit out. But a raw excitement sizzled under her voice that put an almost tangible stench in the air.

"Far from it. A Wilder started this. A Wilder will end it, twenty years overdue."

Courtney reached her own fingers up over the cast squeezing her windpipe. The cylinder bit into the skin beneath her suit. An idea rocketed through her.

"Dr. Campbell," she rasped. "Don't take the offer."

W blinked. Jeanine started a little too, as if forgetting her leverage could speak.

"Listen." Courtney scraped for breath against the grip around her throat. "How many people have spent their lives for this project so far? Give me the number."

W's eyes tightened on hers. She lifted her gaze to the ceiling.

To the blinking red camera in the corner.

The one that had rotated, ever so slightly, in their direction.

"What does that matter?" Jeanine snapped.

"You said you had a legacy. How many Changers have died for this serum? And how many of your own scientists have you lost?"

"I told you it doesn't matter," came the growl behind her ear. "We were all prepared to count the cost."

"My father wasn't. I wasn't. None of those Changers—*people*—you euthanized signed up for this. AITO's told everyone on the outside they're giving their lives to find us a cure. But I don't see any of you falling victim to this epidemic. That means… you've either got a secret cure, hoarded here to protect yourselves from us… or there's no virus at all. You've been lying to ev—"

The arm tightened so hard around her neck the words squeaked off, pressure and lights popping behind her eyes. "How much of a fool are you? You've lived in this city. Of course it's not a virus." A sharp breath blasted the hair on the back of Courtney's neck. "You and the rest of the miserable citizens of this concrete jungle have been given the greatest legacy anyone could ask for: you get to be the next link in our evolution as a species. Every one of you that dies advancing that next step for us is a historical giant. You should be grateful."

"Three seconds, Campbell," W snarled. "Let her go or your last shot at a breakthrough dies with me."

"James," Courtney tried to mouth the words, jerking her eyes toward the camera. "Don't…"

"Three," he growled over her. "Two."

"*As much as I would like to see him hit the ground,*" a voice crackled through the room. *"I've got a more interesting offer. How about world fame?"*

The pressure lifted from Courtney's throat, long enough for her to yank down three gusts of air that burned her lungs and came back up as ripping coughs. Once her eyes stopped watering, she strained them sideways to see where W and Jeanine had turned their attention. The speakers overhead buzzed with a familiar voice.

"Yes, hello. Wave to the camera, everybody."

One of the computer monitors buzzed into the flickering image of Jasper's face. Dina and Books leaned in on either side of him.

"That's right, bitch!" Dina's voice crackled overhead. *"The last two minutes of this juicy conversation have been broadcast across the entire state of Illinois. Thanks to AITO's direct link to the outside, and a couple genius keystrokes from our four-eyed friend here, we're about to start trending on every news network in the country. Pretty sure the rest of the world will be picking that up soon."*

"What?" Jeanine barked.

Jasper nudged Dina out of his face. *"You're live, Doctor. Sure you want to pull that trigger?"*

The arm squeezed tighter. Courtney felt the blood in her face swell beneath her skin. She dug her fingernails into the plaster under her chin, but it didn't loosen. Jeanine started to shake.

"For those of you just tuning in," Dina chimed. *"We just got a crystal-clear confession from the leader of AITO herself that there is, in fact, no deadly virus in Orion City. Thanks for waiting till we had the cameras rolling to blurt that out, Doc."*

"To everyone on the outside," Jasper said. *"Here's the truth. I was one of you. I thought this city was full of people dying of disease, overrun by fear and panic. But it's a city of normal people, trying to lead normal lives, caught in the crossfire of extraordinary*

events. We're calling for an outcry of justice. There's a branch of your military conducting illegal and unethical experiments on American citizens without any accountability at all. It's time to disband AITO, and take down the Wall."

"Oh, looks like we've got an incoming call—kinda nice having the only access link to the outside." Dina leaned over Jasper again and pushed a button behind the camera. *"Who's this? Why, hello, General! No, this is Dina. Don't know who I am? That's okay, you will soon—the whole country will know all of us behind this big fat wall. Oh, that's alright sir, I'd be mad too. No, she can't talk at the moment, she's a little tied up. Busy being a media star and all."*

"It's over, Campbell," Books said to the camera. *"Let her go."*

His voice started to swim. So did the fluorescents on the ceiling. Courtney felt a popping reverberate up through the base of her spine, drumming up through her belly and lungs. It twisted. She had no mind to fight it off. The Change ripped through her like an oncoming car. The grip on her throat widened and fell back—something clattered to the ground. Hot and cold smells slammed her senses, blood and fear. She lay where she fell and dragged air into her lungs.

Shouts ricocheted over her head. The woman in the white coat stumbled back from her. Waved up at the ceiling. Voice high and rough and full of cold things. Angry things. Scared things. A buzzy, tinny bunch of noises echoed out from the ceiling. The people standing around the room began to make noises all at once.

On the ground, by the woman's feet, the tranquilizer gun lay spinning to a stop. Chemicals stung her nose. The woman in the white coat reached for it with her unshielded hand.

Courtney lunged forward. Bones and thin warm skin crunched under her teeth. Before her mind could catch up to her body, she shook the hand with a vicious jerk. Salt and iron filled her mouth.

The woman screamed.

She let go in an instant. The lights and scents and sounds scraped over her, swirled in her head, filled her body. She stumbled. Her head was pounding.

Someone was screaming. She couldn't tell who. But the world tipped. She skidded back, paws slipping through a layer of wetness on the ground, too warm and dark to be anything but more of that thick copper scent that clogged the air, carved fear into every instinct, yanked the air out of her lungs and made the world start to spin, to spin…

"Courtney," said a voice.

A touch at the back of her head. She crouched, blood pounding in her ears. Pain speared up from her leg to infect every nerve in her body. She choked on a cry.

"Courtney… come back."

Peppermint. That one smooth smell cut through the mess of scents. Enveloped her, filled her breaths and slowed them down. She closed her eyes.

The Change slid through her more gently than before, turned her bones back around, pulled her muscles back to themselves with one sharp yank, and settled.

She crumpled. An arm caught her before she hit the blood-soaked concrete. Bright lights stabbed into her vision, so she kept her eyes squeezed shut, waiting for the shapes and colors in the room to stop swirling like oil in a puddle.

The smell of peppermint remained constant.

She grabbed the front of his coat and held onto it with all her strength. Her nose met the warm fabric of his shirt. She heard him inhale. The hands that steadied her by the elbows made to set her back on her feet and move her away, but she yanked her arms from his coat and wrapped them tight around him, anchoring him there.

The voices on the speakers faded, as did the noise around them. All she heard was his heartbeat. Thundering out rapid-fire, harsher and stronger than her own.

"Court…"

The whisper choked in her hair. She felt his lungs contract, catching on themselves as he tried to speak again.

"C," she murmured. "My name is C."

His breath snagged. The arms at her elbows tightened, squeezing her to his chest. She felt the hard bridge of his nose meet her shoulder.

Her ears started ringing.

The sound of his heartbeat was the last thing to fade away.

19. THE HORIZON

T HE PAVEMENT STREAKED by. *A shapeless blur under the tires, that flickering yellow lines zipping in and out of the headlights' glare. Sunlight fading, rosy-golds swimming into deep blues, a thousand dusty flecks of silver winking down from the night sky. The dip and swell of the hills. And the wind... Oh, the wind. Roaring music on the air, it ran wild fingers through her hair, ripping it back from her scalp and filling her lungs with sweet freedom.*

The ocean. Over the next hill, the ocean for as far as she could see. Not a broken line on the horizon. No walls. No sharp edges, no skylines, no harsh earthly lights bleeding into the stars.

For a thousand miles, in all directions, only the horizon.

◆

"Good morning." The reporter's hair tickled the microphone in the wind, her eyes squinting into the sun. "I'm here live at the Wall of Orion City with an update the entire state has been waiting—"

"The entire country," cut in the reporter beside her.

"—thank you, yes, the entire country—has been waiting for. In the three days since the release of a shocking video from the strictly no-contact zone, the nation has turned an overwhelming amount of attention to this little Midwestern city, which has gone overnight from media ghost to media monopoly. Confusing and contradictory reports continue to circle the internet about the validity of the video, but I'm here with reporter Kayla Bell to confirm the facts of what might be the most televised event in the last decade."

"Thank you, Steph." The second reporter gripped her microphone with gloved hands. "Authorities released footage yesterday confirming reports that, until this morning, seemed like fiction. Police were unable to contain the fires and riots that ripped through the downtown area three days ago. Sources say casualties would've tripled were it not for a group of unique individuals whom the public—both in and outside the city—is calling 'Changers.'"

The cold wash of fluorescents glared off the TV in new places as the image changed. The low volume was barely audible over the faint beep of the monitors.

"The apartment was on fire." A man rubbed his nose in front of the camera, squinty-eyed and frowning. "I was on the floor coughing so hard I couldn't find the door, when all of a sudden the window busts open, we're on the second story, and this hand—this giant freak hand as big as my arm—reaches in and pulls me out."

The image switched. A woman leaned into the microphone. "I was in Chinatown square. Everybody was screaming, people were running, somebody said this guy had a gun. I turned around to grab my daughter and I saw this—this *creature* jump over me, like a jaguar or a leopard. It landed on this man and knocked the gun out of his hand, just held him there until the police came."

"A bear saved my life." A young man shook his head, bouncing on his toes and looking around behind the reporter interviewing him. "Chinatown was a mess. Felt like gunshots were poppin' from all directions. Me and some other guys hunkered down behind a street vendor, you know, one of those noodle carts. Then the thing just explodes. Soup sprays everywhere, glass is flying around behind us and I'm positive we're gonna die. Then all of a sudden the shots stop. I sorta peek around and see this huge animal chewing on a gun bigger than me. He slapped the guy to the ground with one paw. The dude never got up, and the bear took off into the crowd, not hurting anybody except the shooters."

An old man, lines carved deep into his face in a permanent scowl. "I don't care what they're all saying, I know what I saw. The Orion Giant saved eighteen of my neighbors on Eastside. If there's not a plaque with his name on it somewhere soon, I'm gonna start my own riot. He's not a criminal or a freak. He's a damned superhero."

The cameras snapped back to the reporter. "Dozens more eyewitness reports place the masked vigilante known as the Orion Giant at the scene of the fires that destroyed over twenty-three buildings in Upper and Lower Eastside. Authorities believe the arsonist responsible is none other than Reginald Murphy, dubbed several years ago by local media as the Torch. Murphy remains at large. Neither have the authorities apprehended the vigilante, who vanished shortly after the fire department managed to get the blaze under control. Authorities have refused to disclose a statement about the vigilante's involvement in their life-saving efforts, but several witnesses credit the Orion Giant with saving over forty lives."

"Thank you, Kayla," said the first reporter. "Meanwhile, thousands flock to the walled perimeter of Orion City this morning to witness what will be the most media-covered event of the last decade: the abolition of the Quarantine that officials placed around the city over ten years ago."

"Dad, turn it up."

"No, that's loud enough. Your sister's sleeping."

"She'd want to see this."

"Mike, lower your voice."

"*Ugh*."

The rolling chair spun across the bleached white tile to sit directly beneath the mounted TV, Michael's coppery mop of hair flipping over the back of the chair as he peered up at the screen.

A low whistle slid past his lips.

"She's pretty famous, huh?"

Conrad's fingers tightened on the starchy edge of the hospital sheet. He smoothed it out under his daughter's still hand, careful not to bump the IV.

"I wish they'd stop playing that video," he murmured.

"Are you kidding? It's awesome. She's a freaking shapeshifter. My *sister*."

Conrad's eyes slid back to the images flickering on the television. The reporter's voice overlaid a jostling group of people smashed together on the edge of a hastily thrown-up metal fence. Picket signs bobbed over multiple heads.

Keep those freaks in a cage.

SOS to Animal Control.

"Despite heavy controversy over the demolition of the Wall, many have come to show their support and welcome these brave citizens back into the outside world."

Pushing, shoving, shouting. Signs of different tones and colors.

Equal rights for Changers.

Down with the Wall.

"She let go!" A man yelled toward the reporters, jostled by the crowd behind her. "The wolf—that girl who Changed—she could've ripped that lady apart, but she let go of her hand instead of tearing it off. They've got a conscience, they're not animals!"

"They're a bunch of freaks!" came the response from a woman nearby.

The camera refocused on the reporter, who lifted her voice to be heard. "Director Jeanine Campbell and other AITO operatives face charges of human rights violations, while the FBI has launched a full investigation into AITO's military sponsors and their alleged supervisors in the CDC. Public outrage and hundreds of petitions to Congress have accelerated the demolition of the Wall. Initial skepticism surrounding the original video decreased as contact with Orion City officials confirmed the truth. The phenomenon affecting roughly one quarter of the population, known by locals as 'Changers', is neither a virus nor a contagion. Members of the scientific community plan to work with affected citizens to help integrate them back into society. What that process looks like, is yet to be determined."

Conrad's fist contracted and relaxed. He focused hard on the glint of Michael's messy hair, fighting the burn that tightened in his bones.

Affected citizens.

His hand closed gently over his daughter's. The tubing under his palm was cold.

"Dad?"

Conrad turned to see Courtney's dark brown eyes cracked open in his direction. She lifted her head from the pillow.

"Baby," he said, tipping forward. "Don't get up."

"I'm fine." She slid her hand from under his, sitting up against the pillows. Her eyes widened at the TV. "Is that live?"

Michael spun around on his rolling chair and skittered back across the tile toward the bedside. "They're knocking it down, Corny! Like, flat! Completely."

"In sections at a time," Conrad said, voice hollow. Courtney's eyes slid to his.

"Did you talk to the doctor?"

"Yes. You're not allowed out of here for at least another two days, even at the rate you're healing."

Brightness sparkled in Courtney's eyes. She wiggled her foot where it made a tent under the thin sheets. "It doesn't hurt."

"That doesn't mean you can just walk out of here," Conrad said at the same time his son declared, "You can *heal* yourself just like the Orion Giant!"

"Not exactly," she said. "But it's like when I feel the Change and force it not to take over. I focus on my muscles and imagine them sealing up, settling down, especially around my leg... and it feels better."

Conrad shook his head. "I don't have your control."

"Yet," Courtney said. "We're both learning. We'll grow together."

Her eyes flickered back to the TV screen. Conrad's throat tightened. He saw the spark there, simmering behind the brown. A longing familiar and piercing.

"Maybe," he said. He dropped his hand off the bed.

She'd grown beyond him already.

"Knock, knock."

The three of them looked up, and the white lab coat in the doorway caused both Conrad and Courtney to stiffen. The doctor walked forward, tapping his clipboard. His salt-and-pepper hair was disheveled, and the rumpled white coat looked several sizes too big, complete with more than one suspicious rust-colored stain. "You're quite the conundrum, young lady." He stopped at the foot of the bed. "Protocol tells us to keep you here at least another two days. But your injuries have gone from critical to minor in less than seventy-two hours. Ordinarily I'd want to keep you here for observation, maybe even a little study, but we've got a patient who needs this room. She's also just moved out of critical, but we're gonna need to watch her a little more closely. What with her being a felon and all."

Courtney sat up. "A felon?"

"Mm-hm." The doctor flipped a paper over on his clipboard. "Punctured lung, fractured T6 vertebrae and moderate thoracic nerve damage. Paralyzed from the waist down. No more gymnastics, looks like. But she's looking far better than anyone I've seen before with that sort of spinal damage. Got the same kind of interesting tissue regeneration you appear to have. In any case, she'll live." He let the papers flip back again and swung the clipboard to his side. "Not that you're interested in a random stranger down the hall."

Conrad frowned at the doctor's informal stance. But as soon as he glanced at Courtney, he saw his daughter's eyes brighten with tears. She pressed a hand to her mouth.

"Has anyone been to visit her?"

The doctor clucked his tongue. "A rude young man in glasses who tells my nurses how to do their jobs."

From behind her hand, Courtney gave a hoarse laugh. Her gaze sparkled with something Conrad couldn't decipher, but was instantly wary of. "I think you can afford to cut him a little slack. After all, he's made your job a lot easier."

"Oh, but I hate easy jobs." A wink with just a little too much of a gleam behind the doctor's smile. "I plan to quit after this."

Courtney giggled again, a silly sound Conrad had never heard his daughter make. His suspicions flared higher. She started, "You wouldn't happen to know if—?"

A nurse entered, disconnected the IV line, and unstrung Courtney's hand from the tubing. She winced as the tape came off. The doctor watched with shadowed eyes.

"An equally rude policeman also came to see you. Unfortunately, our policy is family only."

Courtney snorted. "Wow. And I'm sure you had a big say in that one."

"Course, darlin'. Nothing gets past me."

"Except Books, of course."

"'Fraid I have no idea what you're talking about."

Courtney shook her head with a lighthearted roll of her eyes. "And what about—?"

"Your coffee, miss," the nurse said. She set a mug down on the bedside tray. Along with over two dozen packets of sugar.

"Questions later, fuel now," the doctor said. "You've got a lot of healing to catch up on if you're going to walk out of here this afternoon."

"Excuse me?" Conrad stood. "This afternoon? My daughter was shot in the leg, she's not going to—"

"Whoa, Dad." Michael jumped off his chair and pointed to the TV. "They're knocking it down! Look!"

Conrad wasn't going to take his eyes off the doctor, whose entire personality seemed to have shifted since he'd last visited the room. But the crash from the TV behind him—and the subsequent roar of thousands of voices—overcame the low volume with a sharpness that prickled the hair on the back of his neck. He turned.

A cloud of dust rolled over the picture. The cameras darkened and blurred as it cleared. Sunlight poured through a jagged bite in the Wall, like a giant had taken enormous teeth to the concrete. The wrecking ball trembled on its pendulum, swinging back around for a second blow.

The crowd roared again. The cameras shook.

"Holy..." Michael breathed.

Conrad stared at the rubble. Behind him, the doctor's voice cut the quiet of the room.

"The whole thing's not coming down. They'll set up a bottle-neck along the Eastern perimeter to monitor citizens leaving. Worse will be the crowds on the outside hoping to get in. Claustro-phobic as it is, I find the desperate crowds to be... easier to navigate when you'd like to be overlooked."

"Are you..." Courtney trailed off. "Will I find you? Before you leave?"

Conrad frowned at the TV. He didn't turn around, but the back of his neck bristled at the doctor's low reply: "Not likely. But if you toe the edges of the crowd on the north side of the exit they've made, before sundown, I'll find you."

That was it. Conrad turned around. But all he saw was his daughter, staring at the door with her brows creased, fist curled in the sheet.

The doctor was gone.

The TV crackled with another resounding boom, followed by an ecstatic roar from the crowd.

◆

Courtney stood on tiptoe, tilting her weight to her left foot as she squinted into the fading rays of peach-colored sunlight spearing in over the Wall. The enormous jagged 'V' blasted into the concrete cast oblong purple shadows over the crowd. At the base of the giant opening, behind the slapdash setup of orange tape and rickety metal guardrails, a line of officials ID'd citizens filing past. One by one, men, women, and children slipped under the yawning shadows and out into the blinding sunset beyond.

A funny tickle began in her stomach, glowing hotter with every person that left the Wall behind. Some people ran once they got outside. Others walked as if in a daze, hand in hand with family and friends, gawking up at the tangerine clouds gliding past.

The East side of the entrance. Courtney let her eyes tick between every head, searching for one gaunt profile. He could be anyone in this sea of noses and eyes and cheekbones. Or... no one.

"You should be on crutches," her father muttered beside her.

"Aw, leave her alone, Dad. She's basically a superhero now."

Conrad folded his arms, brow furrowed as he stared out over the crowd ahead. They stood just off the edge of the line, close enough to catch the tantalizing glimpse of a hillside beyond the Wall, but far enough that people shuffled past without a glance in their direction.

"Why aren't we leaving?" Michael bounced on his toes, yanking on the straps of his backpack at his armpits. "I packed my PlayStation and my basketball shorts and all the beef jerky in the house. I'm ready."

"There are things to put in order at home before we think about leaving," Conrad said.

"Then what are we doing here? Why aren't you home fixing stuff up so we can go sooner?"

Courtney felt the weight of her father's gaze settle against the side of her face. "We're here to see your sister off."

"I'm just here to meet someone, Dad." She glanced at him, but couldn't meet the suspicion in his brown eyes. "I wouldn't leave without a goodbye."

"Court…" His voice wavered under the building din of voices. Something stirred up ahead at the makeshift gate. Motion rippled backward through the crowd, a rumble of energy that made her senses tighten. "Just promise me you'll be caref—"

"Whoa!" Michael launched himself up on the tips of his toes. "They're letting people in!"

Courtney stretched impossibly taller. Her right calf sparked, deep in the muscle, and she dropped back to her left foot with a hiss.

The V-shaped hole had divided into two streams of people. A thicker, swifter line flowed outward. But a trickle of people flowed into the city, faces peering around the crowd with an urgency mirrored on each consecutive expression.

"Who are they?" Michael elbowed her. "Hey, whoa—there's your boyfriend."

Courtney spotted him a millisecond after Michael's words registered. Black curls a head taller than the crowd around him, pushing through the line of people in the wrong direction, apologizing as he was shoved back in return.

The knot in her stomach twisted further. Then she caught sight of the tiny figure behind him, dark bob of hair ducking in and out of sight, small hand encased in his as they threaded their way through the crowd.

"Dina!" Michael called out, waving as they approached. "Hey, Jasper."

They broke through the last grumbling knot of people to stop beside them. Dina let go of Jasper's hand and launched herself at Courtney.

"Ah—ouch, watch the—"

"Sorry, sorry!" Arms still wound tight around her ribs, Dina leaned back so her weight didn't press Courtney's leg. "I watched on the cameras, the whole time." Shaky breath gusted through Courtney's hair. "You brave, stupid, brilliant idiot. I thought you were a dead woman three times."

Courtney squeezed Dina back. "None of it would've worked if you guys hadn't been there to do your part. We all risked something."

Jasper lifted a hand, fingers hovering in the air for a second before settling over Courtney's shoulder. "It was hard to watch. Not being able to do anything. You were..." His throat cleared. The fingers slipped off her shoulder. "Dee's right. You were very brave."

"We visited your friend," Dina said. "Strings. She's gonna be okay."

"I'm trying to work on getting her sentence reduced," Jasper said.

"Sentence?"

"The police unearthed her record after her admission to the hospital. They've tied her to multiple heists connected to the Whistler." Seeing the words building on her lips, Jasper hurried on, "But the part she played in exposing AITO's criminal operations will go a long way in the public's eyes. Since she'll also be tried as a minor, I think there's a good chance the outside courts will go easy on her. There's a huge push to acquit Changers of nonviolent crimes on the basis of human interest."

Dina pulled away and reached out to ruffle Michael's hair. "Time for details later. More important thing: are you guys leaving?"

"No," Michael grumbled. "We just came to watch them knock down the Wall. Dad has 'things to put in order' before we ditch this town."

Courtney looked to her father. "What things?"

Conrad shuffled under her gaze. Glancing over where Michael stood chattering with Dina, he drew inward, nodding toward the Wall.

"Look," he said, voice low enough for only Courtney to hear over the crowd. "See all the people coming in."

Courtney watched the steady press of bodies threading through the tiny opening. She looked back to find a startling sheen in her father's dark eyes.

"One day... maybe she'll walk through, too."

Realization stuck her throat together. "Dad..."

"I believe she's out there, Court." His voice was thick, determined. No tremor of false hope or fantasy, but weighted with sure belief. "I think she made it out of this city. After that day, ten years ago, she got stuck outside the Wall. Went to her sister's after our fight, and... could never come back." He swallowed. "I believe... she never meant to leave for good."

Words wouldn't come. The idea of her mother out there, waiting, watching the news, maybe wondering about coming back...

Courtney watched her father watch the Wall, ten years of longing in the lines of his face.

"Maybe, one day, I'll be brave enough to go and find her," he said. "But until then..." His eyes slid to Michael, to Jasper's hand ruffled in the boy's copper hair, Dina's hands tight on his shoulders, like she never planned to let him go. "No," he murmured, as if Courtney had said something. "No, we're going to stay. There's a lot to get used to. Rubble to dig through, rebuilding to start, and this... Change. I want to do it in a place I know. Michael needs that stability too. But one day, Court." A smile touched his eyes as they returned to Courtney. "One day I'm going to leave. I can see over the Wall now; I know the other side's open and free when I'm ready. And... I'll be here, when she's ready."

For a split second, she imagined it. Staying. Rebuilding in the ruins of the past. Cracked foundations filled in, new beams and walls in place of the old skeletons.

The slim possibility sketched itself into a daydream. Her mother's silhouette, emerging out of the sun behind the crumbling Wall, arms open. Beckoning.

She imagined her father's smile. The years melted off, lines erased as they only ever were around Melody Spencer. She imagined Michael meeting her for the first time in his young memory. Her mother's warm brown eyes finally meeting hers, an embrace circling in, big as ever, strong as ever, safe as if no screams had ever replaced the sound of her lullabies in the dark.

It came like a weight. Creeping back in, tight and cold. The Wall's long shadow became a ghostly hand pressing down.

"Dad, I..."

The reluctant note in her voice leaked out against her will.

Watching the light fade from Conrad's smile, Courtney almost wanted to sink backward into the shadow. Let the city swallow her again. It would be so easy. She could return with them. Back to the familiar shade of an old street, safe now in the midst of an old city rebuilding itself in the light. Piecing together what was lost.

Surrounded by rubble.

She stood tall on her aching leg. "I'm not staying."

The dream of that long, endless road rose up in her mind, yellow dashes streaking by along the asphalt, hills rolling past in a smooth blur. Trees and fields and endless stars, dipping all the way down to a jagged horizon. No Wall in sight.

"I know."

The simple, calm reply rocketed through her. Conrad's smile

remained, dimmer, a little more ragged, but softened with understanding.

"You outgrew this city a long time ago, kiddo. Always had that same restless spirit I did." He shook his head. "Only you've... grown beyond your fear." His voice wavered. "She'd be proud of you. I know I am."

The sound of the crowd, the glare of the sun, the awareness of Dina and Jasper just behind, even Michael... all of it faded. Only her father's brown eyes existed, reflecting her own.

Courtney felt her chest twist like it might cave in on itself. She pushed the Change as far back as she could reach, stepped forward, and threw her arms around her father.

"Dad, I love you."

He gripped her shoulder blades with a strength that trembled. "Be back soon. To stay, or visit, whatever you decide. But we're in this together, remember?"

She squeezed him so tight her lungs hurt. "Always."

"Hey!" Michael's voice—followed by a tapping on her shoulder blade—broke the hug. "I want to visit her, too! We need to get out, Dad. Even if we can't move yet."

Conrad let go of Courtney to lay a hand on his shoulder. "Tell you what. Road trip when Courtney gets back. You pick the destination, anywhere between the coasts. Deal?"

Michael's eyes widened. "California?"

Conrad's grin returned, brighter. "Anywhere. Pick a place with a safari even, so your sister and I can blend in."

Michael guffawed, while Dina looked startled, and Courtney's eyes met her father's over their heads. To hear him joke about the Change... it put a warmth in her chest, replacing the old tightening it usually brought.

"Not to invite myself along, but there's a good one in San Diego," Dina said. "If we're talking bucket-lists and safaris."

"Ooh!" Michael bellowed.

As he and Dina crowded in on Conrad, voices climbing over all the glories of road trips, Courtney found her eyes drawn to the crowd again, irresistible in its flickering shadows and faces. She turned around to check on the fifth member of their little group... and saw Jasper's broad shoulders shrinking back through the crowd.

"Hey, Dad, guys—I'll be right back."

She turned and darted after him, slipping through the press of people. His pace was slower than hers, careful and polite in the crowd, so she caught up to him after a painful, wobbly half-jog.

"Hey—!" Her fingers closed over his sleeve.

He turned.

"You trying to disappear?"

"Uh—sorry. I meant to give you some privacy with your family goodbyes."

She let go of his sleeve. "You're... you're not leaving, are you? Without saying goodbye. I wanted... I mean, I'd hoped we'd leave things on better terms than that."

The edge of his mouth softened. He looked down. "I'd hoped so too."

"Are you going back home?"

He shook his head. "I plan to stick around for a while, help this city pick itself back up. Most of my unit headed for the hills, so there aren't many people left over with an inside view of Orion's weak points, where the most help is needed. I figure I'll stay a few months at least to help them sort it out."

A white knight unstained as ever. Tight as it was, the smile tugging at her lips felt real. Jasper touched her hand.

"I know you've made up your mind. But just know... I don't regret any of it. Knowing you, seeing this city through your eyes. All your questions, even the fights, the answers I never thought about seeking. Wherever you end up, I hope... I hope you find what you're looking for."

She closed her fingers over his. "I did."

His jaw flexed. "Him."

"Me."

He frowned, and she looked down at their joined hands, squeezing his as she sifted for words. "You two had your missions all along. You're as different as night and day, yet just the same. You think you're one man against the world. You think you're alone. A white knight and a dark knight trying to fight a battle bigger than yourself, all on your own. You both taught me one man can make a difference, but I learned something from your mistakes. You have to trust people. Broken people. Then, when your own cracks begin to show, you'll have somewhere to fall."

Lips pressed tight, Jasper let out a long breath. He tugged their hands forward and slid an arm around her, nose pressed against the crown of her head.

"Promise me you'll take care of yourself," he said roughly.

She breathed in his scent, pinewood and rain, sealing it away into memory. She didn't regret him either. Only now, the space inside his arms felt like it belonged to someone else. The image of Dina's tiny hand encased in his warmed her thoughts.

"Promise you'll think about what I said," she said. "You're not a lone savior in this broken city. Those shoes aren't yours to fill. Just like they weren't Oliver's, or W's, or mine."

Jasper stepped back. He nodded. Then his frown returned.

"That girl," he said. "I recognize her."

Courtney turned. Margo stood, a dozen feet away, staring as

people shuffled around her. As soon as Courtney met her dark eyes, she turned and headed off into the crowd.

"Margo!" Squeezing Jasper's hand once, Courtney let go. She started after the dark mess of tangled hair weaving through the crowd. Her leg burned beneath her.

She lost sight of her at the edge of the crowd. The exit loomed, huge and echoing. It felt like a thousand people crammed around the metal fence beside the officials, trickling through one by one. Courtney spun in a slow circle. Margo was nowhere in sight.

"Margo!" She cupped her hands around her mouth. "Mar—"

Her right knee gave out with a spasm. Someone caught her by the elbow before she hit the ground.

"Hasn't anyone ever told you it's rude to cut in line?"

Peppermint.

Courtney looked up into the face of a stranger, blond and broad-angled, brown eyes lit with a spark she'd recognize anywhere. A familiar silver tooth glinted behind his left incisor. Without thinking, she jerked him down into a hug.

She wasn't sure who started the kiss. But in the next moment, unfamiliar lips were on hers, and she had her fingers threaded into soft blond hair, strong hands around her waist, pressing her closer. It was so different. The light stubble on his jaw, the fuller mouth, the fact that she didn't have to stretch quite so high up onto her toes to reach him. Yet it was so… right. It was him. No matter the shape, the face; he was hers. A thrill ran through her as they pulled apart, breaths shared, tingles racing down her spine in a rush of clarity.

He was hers. They could go anywhere from here. The city that had twisted him, scarred him, almost taken him from her… it had no claim on him anymore. Nor her. They were free.

Familiar, foreign eyes studied hers as two large hands cradled her jaw. Courtney chased down the breath that had left her.

"Where's Margo?" she blurted out.

W glanced over her head. "I brought her here to register her with child services. She'll... be better off away from here."

Away from me. A weight settled into her stomach as she heard the words he didn't say. Courtney took one of his hands. "James..."

Like she'd shocked him, he flinched back, hands vanishing from her face. She blinked when he sidestepped her, clearing his throat with a nod toward the exit. "Come on. I've got a contact up here. He can get us through with proper papers, clean records. I've even got a car lined up on the other side."

Courtney scanned the crowd. When he motioned for her to follow, she slipped around the gap in the metal fence behind him and approached the officials.

Margo stood waiting. Courtney's heart skipped, then fell at the sight of the official stooping down to talk with her. Margo shrank back into herself, chin tucked, hands knotted in her peacoat.

"You got an adult with you, sweetheart? I'm sorry, but I can't let you through without—"

Margo's head snapped up. Seeing W, she closed the steps between them and wrapped her tiny hand around his big one. He froze in his tracks.

"This one yours?" The official watched W, clipboard raised. As the silence stretched, his eyebrows drew together. Courtney's eyes darted to the official in the dark blazer next to him, the one with the words *Child Protective Services* printed on her sleeve.

Margo slid closer to W. She looked up at the people behind the paper-strewn booth, reaching up to clutch W's fingers with both hands. She tucked her face into the side of his coat.

"Sir?"

Courtney stepped up beside them. She slid her arm around W's other elbow, and leaned close. "She needs you."

He lowered his chin a fraction, and cleared his throat. "Yes. This one's mine."

◆

The ancient car puttered and groaned underneath them, the air close with the smells of leather and gasoline. Courtney hadn't pulled her eyes from the window for the past twenty minutes. Every hill rolling by glowed a deeper green than the last. Even as the sun faded, the colors seemed more vivid, the air sweeter and more open, the horizon bigger every time she traded her gaze from the sky to the hills and back again.

She hadn't been surprised at all when W had found his contacts within the officials. When he'd produced a set of papers for Margo, for himself, and even for herself. Her new name was Caroline. Of course, he'd picked something with a C. She couldn't remember what fake names he'd given for himself and Margo, and she had a feeling she wouldn't need to.

They'd left the city behind over an hour ago. Ten minutes ago the headlights had filled up a sign with the raggedy state outline: *Welcome to Indiana.* East. Away from the setting sun, road singing under the tires, stars winking into existence one by one on the indigo horizon.

Courtney closed her eyes. Margo's soft snore from the backseat filled her with a warmth that had nothing to do with the rickety old heater sputtering behind the vents.

"What are you thinking about?"

W's voice startled her. The silence had felt so comfortable this last stretch of miles, she'd almost forgotten he had to stay awake to drive. Funny how such a simple thing left one's brain when cars ranked as luxuries.

"I'm thinking I'd love to learn to drive," she confessed.

He glanced over at her. "That might be an amusing endeavor."

She laughed. "Hey, if I can learn to shoot a gun and control a Change, I think I can learn to steer four wheels between the lines."

"I don't know. It's more perilous than it sounds."

He spun the wheel a sudden hard right, and the car lurched under them, weaving across the road. Courtney squeaked, clutching the seat rest.

"Cut it out!"

With a chuckle, W drifted the car back into its proper lane. Not five seconds later, headlights broke over the crest of the hill ahead.

The hum of the tires filled the air between them again.

"I'm glad you didn't give her up," Courtney said. "She's yours. You've known that all along, haven't you?"

His fingers flexed on the wheel. "She deserves so much better."

"James…"

The corner of his nose wrinkled. "Don't call me that."

"What?"

"That name. It's his, not mine."

"Oh." Courtney studied the triple band of stars glowing ahead. Orion's belt. It looked so much brighter out here than in the city. Perhaps… a lot of things were brighter outside the Wall. "Okay, then. Let's pick another one. You always said initials were full of potential. You could be anything. Got a favorite letter? Z? Q? A? What about X, that's kinda edgy."

"What about just W?"

She looked back to see his sharp profile silhouetted against the stars. He'd slipped back to his original face, the one he'd told her once may have been the closest to his real one. She felt the strong urge to reach out and touch him.

"Doesn't that remind you of your father's... label for you? Subject W. You picked up that name in the first place because you were angry."

"Maybe... it used to be. It was a brand at first, fueled my hate for his legacy, served as a reminder of others AITO had dehumanized. Whenever I heard my name, it drove my goals deeper, kept the reason I worked fresh in my mind. Until you first said it." The road hummed beneath them. "Whenever you said my name, I was different."

"How?" she whispered.

Courtney watched the headlights glint off the silver in his eyes. It was too dark to see anything else, but the catch in his voice betrayed everything.

"When you say it, I hear any number of infinite possibilities."

DEAR READER

Wow, my friend! You've stuck with me to the end of *The Walls of Orion* duology, and I'm so grateful I got to share W and C's story with you in its entirety! They'll be back for a cameo in my next series, *Shadow Walkers*, coming soon. I've poured my heart into this duology (originally supposed to be just a quick breather during writer's block with *Shadow Walkers*), but I am beyond excited to share this (even larger) part of my heart with you in this upcoming saga! It'll have action, romance, suspense, a wider cast of characters and deeper world-building rich with folklore and pseudo-scientific magical elements woven together. I can't wait to show you!

Thank you for stepping into my crazy world of The *Walls of Orion* and *City of Loons*. If you enjoy my writing, please leave me a review! They're not only the lifeblood of an indie author; I *love* hearing from my readers and getting to know them. Find me on social media @tdfoxauthor and let's connect! Also, for exclusive content, free stories, character snippets, updates of my next books, and more, sign up for my newsletter at www.tdfoxbooks.com. I'm excited to see you again in my next series, *Shadow Walkers*!

ACKNOWLEDGMENTS

I am so thankful to my family for all their amazing support on this journey of authordom and publication!

A huge thank you to the Acorn team, especially the amazing Lindsey, Holly, and Jessica for your guidance, encouragement, and constructive feedback as I worked to bring *The Walls of Orion* and *City of Loons* to life.

I need to give a huge shout out to my amazing roommates: Steph, Kayla, Emily, and Ginnie, who read this story in all its various stages—from baby to awkward teenager to almost-adult—as I edited, wrote, and re-wrote. Steph, you amazing woman, I can't believe you let me read this entire beast of a story (when it was still one looooong book instead of a duology) to you while you listened, and interjected with all your theories and questions. I'm so grateful to you and all my other friends who read this in its early drafts, provided feedback and encouraged me when I wanted to throw the whole manuscript at the wall and go drink hot chocolate.

Again, I need to give a special shout-out to my Mom, without whom I wouldn't be an author today. Thank you for always pushing me to grow in my craft, challenging me to chase this dream, improve, and never stop growing.

A special thanks to my Uncle Dave and Aunt Steph for your amazing encouragement on my topsy-turvy, up-and-down creative journey. To AJ, who never let me go too long without a fiery pep talk full of heart emojis and golden voice memos, and to my sister Christy, whose no-nonsense, honest encouragement kept me going on my hard days! To my Dad, and to Steven, Mark, Mandy, and my Oma and Opa—thanks for always cheering me on!

Thanks, God, for allowing me to give life to the stories in my head, and for providing for me during the insanity of publishing a book during the 2020 pandemic. Thank you for walking with me through the hard seasons where the inspirations for these stories emerged, and walking me out the other side. I never thought this book would see the light of day—I was in a pretty dark place when it began, wrestling with heavy questions about justice in a world full of gray. But You helped me see the color. And the story that came out of it ended up with a lot more light in the pages than I expected.

To Kelsey, my buddy during this original writing exercise where *The Walls of Orion* began. Thank you for cheering for W and Courtney even while they were still villains! And thanks for giving me the encouragement I needed to move beyond that half-sketched idea of a villain's origin story to a tale of redemption.

And, finally, to all the Loons in my life—you know who you are—thank you for your friendship full of laughs, shenanigans, and crazy adventures! If I listed you all, we'd run out of pages.

ABOUT THE AUTHOR

A world romper from the Pacific Northwest who quite enjoys the label "crazy," T.D. Fox supplements a hyperactive imagination with real life shenanigans to add pizzazz to her story endeavors.

Armed with a bachelor's degree in Intercultural Studies, her favorite stories to write usually involve a clash of worldviews, an unflinching reevaluation of one's own internal compass, and an embrace of the compelling unease that arises with vastly different worlds collide.

When not recklessly exploring inner-city alleyways during midnight thunderstorms in the States, she can be found exploring rainforests without enough bug spray somewhere along the equator.

Made in the USA
Las Vegas, NV
19 August 2021